Praise fo

Double-Crossed

"[I]f you're a die-hard Ali Vali/Cain Casey fan and read every book, you'll be incredibly happy with this one and will be thrilled to find a new series to follow in the same universe."—*C-Spot Reviews*

"[An] action-packed mafia entertainment with a dash of romance. It's quite good fun."—*reviewer@large*

"[T]here aren't too many lesfic books like *Double-Crossed* and it is refreshing to see an author like Vali continue to churn out books like these. Excellent crime thriller."—*Colleen Corgel, Librarian, Queens Borough Public Library*

"For all of us die-hard Ali Vali/Cain Casey fans, this is the beginning of a great new series…There is violence in this book, and lots of killing, but there is also romance, love, and the beginning of a great new reading adventure. I can't wait to read more of this intriguing story."—*Rainbow Reflections*

Stormy Seas

Stormy Seas "is one book that adventure lovers must read."—*Rainbow Reflections*

Answering the Call

Answering the Call "is a brilliant cop-and-killer story…The crime story is tight and the love story is fantastic."—*Best Lesbian Erotica*

"Is there anything better than a smoking hot butch woman in uniform?… If you enjoy stories with stakeouts, gun-slinging butch cops, meddling family members coupled with murder and mayhem around every corner, then this story is certainly for you."—*The Lesbian Review*

Lammy Finalist *Calling the Dead*

"So many writers set stories in New Orleans, but Ali Vali's mystery novels have the authenticity that only a real Big Easy resident could bring. Set six months after Hurricane Katrina has devastated the city, a lesbian detective is still battling demons when a body turns up behind one of the city's famous eateries. What follows makes for a classic lesbian murder yarn."—*Curve Magazine*

"The plot is engrossing and satisfying. A fun aspect of the book is the images of food it includes. The descriptions of sex are also delicious." —*Seattle Gay News*

Beauty and the Boss

"The story gripped me from the first page...Vali's writing style is lovely—it's clean, sharp, no wasted words, and it flows beautifully as a result. Highly recommended!"—*Rainbow Book Reviews*

Balance of Forces: Toujours Ici

"A stunning addition to the vampire legend, *Balance of Forces: Toujour Ici* is one that stands apart from the rest."—*Bibliophilic Book Blog*

Blue Skies

"Vali is skilled at building sexual tension, and the sex in this novel flies as high as Berkley's jets. Look for this fast-paced read."—*Just About Write*

Beneath the Waves

"The premise...was brilliantly constructed...skillfully written and the imagination that went into it was fantastic...A wonderful passionate love story with a great mystery."—*Inked Rainbow Reads*

Second Season

"The issues are realistic and center around the universal factors of love, jealousy, betrayal, and doing the right thing and are constantly woven into the fabric of the story. We rated this well written social commentary through the use of fiction our max five hearts."—*Heartland Reviews*

Carly's Sound

"*Carly's Sound* is a great romance, with some wonderfully hot sex, but it is more than that. It is also the tale of a woman rising from the ashes of grief and finding new love and a new life. Vali has surrounded Julia and Poppy with a cast of great supporting characters, making this an extremely satisfying read."—*Just About Write*

Praise for the Cain Casey Saga

The Devil's Due

"This is an enthralling, nail biting and ultra fast moving addition to the Devil series...once again Ali Vali has produced a brilliant story arc, solid character development, incomparable bad-ass women in traditionally male roles, leading both the goodies, baddies and cross-breeds."—*Lesbian Reading Room*

"A Night Owl Reviews Top Pick: Cain Casey is the kind of person you aspire to be even though some consider her a criminal. She's loyal, very protective of those she loves, honorable, big on preserving her family legacy and loves her family greatly. *The Devil's Due* is a book I highly recommend and well worth the wait we all suffered through. I cannot wait for the next book in the series to come out." —*Night Owl Reviews*

The Devil Be Damned

"Ali Vali excels at creating strong, romantic characters along with her fast-paced, sophisticated plots. Her setting, New Orleans, provides just the right blend of immigrants from Mexico, South America, and Cuba, along with a city steeped in traditions."—*Just About Write*

Deal with the Devil

"Ali Vali has given her fans another thick, rich thriller...*Deal With the Devil* has wonderful love stories, great sex, and an ample supply of humor. It is an exciting, page-turning read that leaves her readers eagerly awaiting the next book in the series."—*Just About Write*

The Devil Unleashed

"Fast-paced action scenes, intriguing character revelations, and a refreshing approach to the romance thriller genre all make for an enjoyable reading experience in the Big Easy...*The Devil Unleashed* is an engrossing reading experience."—*Midwest Book Review*

The Devil Inside

"Not only is *The Devil Inside* a ripping mystery, it's also an intimate character study."—*L-Word Literature*

"*The Devil Inside* is the first of what promises to be a very exciting series…While telling an exciting story that grips the reader, Vali has also fully fleshed out her heroes and villains. *The Devil Inside* is that rarity: a fascinating crime novel which includes a tender love story and leaves the reader with a cliffhanger ending."—*MegaScene*

"*The Devil Inside* by Ali Vali is an unusual, unpredictable, and thought-provoking love story that will have the reader questioning the definition of right and wrong long after she finishes the book… first time novelist Vali does not leave the reader hanging for too long, but spins a complex plot of love, conspiracy, and loss."—*Just About Write*

"[T]his isn't your typical 'Godfather-esque' novel, oh no. The head of this crime family is not only a lesbian, but a mother to boot. Vali's fluid writing style quickly puts the reader at ease, which makes the story and its characters equally easy to get to know and care about. When you find yourself talking out loud to the characters in a book, you know the work is polished and professional, as well as entertaining. Ever just wanted to grab a crime boss by the lapels, get in their face, and tell them to open their eyes and see what's right in front of their eyes? If not, you will once you start turning the pages of *The Devil Inside*." —*Family and Friends Magazine*

By the Author

Carly's Sound

Second Season

Love Match

The Dragon Tree Legacy

The Romance Vote

Girls with Guns

Beneath the Waves

Beauty and the Boss

Blue Skies

Stormy Seas

The Inheritance

Face the Music

Call Series

Calling the Dead

Answering the Call

Forces Series

Balance of Forces: Toujours Ici

Battle of Forces: Sera Toujours

Force of Fire: Toujours a Vous

Vegas Nights

Double-Crossed

The Cain Casey Saga

The Devil Inside

The Devil Unleashed

Deal with the Devil

The Devil Be Damned

The Devil's Orchard

The Devil's Due

Heart of the Devil

Face the Music

by

Ali Vali

2020

FACE THE MUSIC

ISBN 13: 978-1-63555-532-5

This Trade Paperback Original Is Published By
Bold Strokes Books, Inc.
P.O. Box 249
Valley Falls, NY 12185

First Edition: April 2020

Credits
Editors: Victoria Villaseñor and Ruth Sternglantz
Production Design: Stacia Seaman
Cover Design by Tammy Seidick

Acknowledgments

Number twenty-five. Thank you, Radclyffe, for your support, your friendship along the way, and letting me indulge my imagination—I wouldn't have reached this milestone without you. Thank you, Sandy, for all the great titles you come up with, this one included, as well as all your hard work on all our behalves. Thank you to my BSB family for being there through everything.

Thank you to my editors, Victoria Villaseñor and Ruth Sternglantz, and all you do to get me over the finish line. You're the dream team for sure. Vic, you make me laugh as we work our way through these books, which makes the process of learning new things a joyful process. You're a gift, my friend. Ruth, thank you, buddy, for being an awesome finisher. You've been a great friend and it's an honor to work with you. Thank you, Tammy, too for the great cover.

Thank you to my beta readers Cris Perez-Soria and Lenore Benoit. You guys and your input definitely make all the difference when I need it most. You guys rock.

The best experience of finishing twenty-five books is the great people I've met and the experiences it's brought me. Telling the stories important to me is a privilege, but the friends I've made along the way has been the best part. Thank you to every reader who's sent an email, stopped by to say hello at an event, and supported me from the beginning—every word is written with you in mind.

To C, thank you for all the adventures and all the ones yet to come—*Verdad!*

To C
and
To the romantic in all of us

CHAPTER ONE

Damn, damn, damn, damn...fuck. The string of curses running through Victoria Roddy's mind was a mantra that kept her from screaming until she passed out, or running into the great beyond to start living as a hermit in the first cave she came across.

"Damn it to hell, kid. Is she ready?" Bryce Benton asked Victoria with barely concealed aggravation.

Victoria glanced at the door to the studio's bathroom and tried not to grimace. There really wasn't anything to say that would sound believable, and she wouldn't lie or make anything up to try to con her mother's longtime guitarist. Bryce had been there from the beginning and hadn't retired to his goats and chickens because Victoria had begged him not to.

In the last couple of years he'd been her ally in trying to keep her mother, Sophie Roddy, in check so they didn't miss any professional obligations. Sophie was country music royalty and the reigning queen of Nashville, but it was hard to see the glamour when she had her head in the toilet and mascara smeared around her eyes.

"She's not feeling well." The statement was the one she'd said with more frequency in the last year. "Give me ten minutes, and she should be good to go."

He shook his head and leaned against the doorframe. "I love you, kid, but it's time for either rehab or a vacation so she can drink herself into the oblivion she's gunning for. Some of the guys are starting to put feelers out for new gigs, and I can't blame them. I owe it to you to give you a heads-up. Pretty soon the band is going to be me and the crazy guy that plays banjo over on Main." Bryce put his arms around her when she couldn't hold back the tears over the whole situation. "I know you love her, but it's time to stop covering up all the stuff that's not your fault."

"She's my mother, Bryce. You know I can't do that." She took a deep breath and kissed his cheek before stepping back. "Give me ten minutes."

"This is going to be a long day, sweetheart. Blowing off a time in the studio is one thing, but tonight we're going to the Opry. She's got to be ready. That's a big stage to fuck up on."

No matter how famous an artist was, they were as awed as a newcomer when it came to walking out onto the Grand Ole Opry stage and into the circle. That six foot section that had come from the mother church of country music, the Ryman, gave the new building some of the tradition and magic of the old place. Her mother had been there dozens of times in her career, but tonight's performance was about to give Victoria hives. Drinking was one thing, but her mother's new boyfriend Weston Cagle had introduced a cocktail of pills for Sophie to chase down with her drink of choice, Cinclair Whiskey.

"She'll be ready." She said it, but there was no part of her that believed it.

Sophie's life of recording, touring, and performing was the only thing Victoria had ever known because Sophie had dragged her along for all if it, although all she'd really wanted was to stay with her grandparents. The only normal life she'd carved out for herself was the four years she'd gone away to college, but her absence had knocked the wheels off her mother's runaway train.

Any dreams of pursuing her love of playing her own music had been sidelined when Sophie's manager quit a month after Victoria's graduation because he'd been fed up with Sophie's behavior. Victoria had taken over, but the last three years were about to drive *her* to drink as a way of escaping the hell her life had become.

No time to dwell, so she opened the door to Sophie's moaning and retching. "Are you okay?"

"What have I told you about this fucking early morning shit?" Sophie got off her knees, staggered to the sink, and stared at the running water like she didn't know what to do with it.

"It's one in the afternoon, and we got here twenty minutes ago.

We were already an hour late, and it's really not fair to the guys." She handed Sophie a wet paper towel and crossed her arms. "You realize you're the headliner at the Opry tonight, right? You need to get it together."

"And you need to reel the judgment back…a lot," Sophie said, taking a moment to spit out the water she swished around her mouth. "You know I'm a damn professional who doesn't need anyone to tell me my goddamned job."

"Your job's been waiting for you for over an hour, and I'm shocked they stuck around. Why is it you're the only one who doesn't see that you're killing yourself?" Her mother rinsed her mouth again and glared at her, making her bloodshot eyes really stand out. It was like looking at a racoon having a piss-poor day. "Get mad all you want, but it's the truth."

"Let's go before the world comes to an end, since that's how you're spinning it. I just wasn't feeling well, and y'all all act like it's a crime." Sophie smoothed down her platinum-blond hair that was a shade or four too garish to be her natural color and circled her shoulders as if to relax them. The big hair that was her mom's signature and the moves she was making only highlighted how thin and frail she looked.

Sophie totally schmoozed the guys in the control room like she always did, but the band didn't appear at all enamored. They seemed furious until they began, and Sophie started singing. The song that'd probably be the first single off the first album her mom was putting out in four years sounded fantastic with her iconic smoky voice.

Weston had floated a few songs and expected them to be chosen because of his relationship with Sophie, then got angry and disappeared when they were rejected. He'd made himself scarce around rehearsals and such, and he'd handed Sophie a bottle before they'd left the house. Victoria wanted to throw it away, but that would only start another argument when her mother found it missing.

"That was wonderful, ma'am," the guy in the control room said, seeming really starstruck. They wouldn't start recording until the producer arrived. This session was for the benefit of the mixer and audio guys, to get things tweaked, and would hopefully make things go smoother when whoever Sophie's longtime label, Banu Records, sent over arrived.

"Quit with the ma'am stuff. It's Sophie." Her mother had a way about her that made it easy to gather new fans, no matter how young or old they were.

"Thank you, Sophie, and we'll go ahead and take it from the top. We're hoping to get through two today, and the rest in the couple of weeks Banu set aside for you."

Victoria was encouraged as Sophie drank four bottles of water and a cup of coffee while they worked and didn't take long in the restroom when she excused herself. Sophie actually appeared sober by the time they wrapped, a little after five. That gave them time to have dinner before they headed to the Opry.

"I'm not hungry, but I do need to lie down for an hour. You should've thought about the strain of a day like this before you scheduled stuff." Sophie leaned back and closed her eyes in the passenger seat as Victoria started her car. "You've been here long enough to know better."

"I do know better, Mom. This was to warm up your voice for tonight. I know how you feel about the Opry over any other venue."

"Shut up—stop being patronizing, and bring me home." Sophie was acting like a petulant child, and it was about to get worse. Victoria could feel it in her gut, like an old man could feel rain coming in his arthritic joints.

"Mom, we don't have time to go back to Brentwood. If you need to lie down, you can come to my place." Once Weston had moved in with her mother, she'd found an apartment in town.

"Call Weston and have him meet me there, then. He can bring me tonight."

The word *fuck* replaced the string of damns in her head, and she took a deep breath to calm her thoughts. "Mom, do you think that's a good idea? You and Weston like to have a good time, and tonight isn't about that."

"Let's remember our places, okay? And you could do with a little fun yourself. All you need to do right now is keep my schedule and make sure everyone's paid. That's it. I'm responsible for me, and it's been me who's gotten this far."

Victoria sighed at Sophie's cruelty. Only an unlucky few got to see this side of her, and Victoria always got the brunt of it. "Sonny Liner gave you a warning after what happened in Baton Rouge. Do you remember that?"

The way Sophie grabbed her arm and tightened her fingers made Victoria swerve the car. "Sonny Liner knows as well as I do that the Banu label would be shit without me as its cornerstone. If you're smart, you'll shut up about Baton Rouge. There was nothing to that except bad timing."

"I don't think he was kidding, but you know best, so I'll remember my place." It was an unkind thought that came to her as she said it, but if the head of her mother's label finally got fed up with her, they'd cancel her contract and Victoria would be free.

"Don't get dramatic on me, sugar. Spending all day locked in a studio puts me in a bad mood, but I'll feel better after a nap." Sophie relaxed her hand into more of a caress, but as usual, it was too little too late.

"You know best, and you have a key, so I'll see you later. I know you hate me saying it, but try to remember how important tonight and this album are. Tonight is the beginning of the PR buildup Banu is doing before it's released. You've *got* to be on your A-game." There was no way she was going to hang around and get yelled at for the rest of the afternoon. Her mother liked reminding her that she was an adult and responsible for her own decisions, and those decisions had landed her on top of the charts. And to add to that, Weston gave Victoria the creeps.

"It'll be a show no one will forget." Sophie opened the door before the car stopped, having spotted Weston lounging on Victoria's front steps.

"That's what I'm afraid of."

❖

"How can you say no?"

Mason Liner glanced up at the waitress before turning her attention to the young guy who'd begged for a meeting. She couldn't remember his name. "Look, I appreciate your enthusiasm for your girlfriend—"

"She's not my girlfriend," he said with the indignity of an old church marm in a whorehouse on a Sunday.

"Kid, never start any negotiation with bullshit. You love this girl, and good for you, but the last thing Nashville needs is another Taylor Swift lookalike in everything but the height and talent. Get her a few gigs on Broadway, then give me a call, but try some voice lessons first." She put her hand out for him to shake, hopeful he'd recognize it as closure to their meeting. It was doubtful any of the bars along the famous street that was Nashville's entertainment district would hire this girl to do anything but bus tables.

"The regular, Mason?" the waitress asked when she came back. They'd both watched the slow walk of rejection the guy had done, but that wouldn't be the last time he'd do it, so it was good he was getting some practice in.

"Let's mix it up and have it with fries this time." She smiled when the woman kissed her before going to put her steak order in.

That order and the table where Mason was sitting had been her Friday night ritual for the last six months. Skull's Rainbow Room wasn't at all a new place in Nashville, but a lot of the locals sometimes forgot it served up great food as well as good entertainment. On Fridays, though, after the band and the dinner service, they'd added burlesque, and Madame Belle Lenox was the only woman she'd ever known who'd turned down a recording deal.

What *Mason* hadn't turned down was an invitation for a drink at Belle's place the first night she'd come to see the show, and that had turned into a mutually satisfying relationship with very few of those annoying strings that usually came with spending time in a woman's bed. Belle was a little older than her, but the way she worked a crowd and danced made you forget everything but Belle.

Her cell phone flashed on the table, and she was surprised to see her father's name on the screen. Friday nights were usually his time to sit in his recliner in his boxers, eat wings, and drink a few beers with her mother. Business was put on the back burner on Friday nights.

"Hey, Pop."

"How's my little Buckaroo?"

She laughed at the nickname and at how her dad's voice made her happy. "Good, I'm having a steak at Skull's, and we put the finishing touches on Colt Kenny's tour. All I need is an opening band, and we can start advertising." She nodded at the waitress as she put her plate down, and Mason immediately salted everything on it. "And I'm an inch taller than you, so keep that in mind when you call me *little* anything."

"Little Buckaroo sounds better than big Amazon, so keep that in mind."

Mason heard her mother laughing in the background.

"You should thank me for your good looks, and hopefully you can do it in person tomorrow. Are you free around ten?"

"For you I'm always free, Papa. I'll come earlier than that and bring some doughnuts."

"Good. Just one more thing, and I hope it's not messing up your night, but I need you to head to the Opry and catch Sophie's set. The studio called me today, and we might have some problems on the horizon when it comes to Ms. Roddy, and that's going to be one of the things we need to talk about tomorrow."

"I'll be happy to, Pop," she said, even though it was the last thing she wanted to do. "I'll see you in the morning. Do you need anything else?"

"All I need is to see you and that brilliant brain of yours you got from your mama. The great hair and eyes—that's all me."

"At least you have me to remind you what great hair used to look like."

"You're killing me, kid, so bring those doughnuts as well to make it up to me."

She laughed at that too as she stared at the black-and-white checkered linoleum stage floor where Elvis, then a nobody, had been given a chance to perform. Skull's had been the first stop for a lot of famous names, and another reason Mason liked it. And all the women backstage ready to dance weren't a bad reason to visit either.

Belle came out an hour later with her signature big yellow feathered boa and prowled the stage as she sang, looking like the truest definition of a sexy woman. The boa dropped on Mason's head as Belle winked at her, but every pair of eyes in the room stayed on Belle. Her body in a sheath dress was something songs should be written about.

The show was an hour long, and Belle's girls packed the place and kept the patrons drinking. Skull's was a Friday night must if you wanted a change of pace from the row of honkytonks on Broadway. Mason downed her drink when the manager waved her over to the end of the bar. The next show wasn't for another hour, and the band started up again to fill the time.

"Belle said to go on back," the guy said, shaking her hand. "And thanks for the recommendation on the band. They've been a good addition, and the folks really like them."

"Let them start playing their original stuff." She waved to the lead singer who'd lifted his hand after noticing her. "Trust me, everyone will love them as much as the old standards they're doing now, and they won't be around for free much longer."

"You signing them?"

"Not yet, but they have potential, and they have that connection with the crowd you can't teach." She stayed for the beginning of their first song before heading to the dressing room past the storage area.

Belle was in a bustier and fishnet stockings held up by garters when she opened the door, and Mason couldn't help but stare like a horny teenage boy. "How is it you get better looking every time I see you?" Belle asked.

"It's all the dim lighting in these places. It works to my advantage." She gladly stepped forward when Belle tugged her by the belt and pushed her down on the couch. "You were as gorgeous as ever, and that voice of yours gives me shivers."

"Hopefully that's not the only thing that gave you shivers, lover." Belle straddled her lap and threaded her fingers into her hair. "You looked so delicious sitting there that I can't wait for you to bring me home."

"Oh yeah?" She untied the top of the bustier and worked it down to expose even more of Belle's cleavage. "What can't you wait for?"

"First I want you to touch me, since I could almost feel your hands on me the way you were staring, and then I need you to fuck me. And I really need you to do that right now, baby."

Mason glanced down, enjoying the way the black garters contrasted against Belle's legs, and how sexy she was with only that and the bustier on. "Are you wet?"

"Mason, you might get pinched for silly questions. Give me what I want."

Belle lifted onto her knees a little when Mason ran two fingers from the opening of her sex to the top of her clit. That made Belle hiss and pull her hair hard enough to cock her head back so she could kiss her.

"You want it fast or slow?" The way Belle was chasing her fingers with the movement of her hips made it clear.

"Are you going to fuck me or talk me to death?" Belle bit her bottom lip before sucking it into her mouth. "God," she said as she stilled when Mason filled her up. "You always know." Belle moaned when Mason stroked her clit and pressed their foreheads together. "Fuck...fuck me."

Mason slid her fingers out and in rapidly, making sure to hit Belle's clit every time. The sight and feel of her made Mason hard, and she wasn't stopping until Belle came on her hand. "Let me see you."

Belle leaned away from her and tugged the blood-red bustier down until it was well below her breasts, and she moaned when Mason sucked one in. "Yeah, baby, harder." Mason pressed into the sofa and put her hand behind Belle's head so she could lean back, giving her room to really move her hand. "Like that, oh, fuck me, like that," Belle said with her eyes closed. Belle's hips pumped in rhythm with Mason's thrusts, and it didn't take long before Mason felt Belle grip her fingers in the most intimate of ways.

"You aren't Nashville's most sought after producer and record executive for nothing, baby," Belle said, squeezing her fingers one more time after she came. She leaned forward and kissed Mason before letting her hand go. "You certainly know how to produce all kinds of things in me."

"Thank you, and if you form a fan club, I want to be nominated for president."

Belle got off her and slipped into the bathroom before coming out in the costume she'd started the show with.

"Are you in pain, babe, or you want to wait?"

"You're a hard one to say no to, but I have to leave early. I promised my father I'd run an errand for him, so I have to get going."

"No time for me to return the favor?" Belle asked as she reapplied lipstick.

"Believe me, I'd like nothing better, but I have to go. Are you okay for a ride?" She usually gave Belle a lift home, but she doubted the night would end anytime soon.

"I'll ask one of the girls, and remember, I owe you one." Belle kissed her and pressed their bodies together.

"That I won't forget, and believe me, the chore Sonny assigned me will be doubly hard considering how hard *I* am at the moment." She laughed and slapped Belle's ass. "Have fun tonight."

"And you try to do the same."

"I'll do my best, darlin', but I very much doubt it." From what her father had said about Sophie, and what she remembered of her past behavior, the rest of her night wasn't going to be fun at all. "I very much doubt it."

Chapter Two

The Opry was filling with both tourists and locals alike who were there for the variety of acts the place delivered for every show, and backstage, the stagehands were working hard to get everything together. Victoria loved the history and tradition of it, and the way people still embraced it. Some of it was corny, but in the end it was all about the music.

"Where's Sophie?" Bryce asked when he joined her right offstage.

"She should be here by now. Weston texted they were on their way. Traffic, maybe?" She went from enjoying the atmosphere to full-blown anxiety.

"Are you sure that's all it is?"

"Let me go find out." The entrance for the performers was behind her, and as she headed for it, the show started. There was a new band opening, but they were only doing two numbers before Sophie would be introduced for her first set. Once the show got started she'd come out again a few times before they wrapped up. Sophie should have been there way before now.

"Did Sophie Roddy arrive?" Victoria asked the doorman. "I'm her manager."

"She hasn't checked in yet."

Shit, she should've stayed with her. She headed back to her purse for her phone. Maybe Weston or her mom had called and she'd missed it. "She's not here," she said to Bryce as the opening band finished their first song. Weston's phone went to voice mail, as had Sophie's. Why the hell did her mother do this? She had everything, and she was throwing it all away.

The band was done, and the night's emcee asked them a few questions before introducing Sophie. Bryce and the guys had gotten into place and started playing, and he shrugged when he glanced her way, then winced when he looked over Victoria's shoulder.

Her mother swayed past her as she stepped out to a sea of cheering people. She saw the impending disaster when her mother couldn't make it to the microphone in a straight line. Bryce didn't stop playing, but Victoria could see his worried expression when Sophie finally made it, though she almost fell backward when she ripped the microphone off the stand.

"Hey, everybody." Sophie was slurring her words and teetering like she wasn't on steady ground. Her speech and her movements seemed to chill the crowd, and silence descended. "Let's get—" Sophie turned quickly and lost her balance, sending her stumbling backward.

There was a collective gasp when Sophie flew off the stage, landing on the floor right in front of the first row. Victoria ran to the edge of the stage and blew out a breath when she saw Sophie was breathing. But her eyes were closed and she wasn't responding, no matter how much Bryce yelled at her from where he knelt beside Victoria.

The stage manager called for help and brought out a blanket to hold in front of Sophie to protect her from the people taking pictures and video. Victoria was lowered down with Bryce to where Sophie still lay, and she couldn't stop the tears of disbelief. There would be no glossing this over. Her mother's career was over.

"Vic, we need to move her," Bryce said.

Her gaze stayed on her mom's chest as she knelt next to her, holding her hand. Losing a career would be a small price to pay if her mom lived, and that's what she was praying for. "Help is on its way, and I don't want to hurt her more."

She heard running along the wood floor of the stage, and an EMT was next to her a second later. They worked to stabilize Sophie and were able to leave by the side of the stage. Victoria heard the emcee ask everyone to pray for her mother and that the evening's show would continue. Who gave a crap about that?

Bryce gave her a ride to the hospital, since she was shaking so badly after watching the EMTs speed away with their lights and sirens on, as if time wasn't on their side. They followed when they rushed Sophie into the ER, where a doctor administered medication to counteract the effects of whatever Sophie had taken. It took a few minutes before Sophie started to show signs of life, and Victoria had to sit, her knees were so weak.

She couldn't quite pinpoint what to feel, considering both relief and terror were at war in her chest. Her mother didn't seem to care anymore, but Victoria couldn't get to that place. Sophie was her mother and she loved her, but watching this decline was making her ache, and there was no cure for it. Her desire to be enough for her mother flitted through her head again, but nothing in the world would grant her that, so she concentrated on Sophie's face.

"What happened?" Sophie opened her eyes and the nurse stopped her from ripping out her IVs.

"You overdosed. That's what happened." She didn't want to yell, but the stress of the day was almost too much to handle. Anger won out over fear. "And you picked the perfect place to do it. Well done."

"I wasn't feeling well." Sophie spoke softly with her hand over her eyes.

"Stop it," Victoria yelled louder. "Stop fucking lying to me, to the people who love you, and, more importantly, to yourself."

"None of you understand *shit*." When guilt and sympathy didn't work, Sophie always went straight to hostility.

"Give it a rest, Mom. No one's falling for this—"

"Am I interrupting something?" A tall woman who didn't look like a doctor simply walked in, and she didn't seem apologetic about doing so. "Haven't you made enough headlines for one day? You should know the drill by now about keeping a low profile until all this blows over. You've been in the business long enough to know that little tidbit."

"Who the hell do you think you are? Get out—this is none of your business." Victoria stood and pointed to the door. "Get out," she said, when all the woman did was give her a condescending smile.

"Sit down and take a breath before you hit shrill, babe. Believe me, it's not a flattering look."

"Fuck you." If what had happened was the crappy ice cream sundae, this asshole was the cherry on top. "Get out or I'll get security."

"You want to break it to her, Sophie, or shall I?"

"Sugar, sit, and let's see what our future's going to be," Sophie said, holding her hand out. "I must be in big trouble if they sent the right hand of the music god. How are you, Mason, and how the hell did you get here so fast?"

"Slightly better than you, Sophie, and I was rerouted here on my way to the Opry to watch your set tonight. What the hell happened?"

"I wasn't feeling well."

The woman smiled, making Victoria think she was an idiot as well as an asshole if she was falling for this. Victoria managed Sophie's schedule and events, but when it came to the business side of things, her mom had insisted on handling everything. It meant Victoria didn't know many of the business contacts her mother made. Clearly, this was an important one she'd missed. She knew Sonny and some of the other execs, but she hadn't heard of anyone below him.

"You barely made it through a show in Biloxi because you were flying higher than Elon Musk's Dragon, and you completely missed the one in Baton Rouge. Sonny covered all of it up because he loves you. That love, though, had some stipulations that you agreed to, and tonight you screwed the poodle on your promise."

"Come on, Mason. People are probably praying for me, and they'll forget about it when I sing again. Everyone loves a comeback story."

Mason took her phone out and start tapping something out as if she was bored. The video she pulled up showed Sophie staggering, then taking a header off the stage. "You're trending on three different social media sites, and the comments have not been kind."

"Do you and Sonny have any idea who the hell I am?" Sophie practically spat the question, and the damn smug smile was back.

"We thought we did, but let's see," Mason said, glancing down at her phone. "Turns out you're a big-haired, tacky, has-been drunk," Mason read. "Here's a good one—*Sophie, get your head out of your ass and head back to the farm. Put us out of our misery.*" Mason looked up. "Those don't sound like prayers or pity."

"There's no reason to pile on," Victoria said, having an urge to defend her mother even though it was all true.

"If you're here to dump me, Mason, get on with it." Sophie acted like she didn't need defending, and Victoria blamed it on the residual impairment of whatever the hell she'd taken. "I'll be signed by someone else tomorrow morning."

"Good luck, then, but let's all agree you were in breach of your contract and save us all the time and aggravation of any kind of legal action." Mason stepped closer to the bed. "I was here to offer you another chance, but it sounds like you're not interested in that."

"All you give a shit about is the money, so save the act." Sophie was getting more venomous by the minute. "You're going to be sorry when I get the new album out and start giving interviews. I'm not holding back on your father, or you."

"Banu owns the rights on three-fourths of the songs, so there'll be no new album until you come up with new material." Mason held her hand up when Sophie appeared ready to rev up again. "I'm not your enemy, Sophie, and you have a short window of time here."

The statement seemed so final, and it was probably true, but Victoria wasn't a fan of the messenger Banu had sent. Mason, whoever the hell she was, was a good example of what was wrong with the music industry. They acted like music gods who cared way more about the profit and nothing about the music.

She followed Mason out and stopped her in the hallway. "In the future, come to me first. I'm her manager, and I'm responsible for her." Mason didn't face her until she stopped talking, but then she turned around, as if waiting for her to keep going. One look at her, and Victoria wished she'd kept walking. The messenger might've been an asshole, but she was extremely attractive, making her level of anger hard to maintain. "That wasn't professional, and Sonny Liner is going to hear about this."

"Why do you think I'm here, sunshine? Sonny Liner already heard about it, and he's pissed. If you *are* responsible for her, you need to up your game." Mason turned and started walking but stopped again when Victoria grabbed her sleeve. "If you don't start making the tough calls, then you won't have to worry about them any longer. Are you blind as to what kind of trouble she's in?"

"Mason, isn't it? You don't know shit about me or Sophie Roddy, and if I can talk her into it, I'll definitely have her sign with someone else once this blows over. If you're running your business by what people say on social media, Sonny Liner will fire your ass by morning."

Mason actually chuckled, making the skin around her eyes crinkle as if she really did find her humorous. "Do you really think so? Maybe the social media stuff and your scathing review of my professionalism will convince him I'm not cut out for this, and I can finally sleep in whenever I want to." Mason stared down at her hand, still gripping

Mason's sleeve, and her fingers automatically opened. "Until then, keep Sophie away from the media, and refrain from giving any statements. But I'm not responsible for you or Sophie, and I can't keep you from committing career suicide. Well, more than you have already."

"She's Sophie Roddy, and she built the Banu label."

"Just because Sophie keeps telling you that, over and over, doesn't make it true."

The way Mason exhaled made Victoria think she was about to lose patience.

"Actually, she is a big-haired, tacky, has-been drunk. Hashtag #bighair will be trending by tomorrow and will be forever synonymous with Sophie Roddy. Call me crazy, but I'm not thinking that's a good thing."

"Fuck you and Twitter."

"That's the best insult ever—I'll have to remember it." Mason sighed. "There's a very small window of opportunity here to get her healthy. Forget about the music for now and concentrate on her. Your assignment is to remember everything I said."

"Believe me, asshole, I'm not forgetting a word."

Mason waited until morning before thinking about her father and his reaction to what had happened. After leaving the hospital it was a tie as to what had her most on edge. She was horny after having to leave Belle before she'd wanted to, and she was aggravated at the insulting little bitch who obviously had no clue who she was. But then, Sophie wasn't on her list of responsibilities, so she didn't really know that much about her or anyone in her orbit. At her father's urging, she'd spent a few years in LA expanding their talent pool outside country music. Her three years in California had kept her out of the country music scene in Nashville until only very recently, and after meeting Sophie and her representative, she was happy to have been out of that loop. She wasn't wasting time finding out if Sophie was serious about leaving their label.

She drove into Nashville to get her dad a variety of choices from Fox's Donut Den before turning around and heading back to Hendersonville. Her parents had decided to go north of the city instead of south like most of the big names who'd settled in places like Brentwood and Franklin.

Mason's horse ranch was ten miles from her parents' place, and they were her closest neighbors. The Blue Heaven Ranch already had that name when she bought it four years before, but the *heaven* part fit, and she'd kept it. It was still an adjustment living out there with all the rolling hills and quiet, but after the first month it was hard to think of anyplace else as home.

She'd learned the ins and outs of the business from her dad, who she talked to daily, along with a few of his friends. It was an education that had started early and wouldn't end until Sonny took his last breath. That anyone would think he didn't care about the music infuriated her.

They worked together, and she was happy Sonny still loved being *the* Sonny Liner. That was why yesterday was so refreshing. Once people heard the name Mason Liner, ninety-nine percent of the time their attitude changed from ambivalence to kiss ass. Sophie's manager was the one percent odd man out.

"Yo, Mason," Wilbur Corsot, the young guy behind the counter, called out when he saw her toward the back of the line. "You want the usual?"

"Double it, my man, we're having guests." She was going to have to start mixing it up if practically everyone in town knew her usual. "Don't forget my mama's box."

"And have Miss Amelia call my daddy?" Wilbur laughed as he worked. "No way, I don't need that kind of negativity in my life."

"How are the guitar lessons going?" She got her wallet out as he bagged her order. The kid played some good blues, but he needed to perfect some stuff before she'd agree to place him somewhere he'd have a career doing something he loved. Her deal had been lessons until he reached the level she wanted. "You skipped last week."

"I skipped *you* last week, Mason, not the lessons. It was Granny's birthday, and I figured you'd be cool with me not meeting up with you."

"I'd have been cooler if you'd called." She handed over three hundred for the fifty dollar order. "No artist is ever going to be cool with no call because they're not as wonderful as me. Shit like that will get you fired." Her joke made him release the breath he'd been holding, and he fist-bumped her for the tip that would pay for next week's lesson.

"Sorry, man, and it won't happen again. Like, ever, you know?"

"I know, and come by next week if you have time. There might be some people you want to meet." He carried half her order to the new Sierra she was driving.

"Tell me it's not all twangers." That was Wilbur's name for the straight crying-in-your-beer country guys.

"With a name like Wilbur, don't throw stones, son." She hugged him. She waved to his father, who'd just arrived. "Go take care of the old man, and call me."

"You got it, and nice ride."

"I'm trying to butch up my image since a girl told me and Twitter to fuck off. I must look like a cream puff for that kind of insult."

"Any more butch, bro, and you'll need to shave. Hey, is Sophie Roddy one of yours?"

"Momentarily, why?"

"That was some messed up shit last night, and she's blowing up Instagram and everything with that dive. Good luck with that and drive safe."

She headed to her parents' place figuring her father had gotten Woody, the company's fixer, back in town for this. The music and finding talent were her strong suits, but pure PR and how to weather a shit storm weren't her things. She punched the code to the gate and headed down the long drive to the six car garage.

Her parents' original house was still on the property, but her father had given in to her mother's wish for a new one, and her mom had created a beautiful new place that had great views of the Cumberland River. The great thing about the land right outside Hendersonville was that the river widened, giving it an almost lakelike feeling, that gave you a sense of peace hard to find anywhere else.

Mason's place was situated the same way. Her bedroom had a deck that overlooked the river and was one of her favorite places in the world. Every so often she visited her parents by way of the water, coming by boat. She stared out at the river, thinking the reflection of the sun made it shimmer.

"It's mesmerizing, isn't it?" Amelia Liner came out and put her arms around Mason's waist. Her mother was a petite woman who loved the outdoors and had retained the beauty that drew people to her, just as it drew in her dad. Their marriage was one of those rare relationships that made most people envious.

"You know it." She kissed the top of her mom's head and smiled when Amelia squeezed harder. "How is he?"

"He's calmer, which might save someone from a punch in the nose, but I can't make any promises. He got a call from Justin Sullivan at Brookline about thirty minutes ago, and it didn't go well."

"Sophie shopping a new label already? It wasn't my unprofessional behavior last night that sent her running into Justin's arms, was it?" They walked down to the swing by the water. The rest of the day would come soon enough to trigger a major case of indigestion, so a moment of alone time was in order. "Sophie's new manager chewed me out and threatened to report me to my boss. She had that beautiful-when-angry thing going, but she really didn't like me very much."

"My kid unprofessional? No way, that I won't believe," Amelia said, taking her hand. "Though your father did get a call about that and screamed at whoever it was so loud I might have to replace the windows in the sunroom."

Mason laughed and bumped shoulders with her mom. "Ah, you know I can be an ass if I put my mind to it, but Sophie and her people are in some major denial. That's what I was trying to get across, but it was like talking to a really dense brick wall."

"You realize we can't cut her loose without looking heartless, right?"

She nodded, having come to the same conclusion that morning in the quiet of her deck. Sophie Roddy was a mess, but she was Sophie Roddy. "Does Dad know that?"

"That's where you come in, Buckaroo. You came out screaming your ass off, with your coal-black hair and sky-blue eyes, and my first thought was *uh-oh*. You're a carbon copy of the love of my life, and that's exactly the title you share with your father, but you have loads more patience than he does. You'll have to do some convincing, I think."

"You know this isn't going to be easy. The videos out there will make people think twice about investing in Sophie. Who wants to buy concert tickets to watch someone forget the lines of the song they've been performing since the womb?" She rocked them on the double swing and tried to put off what had to be done.

"I have faith in you, honey, and this is about more than how we'll look in all this. These days it's easy to toss people away like an old newspaper because that's what society does, but I'm positive there's a lot of people like me out there." Her mother straightened and kissed her cheek.

"What do you mean?" They walked back to her truck for the treats she'd brought.

"I fell in love with your father while we danced to Sophie's beautiful voice, and I have plenty more dancing to do. She's an icon, and people will remember all she gave them." Amelia kissed her cheek again and smiled. "All you need to do is convince your father of that."

"Sure. I'm sure that'll be as easy as downing some of these doughnuts, especially if Sophie or her manager told *him* to fuck off."

CHAPTER THREE

Fuck." Sophie threw the phone hard enough to break against the wall.

"Baby, you need to shut it down for a while," Weston said, wrapping his hand around her bicep. He tried leading her into the bedroom, but Victoria shook her head and blocked his path.

"What she needs to do is try and fix this." She stared at her mother and was truly disgusted by what she saw. "Unless this is how you want to end your career."

"You're as screwed in the head as Sonny Liner if you think I'm going to beg." Sophie seemed to have lost her ability to talk in a normal tone. "It ain't happening."

"I guess you can go and do whatever you want, then, but I'm done." She was tired, exhausted really, and it wasn't from the sleepless night. "I'm done."

They'd left the hospital against the doctor's objections, and Sophie had been quiet as Victoria drove her to the big house in Brentwood. It wasn't very old, and in truth it was the first home Sophie had ever had since she'd left her parents'. Most of her career and life had been about touring and not setting down roots. Her gold and platinum albums were on the walls, her awards filled the built-in bookshelves, and pictures of them all over the world were scattered throughout the place.

It was a beautiful house full of the things that had marked Sophie's success, but it didn't feel like a home. To have that, it needed Sophie wanting to be there, and her constant restlessness was never going to allow for that. It was like her mom had lost something essential to her, and no amount of searching had turned it up. To numb the loss, she'd turned to Weston and his special way of handling things.

"You walk out, sugar, and there's no coming back." Her mother was in the circle of Weston's arms, and his expression of triumph wasn't lost on Victoria.

Weston was nothing but a leech, and her mother's bank accounts were what he wanted to suck dry. "I'm okay with that. Are you?"

Sophie shrugged Weston off and came forward so quickly, Victoria really thought she'd hit her. "After everything I've done for you? All the sacrifices I've made? You've always been so ungrateful."

"Don't rewrite history to keep yourself on the cross, Mom. You've lived your life the way you've wanted, and you've never denied yourself anything." Being the peacemaker was a mantle she was ready to shed, and she'd have to learn to live with whatever came of leaving. "I'm going, and if it makes you feel better, go ahead and blame me. Just think, now there'll be no more nagging about anything. You're free to fall off any stage you want."

Victoria turned to go but stopped when the phone rang. "Roddy residence," she answered robotically, unable to help herself.

"Sonny Liner's office for Sophie Roddy," a woman said. "He'd like to invite Ms. Roddy to his home for a meeting. Would she be available around five this afternoon?"

"Let me check." She put the caller on hold and relayed the message.

"See, what did I tell you?" Sophie said, laughing. "Tell him he can go fuck himself."

"Ms. Roddy isn't available this afternoon, but we'll be in touch." She hung up and walked out. Whatever came next was up to her mother. The scenic drive back to the city made her go slowly, and she finally stopped at an overlook on the Cumberland River.

The ripples that outlined the current made her think of her own life, and how she'd had as much chance of carving her own way as a leaf in the fast-moving water. All those afternoons with her grandfather teaching her how to plant a garden, or her grandmother and her homemade cobbler, were like a different lifetime.

"Time to start living and thinking for yourself." She spoke the words to the wind and tossed a rock into the river as a reminder that she didn't want to get sucked back into her mother's life.

There was enough money in the bank to give her time to decide her next move. Granted, she'd been her mother's manager, but she'd only been responsible for the tours and studio time. If she no longer worked for her mother, what would she do? Where could she go? The options and release left her breathless.

Her drive home helped relax the tension across her shoulders, and finding her best friend, Josette, waiting on the steps leading up to her apartment with a bag of takeout completely brightened her mood. Josette was a bartender at the Whiskey Bent Saloon, and they'd met when Victoria had sat in on the piano with the band one night.

"You've sounded bummed lately, so I'll trade you a beer for a Prince's hot chicken sandwich." Josette held up the bag and shook it.

"God, I love you. You're always guessing what I want most in life, and right now it's that sandwich and you." They climbed the stairs arm in arm, not in any hurry. "If I had champagne, we'd have that, but beer will have to do."

"Are we celebrating something?" Josette got plates and napkins, having been there often enough to know where everything was.

"I quit my job, and Sophie is headed for retirement. It'll be up to whoever to break it to her, but thankfully it won't be me." She laughed at Josette's stunned expression.

"Are you serious?"

"Don't lie and tell me you didn't see or hear about that fucking slow-motion breakdown she had last night. If you didn't, you're the only one in Nashville, since we got schooled on social media happenings by the asshole Banu sent." She took a sip of her beer before taking a huge bite out of her sandwich. "The bitch seemed to take some perverse pleasure in reading us the negative comments on the viral videos."

"I did see it, at the bar, actually." Josette took her own bite, but it seemed more like a way to stop talking than to actually satisfy her hunger.

"What?" She stared at Josette, and she could swear it made her chew slower. "Come on, tell me. It can't be any worse than last night."

She swallowed and shrugged. "The videos of Sophie showed up on the news last night all right, but they weren't shot by some yahoo with a phone. It appeared to be the Opry's feed, complete with close-ups."

"That's probably why Liner wants to meet with her." She put her sandwich down. Her appetite had disappeared at the news. "You know Sophie is a pain in the ass, but I love her. I can't help it."

"I know, sweetie, but from that close-up they got of her, she looked totally out of it. Maybe if this forces her to get her shit together, she'll at least be alive."

"It was horrific." Victoria could still see her mother falling off the stage to the floor below, and it made her stomach lurch. "And she acted like we were crazy for making a big deal out of this. She needs to get her shit together, and the first step is sending Weston packing, but she'd let me go first. Hell, she didn't exactly put up a fight when I told her I was going." Maybe she wasn't responsible for Sophie any longer, but she had to call and warn her before she shot her mouth off. The two labels she'd called for her mom that morning didn't want to have a conversation.

Josette reached for her hand and peered at her with a mixture of sympathy and pity. "If she was still a gold mine like Colt Kenny, believe me, her label would be on television swearing on their mama's head it was an allergic reaction to something, but Sophie's got to know Liner's not going to pull out all the stops for her. She's a legend, but a legend with waning sales."

"You think I don't know that?" She didn't want to get angry at Josette, but no one really had any idea of the extent of the problem. The drugs were killing her mother, and there was nothing slow about it. "Rehab doesn't work unless she buys in, and the great Sophie Roddy doesn't think there's a problem. The problem is everyone else."

"I totally get that. Now tell me how you're doing?"

"I'm nauseous from the roller coaster my mom's life is, but fate is conspiring against me to keep me from leaving." Leaving was the only option to keep sane, but a lifetime of guilt if her mother died wasn't worth the gamble. If something happened, and it *was* going to happen, and she wasn't there, it would be totally on her. No one would ever convince her otherwise, no matter how rational their argument. She was in this train wreck to the end.

Josette laughed and hugged her. "If that's your opening, then it's downhill from here. Keep repeating the words *tough love*, and let your mom find her way. If you don't, all you're going to do is make yourself sick."

They talked and finished lunch, enjoying their time to catch up. Josette left after getting her to swear they'd get together soon, and she promised to keep an eye out for anyone needing a piano player.

She took a nap with the television on HGTV, not wanting to see any coverage of what had happened to her mother. Being there in person had been bad enough. It was the incessant buzzing of her phone that finally woke her to the dark apartment. She'd slept way longer than she'd imagined, and the caller quit then started up again.

"Victoria?"

She squinted, trying to read the clock on the microwave. It was almost nine, which meant she'd be up all night after her four-hour nap. "Who is this?"

"It's Weston." He sounded out of breath and anxious, and neither was good. "It's Sophie. You'd better come."

"Where is she?" She scrubbed her face with her hand, hoping it would make her more alert. "Where is she, Weston?" She spoke slowly and with the kind of authority that would hopefully cut through whatever high he was on.

"She's on the bed and moaning, but I can't wake her up. You need to come."

"I'm on my way. You need to tell me what she took, and don't fucking lie." She grabbed her keys and wallet before taking the stairs so fast she thought she might trip and fall. "Put whatever it was on the nightstand."

"Okay, but we don't have prescriptions for none of this shit."

"That's never stopped either of you before." The call disconnected and she wondered if it was from the dead zone or if Weston was planning to run so none of this would come back on him. She dialed 911 and told them what she could, and to break in if that's what it took. There was no way she'd let her mom die. Not like this.

The ambulance was outside when she got there, and she ran up to the master bedroom, praying she wasn't too late. "Is she breathing?"

An EMT sitting on the bed holding a pill bottle nodded. "She is, but a few more minutes, and we'd have been too late. You know how many of these she took?"

He handed her the bottle, and her heart twisted at the fact it was empty. Her mother couldn't have been that stupid, but Weston had taken advantage of her ignorance, and there was no going back. "Where's the guy she was with? Did he let you in?" The need to sit was overwhelming at the sight of her mother's still body on the bed. Her worst fear had taken less than a day to come true, and she wanted to scream from the frustration of her own weakness, of her mother's stupidity, and with the whole damn situation.

The thought of this being the rest of her life made her close her eyes. It depressed her, but this wasn't the time to dwell. No matter what she wanted, it would always have to wait until she dealt with her mother's problems.

"There was no one here and the front door was wide open, so we came in. We're going to have to transport," the EMT said as that precise order came over his radio. "You can follow us."

She walked down with them, holding her mom's hand until they reached the stairs. Sophie was her only family, and if she died, none of what she left behind would matter. Victoria would be alone. Her hands shook on the steering wheel. Her mother had never looked so close to death before, and Victoria's emotions were a storm of chaos. Anger, frustration, despair, fear…they crashed into one another, melding and choking her.

It took the doctor an hour before he came out and told her Sophie was stable after they'd pumped her stomach and given her something to counteract the drugs in her system. "I hope she realizes how very close she was to this turning out differently. Your mother needs help, and she needs it now."

"I've tried, believe me, but she doesn't think there's a problem. Even when she nearly dies." The waiting area was packed, but she was utterly alone. Her grandparents were gone, and her father had run the minute Sophie told him she was pregnant. At least, that was Sophie's story when Victoria had been old enough to ask.

"Hopefully, between the two of us, we can convince her otherwise." He placed his hand on her shoulder and squeezed. "You can go on back if you want."

She followed him and took a deep breath before going in. "Hello, Mom."

"Do you want something?" Sophie asked in a voice so raspy Victoria barely understood her. "What are you doing here? I thought you were done. So, what?"

"You almost died, that's what. I could've lost you, and you don't seem to care." She hardly ever cried, but she couldn't help let the tears fall. "Wake up before it's too late."

"I swear, you're like a broken record. Where's Weston?" Sophie was acting like she was waking up from a nap and was ready to go out for drinks and dinner.

"He called me, then he took off. He's a prince of a guy." She sat and Sophie followed her with her eyes. "He was nice enough to leave the front door open for the EMTs."

"Why do you care?" Sophie slurred her words as if the high hadn't worn away yet.

"I'm here because I love you." She wiped at her face, trying to stop crying. Her mother probably thought those were empty words, but she felt the truth of them to her core. Love was the one thing she couldn't let go of, but it also bound her to see this out no matter the outcome. Eventually, she'd have to examine the truth of why she couldn't let go and look at the damage it was doing to her own soul. "But we need to talk about the future." That Sophie stared at her without a word encouraged her. "And we can have a good future if you listen for once."

"You don't understand. You don't understand anything."

"Then make me."

After a long silent moment filled only with the beeping of the machines around them, Sophie started talking. Victoria didn't think what she was saying made much sense, but all the insecurities and experiences she'd never shared with anyone were clearly what had driven her to numb her life with drugs and whiskey.

"Jesus." Victoria held her mom's hand as Sophie cried softly, looking like an old woman who'd lost everything, and nothing like the country superstar the world knew.

This was going to take so much more than rehab, but she wasn't giving up. "We'll get through this together, and I'll be right beside you, but you'll have to do the work." They were words she'd said before, but she couldn't deny the flicker of hope that this time, things would be different.

The original house built on Mason's property was a dilapidated mess when she'd purchased the land, but she'd made numerous trips home during the renovation of the old house, as well as the construction of the new house up the hill. She loved the house she'd constructed to her specifications, but she also spent a lot of time in the old place that was now a one-room guesthouse, though she used it more as a studio and office. It was nice for those days she didn't want to go into the city. And it wasn't all that far from her parents' place, which was a bonus.

Her job would always revolve around the business part of Banu, but she'd taken her father's advice to her soul. Sonny Liner wanted to find talent and introduce it to the world, but it always had to be about the music. You had to believe in music as well as the people.

She was reviewing contracts with Sophie Roddy's greatest hits playing in the background, and she had to stop every so often to listen to the true beauty of Sophie's voice as well as the depth of her lyrics. Sophie probably hadn't written the lyrics, but it had to be someone close to her. It wasn't a stranger, since Sophie had to put too much heart in the songs.

"You should listen to your own stuff sometime," she said to an empty room. Sophie Roddy had a gift, and it'd be a lasting one to her fans. The sad part was Mason truly believed Sophie had so much more to give.

Her cell ringing made her turn the music down and answer. "Something wrong?" She and her father had spent the day together, and Sonny wasn't a fan of the phone.

"You're such a pessimist."

She made one final note in the margin of the contract before leaving it for her assistant to deal with. "Sorry, were you in the mood for a sensitive chat?"

"Kid, you know everything about me, and you know how nuts I am about you, so that's a no on the sensitive chat."

"Then what's wrong?"

"I need you to come back. I want you to handle something for me, and while I promise I won't interfere, we need to talk about it before you start."

"Give me a few minutes and I'll be there."

She put her boots back on and walked up the hill in the dark to the main house and her truck, not wanting to keep him waiting and wondering what he had in mind. Her father had brought her back from California earlier than they'd planned, and she hadn't questioned it. Now she wondered if she should've. Maybe he was sick or something and had waited to talk about it.

Woody's car was there, and it made her want to turn toward home again. Anything that required PR on Saturday night wasn't going to be fun. "Did you guys want to keep up the party?" She found everyone in the kitchen and took the time to kiss her mom's cheek.

"Shit like this does make me want to drink, Buckaroo, but it ain't from no sense of fun," Sonny said with a long sigh. "Come on, let's get comfortable."

They headed to the big den, and she took the seat next to the sofa. "Something happen? I only left an hour ago."

"It's Sophie Roddy," Woody said.

"What about her?" Mason had called more than once and gotten no answer until the woman basically gave her the don't call us—we'll call you line. "If she's smart, she's at home coming to grips with her new reality."

"What reality is that?" Amelia asked appearing curious.

"She's a legend who fell off the stage at the Grand Ole Opry," she said with exaggerated slowness. "And she fell off that stage, of all places, because she was drunk, high, or both. Once the laughter dies down, the pity will kick in, and it'll be just as bad. Believe me, the first *oh, bless her heart* she gets will be it." What she was saying was true. People like Sophie were legends for a reason, but their downfall was often of their own making.

"You think she's done, then?" Amelia asked. Her father and Woody stayed quiet.

"Mom, you, Dad, and Mr. Woody know way more about these kinds of things than me, and have more experience with how to handle them, but I think, eventually, folks like Sophie become a bucket-list checkmark."

Sonny laughed at that, and Amelia slapped him in the stomach. "I'm not sure I understand."

"She's in the same league with Cash, Haggard, and Nelson, but unlike them, she stagnated. Her music has become secondary to her lifestyle of booze and drugs, and instead of staying relevant, she's become the type of artist people put on their bucket lists, so they can say they saw her before she killed herself." She could tell that wasn't what her mom wanted to hear, but it was the truth. "People are going to want to go to anything she's involved in, if only to see if she takes a flying leap off the stage."

"She's not worth fighting for, then?"

"If she gives a damn, then yes. If she wants to keep boozing, then no. Trying to help someone who doesn't want to change anything is like beating your head against the wall and not expecting to have a massive headache."

Amelia nodded and so did Sonny.

"She's in the hospital recovering from what sounds like another overdose, and it's going to take the media and the tabloids about a second to figure out that's what's happened."

Mason stared at Woody, not believing what he was saying. It was like Sophie wanted to fast-track her demise and not just her music career. "Already? Is she okay?"

"She could be," Sonny said. "That's for you to help her decide. Sophie's pissed at me and won't talk to Woody, so I'm leaving it up to you to work through this one. Is she worth saving? That's the answer I want from you, and I need it soon. But you'll need to sit with her, talk it out, before we can say for certain. I want you to look her in the eye before you make that choice."

"How soon?"

"Couple of days, Buckaroo, but I've got faith in you to get it right."

The way her father said it so matter-of-factly made her think he was kidding. "That's a joke, right?"

"Not a joke, and you're already wasting time," Amelia said.

The distinct vibe she was getting was that the right answer wasn't letting Sophie go or letting her sink. "*Okay*," she said, elongating the word. "Is she at the same hospital?"

"Yes, and if you don't mind, I'll tag along to see what our game plan's going to be," Woody said. "She won't talk to me, but at least I'll know what's going on."

"Our game plan is to be real honest, Mr. Woody. I doubt the public's going to buy she has the flu and overdid it on the NyQuil." She slapped her hands on the chair arms before standing and saying goodbye. The best course of action was to lock Sophie away somewhere until she was sober and had a plan to stay that way.

❖

"Hey, good-lookin'." Belle always answered the phone like she was working a sex line. "I missed you when you didn't come back."

"I didn't come at all, and hearing your voice is most certainly reminding me of that sad truth." Mason slowed for the gate to open, then punched the accelerator and headed toward Nashville.

"That's easily remedied, stud, and you know my address."

"I wish that's why I was calling, but I need you to put on your counseling hat and do me a favor." She stayed vigilant for deer on the road, but her brain was trying to work out a solution.

"You know I'm trying to retire from that, but it's you, so I'll do my best if what you need is advice. Please tell me it's not for you personally, though."

"My addictions are beautiful sexy women and good music, and I don't need rehab for either. I'm talking about Sophie Roddy."

There was a pause, but Belle didn't hang up right away, giving her hope that the first plan that had come to her would be feasible.

"I saw what happened, and I was really sorry for her. Her song 'Standing' is one of my favorites."

"You do it justice in your show."

"Stop buttering me up and tell me what you want."

"I'm on my way to Vanderbilt. She had to be rushed there, and someone alerted Sonny."

"That's sad, and a horrible invasion of her privacy."

She smiled at Belle's overprotective nature. "It was, and I agree on the sad part, but you know as well as I do that the vultures who live for this kind of crap will have a picture of her in the worst possible shape by tomorrow. People suck, but downfall stories sell."

"What do you want from me?"

She sketched the general contours of her plan. The best thing for Sophie would be isolation for however long it took, but Mason couldn't do it alone. "Don't decide right now, but Sonny gave me two days. I could use your help."

Belle laughed. "Are you doing this because you want to make points with your boss, or is it something else?"

"The first girl I kissed is a moment I'll never forget," she said, remembering the hot summer day on her daddy's ranch. "She had on denim shorts, a tank top, and strawberry lip gloss. We were by the river with a picnic and the song on the radio was 'Only You.'"

"Sounds memorable," Belle said softly.

"I think about that moment every time that song comes on the radio, and I think there're plenty more people out there who are waiting to make the same memories. And plenty who have memories like mine." She parked by the emergency room. "The company will be mine one day, but I don't deserve it if I don't even try."

"You're a hard one to say no to, stud, and I'll take care of what you want. I'll need about an hour, and a doctor's assurance it's okay for her to leave. Give whoever is in charge of her care my cell number, and I'll take over."

"Start thinking of a way for me to repay you."

Belle laughed longer this time. "Oh, I have a few things in mind, but remember, I'm in charge. Make sure her people know to stay away until we're done. If they don't, this won't work. And tell Sonny it took God more than two days to create the world. At least, that's what my pastor was always trying to tell me."

"I'll do my best."

"You always do."

The drive home gave her time to think of the best approach to deal with the first problem she'd encounter, and that wasn't Sophie. It was Sophie's angry manager. The woman had defended her client even though she didn't seem to realize the danger of protecting Sophie from the consequences of her actions, but there was something about her that made Mason smile.

She loved women, all women, but some had a way of grabbing her attention by virtue of the way they walked through the world. Sophie's manager was fierce, and her anger really set off her beauty, pinging Mason's *hey, look at me* response, making her attractive in ways that had nothing to do with beauty.

"Forget it, Buckaroo," she said to herself. "If she hated me before, it's only going to get worse in about twenty minutes."

But what the hell was life about if not for impossible challenges?

CHAPTER FOUR

Sophie fell asleep after her talk with Victoria, and Victoria was happy for the few minutes of quiet. She needed to think about everything her mom had shared with her and all she'd learned about what made Sophie tick. Of course, it could all be a con to get out of the hospital and back to Weston, and Victoria's cynicism made her gravitate to that possibility rather than to the possible sincerity of her mother's words.

"I wonder where that little asshole is," she whispered as she gazed at her mother. She thought of all those years on the road and the numerous towns and countries they'd visited. It wasn't the life she'd have chosen for herself, but it hadn't been without great adventures. All of that seemed like it fell away from Sophie's mind the day Weston came along with his bag of surprises.

She made a note to freeze all her mother's accounts to prevent any withdrawals if Weston wanted to hit the road in style. The idea of moving on to live her own life had to be buried for now—her mother needed her. Bryce walked in before she could make many more notes of things that needed taking care of, and she felt centered when he hugged her.

"What happened?" Bryce asked, taking his hat off and holding it in front of him like a shield when he stepped next to the bed to look down at Sophie.

"That asshole Weston called me," she said softly, telling him the whole story. "She's never been this bad, and I don't know if she can go through it again. She almost died." She pressed her hands to her mouth to prevent the sob from coming out. "Damn, it's like she forgot she was here last night."

Bryce nodded, but a knock on the door stopped him from saying anything as he went and opened it. It was the Banu exec from last night.

"Hey. Can I talk to you or whoever is in charge of Ms. Roddy's care?"

"What are you, a fucking asshole with no heart?" Victoria's tears dried up, and she slammed her hands to Mason's chest hard enough to make her take a step back. "She was right. Sonny Liner *is* an asshole if you're here to either lecture her or let her go. Would you like to spit on her too?"

"Honey, wait," Bryce said, holding her back from hitting Mason again. "I'm the one who called Sonny. You can't do this alone."

"Why?" she asked, not understanding Bryce's motive. This was a betrayal and nothing less. "Why would you do this to her?"

"Why not hear me out before you have me shot and fed to the hogs." The remark could've been condescending, but Mason's handsome face held no trace of malice or ridicule.

"Go on, honey, and I'll stay with her in case she wakes up. She won't be alone," Bryce said.

"This won't take long."

She followed Mason down to the elevator and to the cafeteria in tense silence, where they both got coffee. Her time as her mom's manager hadn't given her the opportunity to meet the infamous Sonny Liner, though she obviously knew of him, but his henchman, or henchwoman, was incredibly attractive. The career killer he'd sent looked like a softer version of the Marlboro Man with her white shirt, jeans, cowboy boots, and gorgeous tanned face. The tan really set off the black hair and sky-blue eyes.

"Maybe we should start with introductions that go beyond I work for Sonny and you work for Sophie." Mason smiled and the dimples completed the whole perfect package. "I'm Mason Liner, and I work for Banu."

"Any relation to Sonny?"

"Sonny's my father, but I don't get any slack for it. If anything, I'm expected to do double the work."

"Victoria Roddy." She ignored the offered hand, not feeling especially social, not that she ever did. Mason lowered it and took a sip of her coffee instead.

"Any relation to Sophie?"

"She's my mother, and you need to understand she's more than a client. I'm not going to let you destroy her. What are you even doing here?" She combed her hair back and kept her hands on her head. "Sophie's not that much of an embarrassment, is she?" It was a stupid question, and she knew it. A drunk star falling off a stage wasn't something any label wanted.

"Miss Roddy," Mason said in that same even manner she'd used in their brief encounters. She was controlled but she also sounded warm. "These days an addiction problem isn't the end of the road the way it perhaps once was, and my being here is to offer my help. The last thing I want is to be the cause of Sophie's downfall."

"What can you possibly do to help her?" This was taking way too long, and she needed to get back.

"Sonny put me in charge of how we move forward."

She slapped the tabletop with her hands and stifled the urge to scream. "And the easiest thing is to drop her, I'm guessing."

"How about you listen for a change, instead of attacking?" Mason lost her smile and, with it, the dimples. "I'm not your enemy, and neither is my father."

"Then what? What's your brilliant plan that you think I haven't tried yet?"

"Your mom is one of the greatest talents to ever grace the stage, and I don't want to see that end or to see her gift pissed away by booze and pills." Mason spoke softly and waved over someone Victoria actually recognized. "All done, Mr. Woody?"

"The hospital administrator's been advised of the severe consequences of violating Ms. Roddy's privacy by anyone looking to make a quick buck." Woody smiled at her, and she couldn't help but reciprocate. He'd always been really nice to work with. "Also, Ms. Lenox is here and waiting for permission to speak to the doctor."

"What are you talking about, and who's Miss Lenox?" It was almost like the ground was shifting and she was having trouble getting her footing.

"She's a trained detox and addiction therapist with a unique practice. My hope, only if you agree, is to have her work with your mother privately, along with her team."

"My mother will never agree to that." That was the simple truth, and not even the fear of losing everything was going to change her mom's mind.

"She needs to tell me what she wants her future to be, but only after the drugs and everything else are out of her system for at least a couple of weeks."

Mason was talking but had no clue what the hell she was saying. Sophie was going to tear her to shreds, and that might be the only entertaining part of this whole fiasco.

"It'll probably take at least a month for her to get to that point," Mason continued.

"Unless you lock her up somewhere, she's never going to agree to that. You have to have a clue before you start spouting off about her telling you anything." Victoria finally laughed at the absurdity of all this. "Are you forgetting, we met last night?"

"I haven't forgotten anything. Did you forget what I said to you?"

Saying exactly what was on her mind probably wasn't a smart move, but Victoria wasn't as career minded as Sophie and every other wannabe who probably creamed their pants for Mason Liner and her goddamn dimples, but what the hell. "When someone is as big an asshole as you are, Ms. Liner, it's hard to forget."

"If brutal honesty gets you in this big a twist, you're really going to hate the next part," Mason said, but the smile and the dimples were back. "And I have to compliment you on your insults. You've got a real talent in that department."

"What's your brilliant plan?"

"I want to lock your mother up in order to sober her up. Take her somewhere isolated, away from the press and other people," Mason said, completely serious.

At least she thought Mason was being serious. "You're kidding, aren't you?"

"No, and I need your help."

The day had gone from truly crazy to bizarre. "She can barely stand me now," she said, thinking how sad that was. "I can just about imagine what will happen if I help you do that."

"Which would you prefer? A dead Sophie or an angry Sophie? There's no fixing one of those if that's the road you take."

"Are you going to be this blunt the whole time? A few weeks of you, and I might need therapy myself." There was no question that her mom was in serious trouble, but she didn't know if this was the right choice.

"I realize you think I'm a total asshole—biggest asshole ever, I believe you said—but I'm on your side when it comes to this. Your mother's important, and it has nothing to do with money or her contract with our label." Mason's face seemed to soften. "She's worth saving, even if she never sings another thing for Banu."

"Thank you for saying that." For a moment, all the fight went out of her.

Mason nodded and sighed. "I'm not trying to bribe you with sweet words. I'm only trying to help you save your mom."

"Where are you taking her?"

"The best place in the world when you have to go through hell."

Victoria thought about this proposition in a different light. If Mason Liner could free Sophie from her addiction, it would also unshackle her to live her life free of the guilt she felt when it came to her mother and all her problems. And Bryce was right. She'd tried to do it alone, and they'd ended up here. She needed help. "Where exactly is that?"

"Heaven."

❖

"We need to wait for the toxicology report to see what we're facing here, but the doctor can at least confirm they got some oxycodone out of her stomach. We won't know if she ingested anything else until those reports come in," Belle said when Mason introduced her to Victoria. "The only reason she's still alive is that she swallowed the pills whole and didn't crush them."

"You think it's more than that? An opioid addiction will be hard enough, but if she's mixing it with other recreational drugs, it'll take more work to get her clean." Mason had no clue about any of this. She'd dabbled a little in alcohol and women, but never enough to lose control of her life. Addiction had been the subject of more than one lecture from both her parents because of who she was and what she did for a living. That power over people's futures made it easy to let go of the reins.

"There's plenty we need to do to get to the root of Ms. Roddy's problems," Belle said, "but the one certainty we have is that she's in trouble. I think we can all agree on that and go from there." Belle reached out and covered Victoria's clenched hands with hers. "She's lost perspective, and that kind of thing leads you to swallow pills that could kill you because you either don't know any better or you simply don't care."

"Which do you think it is?" Victoria asked.

"I have no idea, and it's not my job to guess."

"What exactly will your job be?" Victoria crossed her arms and glared at Belle.

Belle leaned away from Victoria and stared at Mason. Her expression was one Mason had never seen, and she couldn't guess what it meant.

"Problem?" Mason finally said after a long, uncomfortable silence.

"She's either an ally in this, or it won't work, and if it's not going to work, we're all wasting our time."

One of the things she liked about Belle was her straightforwardness, but from her experience with Victoria, straight-shooting about her mother wasn't something she was a fan of. Not in the slightest way.

"If I'm going to be wasting my time," Belle said, "I'd rather do it on something else that'll be a hell of a lot more pleasurable than this."

"What do you want from me?" Victoria said, louder than was polite. "You don't know anything about me or my mother." She stood and left the room, letting the door bang behind her.

"Are you sure about this?" Belle asked.

Mason glanced at the door and shook her head. "Somehow I think my answer should be no, but it's not like I have a choice."

"We all have choices, Mason. I asked already, but are you really doing this for Sophie, or is it something else?"

"What does that mean, and why do I get the feeling you're psychoanalyzing me?" She narrowed her eyes, suspicious of Belle's widening smile.

"We've already discussed *your* addictions."

"What's your point, Dr. Feel Good?"

"That's a really pretty girl," Belle said, as if it explained everything.

"And?"

"Nothing, I'm only making an observation. If your commitment to this is only to the young Miss Roddy, then your plan won't work even if your heart is in the right place."

"Unless you're blind, the young Miss Roddy isn't a fan of mine, and my commitment is to getting Sophie back to a place where she can be comfortable in her own skin. I've got some experience in that area." She'd been an idiot to think a no-strings relationship wouldn't come with, well, strings. Jealous women were gifts from Satan. "All I need to know is if you can do the job."

"I didn't tell you that for the reasons you think, stud." Belle moved until she was behind her and placed her hands on her shoulders. Mason smiled when Belle kissed the top of her head before resting her chin on it. "Victoria Roddy comes with her own set of complicated problems, and she and Sophie feed off each other. In a healthy relationship that's a good thing, but this thing between them only further entrenches their problems. When the solution you pick is drugs and booze, it's a vicious cycle."

"What's Victoria addicted to?" The feel of Belle pressed to her was something she was trying to commit to memory. Once they started down this path, it'd probably be the end of their intimate relationship. That didn't rise to the level of making her sad, but she was really disappointed. Belle wasn't simply a great bedmate, but an interesting woman. They could still enjoy a great friendship, but the sex would be hard to forget.

"If I had to guess? Anger, and she's got an infinite supply of it."

"Hmm." Victoria Roddy did seem like a woman wound a little too tight. The day she snapped she'd probably take out whoever was within a hundred feet of her. "What's she so mad at?"

"The root of a lot of people's problems begins and ends with the woman who gave them life. Not everyone is as lucky as you, Mason. Amelia is a gift God gave you because she knew how to handle the blessing of a child. That obviously can't be said of Sophie Roddy."

Mason thought for a moment, lulled by the way Belle massaged her shoulders. "It's a lot to ask, Belle, but will you help them both?"

"Only because it's you who's asking, and only if you allow me to do my job." Belle held her tighter before letting go completely.

"You're in charge here as much as you are at Skull's, Madame Lenox."

"Good. Your assignment is the young Miss Roddy. Sophie won't have a choice for a while, but her daughter needs to come to me for help of her own free will. The only way to get her to do that is if someone takes her by the hand and leads her."

Mason laughed without humor. "I take her by the hand, and I'll be in a cast for six weeks when she breaks my arm."

"Don't forget who you are, stud, and I'm not talking about your last name. Amelia raised you to be a compassionate soul, and that's what Victoria needs."

Nothing like throwing your mama's teachings at you to get you to behave. "I'll try my best."

"That's good enough for me, and we both need to get to it." Belle kissed her before leaving, and it gave her a few moments to think about what came next. Two days wasn't enough time to give her father a complete update, but that's what she had.

"Suck it up, Liner, and get to it."

It took her an hour to find Victoria, who made a sad picture sitting outside on a bench, alone in the dark. The attractive strawberry-blonde resembled her mother somewhat but not completely, which made Mason wonder who Victoria's father was. The real question was where was he, and didn't he know his kid was in trouble?

"Mind if I join you?"

Victoria didn't turn around, but she did shake her head. "Why are you really doing this?"

The question smelled of distrust and accusation, but she thought of what Belle had said. "How about we make a deal that'll last exactly the time it'll take for us to get through two questions." She held her hand out and waited.

"Depends on the two questions, I guess." Victoria took her hand and held it.

"I'll answer your question about why I'm really doing this," she said, holding Victoria's hand tighter before letting go. There was no way for her to know for sure, but she had a feeling Victoria didn't care for manhandling, no matter the circumstance. "And you answer my question."

"Like I said, it depends on what it is."

"What does your mother mean to you?"

Victoria laughed and combed her hair back, making Mason notice the slight curl in it. "Can we start with something easier?"

She smiled, but not too widely. She didn't want Victoria to think she was taking this lightly. "Nothing says you have to answer right this second, but that's my question. The answer to your question is simple. My father gave me discretion on what to do for your mom. The easiest solution would be to mind my own business and do nothing, but I listened to her music tonight, and it touched something in my soul."

"Get to know her, and she'll kill that as fast as if she'd used a gun." Victoria spoke softly, but the hurt in her voice resonated as much as Sophie's music had. "I'm sorry. That was a horrible thing to say."

"We all carry our pain, Miss Roddy, and it's what we use to shield us from any further wounds. Don't be sorry. Just let me help your mom get back to life without all this."

Victoria nodded, her shoulders hunched like she was protecting herself. "Go ahead and try, but let me warn you about being disappointed. She's my mother and I love her, but her greatest talents are her voice and disappointing people who love her."

"I'll do that, if you promise to stop blaming yourself for all of this."

Victoria finally really looked at her. "Why do you think I do?" Those pretty green eyes filled with tears but they didn't fall.

"Because you're sitting out here crying in the dark. Those tears mean you love her more than anyone in the world, but you don't know how to help her." She took a chance and wiped away the few tears that had finally fallen. "Together we can give it our best, and the rest will be up to Sophie."

"Thank you, but I can't let her go alone. Not to a place I don't know."

"That'll be up to Belle Lenox." If they'd had a moment, the expression Victoria was giving her meant it was over.

"That'll be up to *me*. If you want me to go along with all this, don't forget it."

"I very much doubt you'll let me forget that or anything else." Mason smiled and was relieved when Victoria gave her a small, quick smile in return. She was pretty, but the shadows in her eyes warned of a woman who didn't trust easily, if at all. That wasn't someone she needed to waste time getting to know, but her allure made Mason want to take on the challenge. Okay, maybe *allure* was a little over the top, but Victoria Roddy wasn't a woman easily ignored, and she had Mason's attention whether she liked it or not.

"Shall we?"

Victoria nodded and Mason tried to convince her head that the words didn't go well beyond just the obvious. The problem was, her heart knew better.

Chapter Five

"Get Victoria in here." Sophie pulled the sheet up to her neck as if it would protect her from Belle and the two guys she'd brought with her. "Get out."

Belle was familiar with all the steps Sophie would go through before the recognition of what was happening finally sank in and she accepted nothing was going to change the course they were on. The next month was going to be hard, but not as tough as the next week or so as Sophie's body went through withdrawal.

"Victoria's busy right now, but she signed off on you coming with us. There's no choice in that, and you'll make this easier on yourself if you simply agree." Belle didn't make any moves toward the bed, wanting to avoid a violent outburst.

"Give me my fucking phone." Sophie's screaming brought the doctor to the room. "Get Weston on the phone and tell him I'm ready to go home."

"I'd rather not do restraints, but if that's what it takes, I will. All we need is a clean exit out of here." Belle spoke to the doctor but kept her eyes on Sophie, already missing the life she was working toward.

She'd done this for years, staging interventions and private rehab for the privileged few who achieved the kind of fame Sophie had, but who then handled the stress of it with chemical enhancements to cope with their chaotic lives. Getting them back to sobriety had burned her out, and she'd escaped to Skull's and her girls. When she was onstage, her only responsibility was to her audience, and she didn't have to peel their layers away to figure out what their problems were or how to help them. She lost herself in performance and music. Yet here she was.

"A little sedative will do the trick," the doctor said, "and the laundry area is empty at this time of night, so that's your best bet out." The doctor waited for the guys to hold Sophie down before injecting the small dose that would make the move more manageable.

"I'll have your ass for this," Sophie said, but she was already speaking softly. When her eyes closed, the doctor escorted them out the way he'd mentioned.

There was an ambulance waiting for them, and the EMTs were quick in transferring Sophie from the hospital bed to the gurney. Belle closed her eyes when she was seat-belted into the back, knowing it was at least thirty minutes to Mason's, and she was curious about what she'd find. Her relationship with Mason was about fun and mutual satisfaction, but she wasn't familiar with the rest of Mason's life.

Until this moment, she hadn't given it much thought. What Mason did when they weren't together wasn't something she dwelled on because she knew the parameters of their relationship or, more accurately, their arrangement. Mutual satisfaction was at the center of who they were together, so this was weird. Once she exposed all of Mason's secrets, perhaps it'd make it harder to stick to what they knew, but it was too late to turn back now.

She opened her eyes when they stopped, and she heard the driver talking to someone. Belle glanced outside and saw they were following a utility type vehicle, and it took a few minutes before a beautiful house came into view. The rest of her team were waiting at the front, but there was no sign of Mason.

"Hey, Belle," Cassandra Unger said as Belle stepped down from the ambulance. "We've set up in one of the guestrooms, and there are another three right by it. I went ahead and set the schedule, but I thought we'd take the first week."

Belle had worked with Cassandra from the time they'd graduated together and Cassandra now owned the practice they'd built together. Their specialty had been private, individualized rehab for the rich and famous, away from any type of formal treatment facility, which minimized the chances of anyone trying to exploit their recovery. She and Cassandra still saw each other, though, since Belle gave her dance lessons, but it had been a while since they'd shared anything like this.

"If anything, we get to enjoy how the other half lives while we work." She heard snorting coming from the other side of the white fence close to the drive and went to investigate. Belle smiled when she saw the large black horse staring at them as if they were bothering him and his home.

"That's Zeus, and he runs the place," Mason said as she materialized out of the dark. "He should be in his stall, but we give him the run of the farm." Mason raised her hand, and the stallion pressed his nose to it. "He probably came out to see who's disturbing his domain."

"You have a beautiful home, Mason." She scratched Zeus between the ears, and he whinnied loudly. "Maybe it's time to share it with someone." It slipped out, and she hoped Mason didn't take it as some kind of hint.

"My big boy is a major pleasure hound, so stop before you're out here all night, and I share this place with Jeb." The horse trotted off when Mason kissed his nose and gave him a gentle shove.

"Who's Jeb?"

"That'd be me, ma'am." The tall African American man who'd joined them had a handsome face and a head topped with gorgeous snow-white hair. Belle didn't know him, but she had a sense she'd like him. "I'm Jedidiah Abbott, and I'm Blue Heaven's manager. We got everything you requested, but if we're missing anything, give me a call." He handed over a card with his name and information.

"Thank you, and I'm Belle Lenox. I appreciate the help."

Jeb took his hat off to shake her hand, and smiled when they touched. "Mason did a good job describing you, ma'am, so I know who you are. I'm pleased to meet you."

"I'll have to hear what she said later. Right now I should go see our patient." Belle placed her hand on Mason's forearm and gazed up at her. "Hopefully you're not a light sleeper. Once that sedative wears off in about an hour, Sophie is going to raise forty kinds of hell."

"Do whatever you need to. I'll be okay. I'm going to wait for the delightful Miss Roddy and get her settled before I decide on my sleeping arrangements."

Belle kissed Mason's cheek before walking toward the house. She certainly seemed to know her audience, since both Mason and Jeb stayed quiet until she disappeared into the house. The extra roll of her hips had to be the cause. "It's good to know my glamour works without the pasties on," she said softly, glancing back once before going through the front door.

❖

"You sick in the head or something?" Jeb asked with his hands shoved deep in his pockets.

"Some people certainly think so, but why do you ask?" Mason shook her head, remembering the last time she was alone with Belle and how sexy she was in that bustier, but it wasn't the time to dwell on that. She wanted to get some sleep, but tired didn't seem to trump horny, and she was certainly both.

"I'd be begging that woman to take my ring. She's beautiful."

"She's also smart, kind, and sexy as hell, but she doesn't want my ring, or anyone else's. Belle's a strong woman who knows what she wants, and more importantly, what she doesn't. I'm not it." The quiet was broken by another vehicle approaching.

"You're an idiot." Jeb slapped her on the back and laughed when Victoria got out of her car. "Or maybe you're after something else."

She rolled her eyes at the absurd thought. "Do I look suicidal to you?"

"That little bit scares you?" Jeb laughed as he started toward Victoria.

"Scared is a strong word, but after a few minutes you do feel like running." She lifted her hand in greeting, and Victoria's stony expression never changed. "Can I carry your bags upstairs, or are you going to come and go?"

"Where is she? I want to see her." Victoria spoke as if she didn't hear a word Mason had just said.

"Right this way." Mason glanced at Jeb before walking off. "Meet you down by the west barn at seven. Thanks for tonight."

"The girls did all the work, and you were right. Sometimes running keeps you sane."

She laughed and then guided Victoria upstairs, but they heard the screaming way before that. Whatever was wrong with Sophie, be it withdrawal or cravings, it was making her nuts. The behavior was totally out of control and irrational, but the addict could no more help that than breathing. Mason had only seen it once before, and she prayed, at least for Victoria's and Sophie's sakes, this time the result would be different.

"Maybe you should wait a few days." She wanted to spare Victoria some of the pain this was going to inflict. Not that she hadn't endured enough already, but the coming days were going to be a fresh kind of shit storm.

"Maybe you should worry about yourself, and I'll worry about me."

Then again, maybe Victoria was a masochist without any of the fun parts. "Go right ahead." She pointed to the door before going back down to the kitchen for a drink. The screaming went into overdrive as she got to the bottom step, and from the sound of it, Belle was louder than Sophie. Then a door slammed, and it was back to the Sophie Roddy show.

Both Victoria and Belle had no problem finding the kitchen. Mason poured herself a glass of orange juice, and both of them stared at her as if she was supposed to pick sides. She'd rather stick a fork in her eye.

"Mason, it's time for you to explain to Ms. Roddy how this works. If she's not intelligent enough to follow the rules, I'm out of here." Belle didn't give her a chance to refuse. She walked out and left a pissed Victoria behind.

"Juice"—she held up the pitcher—"and don't." Victoria was going right back upstairs from the set of her shoulders, and Belle seldom if ever kidded about walking away. "Don't go back up there. Belle's methods may not be orthodox, but they work, and you need to fall in. If Belle quits, we're right back to what got us here, and there's no guarantee Sophie survives the next round. What about that do you not understand?"

"She's all I have left. What about that do *you* not understand?" Victoria shot the words at her like daggers. "I'm not leaving her to face this alone. She needs me."

"How about we compromise? There's another option that'll keep you close by but not in the house. Will that make it easier for you?"

"I'm not leaving," Victoria said each word slowly and angrily.

"I know you don't want to hear this, especially from me, but what she needs is to face this alone. She got to this point alone, and that's the only way for her to get out of it. Belle will navigate her through it, but the last thing your mom needs is a crutch. You keep giving her a pass, and she'll keep taking it right to the grave."

"What the hell do you know? You've probably lived a charmed life, with your dimples and big house. What do you know about this kind of pain?"

Victoria apparently had a real talent for finding the vulnerable fleshy parts and driving a knife right through them with no hesitation.

Mason's anger simmered red hot right under the surface, but she remembered her promise to Belle. "I know plenty." She moved slowly, and Victoria seemed wary, but Mason put her arms around her and held her. Victoria was stiff at first, but it didn't take long for the tears to come and totally overwhelm her.

"Oh, Christ." Victoria clung to her in a desperate kind of way.

"I know plenty, and you aren't alone." It was the first of a string of hard days, but compassion might make it easier. "You're not alone."

The rest of the night was spent listening to Sophie scream, then moan when it sounded like she was too tired to raise her voice any longer. Victoria figured whoever was in the house wasn't sleeping unless someone had knocked them unconscious. She'd spent hours lying in the big bed in the room Mason had led her to, but aside from her mother, the house was quiet. Hours before she'd heard the door to the room next to hers close, and she guessed she and Mason were neighbors.

She got up when she heard that door open again as dawn started coloring the sky and saw Mason sneaking by in bare feet. Mason stopped when she cleared her throat. "Good morning—not that there's anything remotely good about it after last night, but I'm sorry for all of this." Victoria was stubborn, but she wasn't stupid. No one put themselves through something like this if they weren't trying to do something good.

"I knew what I was signing up for. Don't apologize." Mason put her boots down and walked back to her. "How about taking a break somewhere quieter?"

"Is it in another state?"

Mason smiled, making those damn dimples reappear. "Was that a joke, Miss Roddy?"

"Blame it on the noise, stress, and exhaustion. Don't get used to it." She kept smiling as she said it and genuinely enjoyed Mason's laugh.

"Put on some shoes, and I'll give you a break."

"Give me a minute." She changed out of her wrinkled shirt and threw on a T-shirt with a sweatshirt over it. "I know I've been a royal bitch since we met, but thank you for doing this. You're probably sick of the Roddy family already, but we appreciate you."

"You don't have to thank me, Miss Roddy. I'm just happy you agreed because you and your mom deserve a chance. It's no one's fault we're here, and you'll see—it'll get better." The outside was cool, and the early light painted the expanse of land in soft pinks.

The vista was beautiful, and she stopped to appreciate the area and the horses that were grazing on the other side of the white fence that seemed to go on for miles. That Mason had money was plain from the house and where it sat, but she wasn't dressed like the lord of the manor—this morning, Mason wore an old denim jacket and scruffy boots. The sweat stained hat completed the look, and Victoria liked this version of Mason better than the executive who'd shown up to deal with Sophie.

"Will my break include some kind of manual labor?" She followed Mason down the hill, feeling her toes getting wet as the dew on the grass soaked into her shoes. It didn't take long for a house closer to the water to come into view, and it appeared original to the property even though it was in pristine condition.

"You're safe from hard work since I'll take care of that, but you do have an assignment for today." Mason walked up the few steps and unlocked the door. "This house was here when I purchased the land, but the insurance folks wanted me to build farther up the hill because of seasonal flooding."

"They should've seen this place before deciding that. It's beautiful, and more importantly, it's still here. That should count for something." The space was open with a bank of windows that overlooked the river.

"The water comes close every year, but thankfully it's never flooded. My mom did a great job of redoing it to fit what I wanted, and it reminds me every day that you shouldn't toss things out because they're no longer a safe bet." Mason opened the door to the back porch and went out. "Everyone told me to tear this place down since it was in pitiful shape, but I love it more than the big house. It was worth saving."

"You're good at convincing me that things will be okay." She wrapped her arms around herself, and the move made Mason lead her back inside to what appeared to be a home office.

"Nah, no one has ever accused me of being that slick. I'm just talking about the house." There were some awards on the bookshelves, but mostly they held books, lots of them, and their spines were cracked, indicating they'd been read. "I find that couch is really good for naps, or for enjoying a good book. Stretch out and close your eyes for however long you want. You're safe from the flood," Mason said, pointing outside where the river level actually appeared low. "There's stuff in the fridge if you get thirsty, and if you need anything, head up the hill to the house. The staff will get you whatever you need."

"Where are you going?"

"Jeb and I are riding fences this morning. Some sections need repair, and he keeps telling me they won't fix themselves." Mason held her hat against her body, resembling a polite cowboy from a long ago past.

"You're full of comments that could be taken another way," she said, sitting on the sofa. "And thanks for this. The quiet is almost deafening. Does that make sense?"

"Perfectly. Take that nap, and I'll be by later, or I can stay away if you need some time to yourself." Mason waved and her footsteps sounded loud on the wood floor of the porch.

She walked to the front to see what direction Mason headed off in, and she stayed by the window until the trees seemed to swallow Mason up. Whatever this place was, it appeared lived in from the piles of paperwork on the desk to the music sheets scattered on the piano in the main space. There were also some guitars on stands with chairs and music stands close to them.

"Recording studio?" she said out loud. That couldn't be it either, since there was still ambient noise even if the place was peaceful.

There was also a great stereo system with a turntable that was state-of-the-art, giving Mason points for knowing the best way to enjoy music. Mason had left a record on the turntable, which made her curious—that wasn't the norm for true LP connoisseurs. That it was a compilation of her mother's greatest hits surprised her, but then it didn't. What Mason was doing for her mother wasn't simply to keep someone under contract. You didn't bring that kind of hassle in without mostly pure motives.

"What's your story?"

She snooped a little more, but nothing too invasive. The desk and its scattering of papers were off-limits, but she stared at it, then followed Mason's advice. She stretched out on the couch and used the soft blanket across the back. It smelled of citrus with a hint of sandalwood, and it reminded her of Mason. She hadn't thought she'd noticed much about her in their short meetings, but obviously her subconscious had.

Her nap lasted three hours, and to chase away the grogginess she moved to the other room and sat at the piano. It was a Steinway and the nicest instrument she'd ever laid her hands on. "Of course it is. Nothing but the best, Ms. Liner."

She closed her eyes and started playing one of the first classical pieces she'd learned, and the music transported her to a better place. That was one of the things she loved about playing, and something she wished her mother would remember. This was better than any drug or alcohol, and it totally filled her soul. There, in the peace and quiet, she felt more like herself than she had in far, far too long.

CHAPTER SIX

Mason put her jacket back on knowing the breeze off the water would cool the sweat she'd built up. It was a nice morning of work where the only things she had to concentrate on were not bashing her fingers with a hammer and talking about fishing with Jeb. She would've kept working, but Jeb gave her a gentle hint about going to check on her guest and offering lunch.

The walk to the river house didn't take long, and she stopped to watch Victoria at the piano. She couldn't hear what she was playing, but she seemed to put all of herself into the music, and the unguarded expression on her face made Mason really look at her. Victoria Roddy was a beautiful woman who was mad at the world, and she wasn't about to let anyone within ten feet of her. It didn't detract from her beauty, but Mason wondered about the passion beneath the anger.

"You don't let anyone in, so no one can hurt you. I think that's your philosophy." She stayed in the trees, not wanting to embarrass her. Or piss her off, which seemed to be a talent of hers.

She waited until Victoria's hands came up almost reverently before doubling back to make it look like she was just coming up from the barn. Victoria had stepped onto the back porch and lifted her hand in a hesitant wave, and it made Mason walk faster. Victoria didn't appear as haunted as she had earlier, which hopefully meant she'd gotten some sleep.

"The couch work its magic?"

Victoria smiled and nodded. "It did, and I appreciate you lending it to me. Is this like your office?"

Mason leaned against the split wood railing, which felt rough even through Mason's jeans—she was loath to change it, since it was original to the house. Victoria had mirrored her pose for only a second before taking a seat on one of the deck chairs.

"I use it as a satellite when I don't feel like putting on grown-up clothes, and I also have people come out to...work through their stuff, when it's necessary."

Victoria cocked her head to the left as if trying to figure out what she meant. "You sound as qualified as your pal up there helping my mother."

"I'm no therapist, believe me. Not in that sense, anyway." She remembered her manners and took her hat off, combing her hair back. "My therapy sessions are more centered around helping artists find what works and taking away what doesn't."

"You're a producer, aren't you?"

Mason wasn't a fan of Twenty Questions, but Victoria was talking and she wanted to keep it up. "That's one of the hats I wear for my father, but not necessarily the one I enjoy the most."

"I'm guessing babysitter isn't it, either." Victoria gave her that slight, small smile that lightened her eyes.

She laughed at that and shook her head. "The music business is changing all the time because people's attention span is as short as the life of a mayfly."

Victoria put her hand up again. "I'm sorry, what's a mayfly?"

"They're insects that only live for a few hours. There's about three thousand species of them around the world, and I think they exist to remind me that we shouldn't waste time on the things that aren't important. Life should be enjoyed and spent trying to help people achieve all they can."

"You're an interesting person." Victoria wrapped her hands around her knees and gazed up at her with an open expression.

"I'm a person with a lot of trivia in my head, but I try to use it in everyday life." She bounced her hat on her leg and moved to sit on the railing.

"What do mayflies have to do with the music industry?"

"The newcomers, as well as some artists who've been around for a while, have to find ways to stay on the charts and on people's minds, but not go crazy trying to do it. It's what makes the Sophie Roddys of the world rare commodities." She was probably boring Victoria to tears but her eyes hadn't glazed over yet. "My job is to make sure our artists stay in the public eye while staying true to themselves and happy."

"I'm not sure I understand," Victoria said, combing her hair back behind her ears and maintaining eye contact.

"Very few people have the ability to change genres of music without paying the price in either public ridicule or by going down in flames. Think of Hank Williams or Patsy Cline releasing a rap album. That's a drastic example, but some people chase the next chart topper at the expense of who they are. Once you lose your identity to chase fame or money, you're already lost."

Victoria nodded and smiled again. "And the new artists out there waiting to be discovered?"

"Those are my favorite people to work with sometimes because it's my job to help them find themselves and chart that course. To figure out who they are as artists." Her stomach chose that moment to rumble. "How about we continue this over lunch? It's what I came to ask you."

The way Victoria glanced over her shoulder, as if she could see the main house, convinced Mason she wasn't interested in going back. "I'm not really hungry."

"I was thinking of going out for a drive, but you can stay here if you like." She dropped down to the porch and waited. "I'd like it if you came, though."

"Do I need to change? Not that I'm a slave to fashion"—Victoria plucked at her sweatshirt—"but I'd rather not go out in this. It's got a hole in it."

"I need to shower since I stink, which will give you plenty of time. Are you okay to go back in?"

"Actually, I feel guilty for spending all this time out here."

She opened the door for Victoria and allowed her in first, and then they walked through the house and left by way of the front door. "I spoke with Cassandra, who's in charge while Belle takes a break until tonight. The real withdrawal has begun, and they've had to replace the IV lines a few times since Sophie's not in a good mood." They started their walk back up to Blue Heaven, and while she didn't want to mess up their afternoon, Cassandra had made a suggestion she wanted to share with Victoria. "Your mom's got a ways to go yet, and there's no reason to make yourself miserable."

"What do you mean?"

"Cassandra said if you'd be more comfortable, you could go home until Sophie's in better shape. She said she's not in any danger, and it can be hard to listen to."

"I appreciate the offer, but I want to stay. I'd only worry myself sick at home."

"That's understandable, and the river house is open to you whenever you like. If I'm not around, the keys are hanging at the back door in the kitchen." They made their way inside where moaning and cursing were immediately heard.

"God, you must find this is so pathetic." Victoria slumped against the wall, her eyes closed.

"Neither you nor your mother is pathetic. Think of this as having the flu. Right now we're waiting for the fever to break, and once it does, we can start working so that Sophie doesn't get the flu again." She put the keys back and started for the stairs. "Granted, getting there will require plenty of this pissy version of Sophie, so get used to it."

"I was about to accuse you of having too much of a sunny disposition, but that last part has your usual blunt way of going about things." Victoria stopped at her door, her smile gone.

"Would you rather I sugarcoat things? I can, if it'll make you feel better."

Victoria looked at her for a moment, then down at the floor. "No, that'd be worse, I think."

It was all Victoria said before disappearing into the guestroom. "She's cute, but murder on my ego," Mason said to herself as she stepped into the shower.

❖

Mason checked her messages for anything urgent before knocking on Victoria's door and finding her in nice jeans and a sweater that showed plenty of cleavage. She had no business looking, but pretty girls and cleavage had a way of overpowering her sense of reason. Victoria was definitely in the unreasonable but pretty category of girls.

"Any requests, or do you want me to choose?" She opened the truck door for Victoria and closed it after her, giving her a chance to think about the answer as she climbed into the driver's seat.

"You go ahead, so we don't get into one of those circular conversations about who picks."

Mason nodded, turned the radio on, and started driving. It took a while to arrive at the Loveless Cafe, and as usual it was packed with what appeared to be mostly tourists. She parked under the trees in the back and got Victoria's door again.

"I haven't been here in a million years. My grandfather loved this place." Victoria pulled her hair back into a messy ponytail and followed her in through the kitchen door.

"It's Sunday, and their hot chicken is good, but the Hashbrown Casserole keeps me coming back." She greeted the kitchen crew before one of the waitresses showed them to a table.

"Sweet tea for you, and your usual." The young woman pointed her pen at Mason, then pressed it to the pad when she glanced at Victoria.

"The same, thank you." Victoria studied the menu but only for a moment. "You're surprising at times, but then I don't know you very well, and you could be this spontaneous all the time."

"I'm like most people, Miss Roddy. I grew up in Nashville and spent a lot of years thinking I needed to get out of here so I wouldn't have to grow up in my father's shadow. Then I got my wish."

"You left, you mean?"

The waitress dropped the drinks off with a plate of biscuits and left them alone again. "I've been in LA for the last three years, and I didn't hate it."

Victoria tore her biscuit open and nodded. "Does that mean you didn't love it?"

"I was working and exploring the area and the talent, but there wasn't anyplace like this. Maybe some people think it's corny, but sometimes corny is what it takes to make you happy." She spread strawberry preserves and butter on her biscuit and took a big bite. "Leaving is what it took to make me find that sense that I belong here."

"There hasn't been much to make me or Mom happy lately, and maybe that's what's added to our problems."

That uncomfortable feeling that seemed to radiate off Victoria like a heater in winter was back.

"Once you know what makes you happy, it's not that hard to achieve."

"That's not so easy sometimes. How do you find happiness if you know leaving to find it might endanger someone else?"

Mason nodded, understanding the underlying issue. "Life gives us all choices, and what we do with those gives the truest sense I've ever gotten about what makes us human." Since her usual was one of their most popular dishes, their food didn't take long to arrive, and she smiled when Victoria sighed.

"What do you mean, exactly?"

"Your mom chose music, and she's been successful, but then she also chose to try to kill herself with pills," Mason said softly since their conversation wasn't anyone's business. "One brought her happiness, I'd guess, and the other nothing but pain. We're all flawed in some way, but we all have to find that balance that makes those horrible choices manageable. A balance that still allows us to be happy."

"You're definitely an interesting person, and I think you're a bit naive." Victoria smiled and touched her hand briefly. "What are you happy about?"

Mason raised her eyebrow. That was a word no one had ever used to describe her, and she wasn't sure how she felt about it. "Right this second both of us should let our happiness center around hot chicken."

"You're also a person with odd ideas about happiness, but what the hell. I'll give the hot chicken a shot." Victoria picked up her sandwich and took a bite. "This is delicious," she said around a mouthful.

"I am, it is, and the rest will eventually work itself out."

Victoria glanced through the crack in the door. Her mother had her eyes closed, but the way her hands strained to shield her belly meant her stomach was cramping.

"You need to let me go, you bitch. Can't you see I'm sick?" She tried sitting up, but the restraints would only give so much. "I need a doctor."

The woman watching her glanced at her watch as if she was bored before she came closer and wiped Sophie's forehead with a cool towel. "What's the name of your doctor? We'd like to talk to the guy who told you it was okay to swallow a bunch of oxycodone pills at once with a bottle of whiskey chaser. He needs his license taken away."

"That's not your business." The cramp seemed to twist into a more intense pain, and she screamed as her body bent as far as it could. "Oh my God, that hurts."

"You need to get through this part before we can start working on what got you here."

"Bitch, you have no idea what got me here or anything else about me." She laughed, but the pain cut that short. "Get my daughter in here, then. I want to talk to her. She'll get me out and back home since you don't seem to understand who the hell you're dealing with."

Victoria dug her nails into her palm when her mother mentioned her.

"You're Sophie Roddy, country music legend. Is that what you're talking about?"

"You're goddamned right, and the law will see this as kidnapping and being held against my will. What's your name?"

"Cassandra, and you've gotten to a point where you can't make decisions for yourself, so your daughter is acting in your best interest. Legally." Cassandra put the towel down and injected something into her IV line. "This will help with the cramps and help you sleep. Take some deep breaths and try to relax."

"I want to talk to Victoria." Sophie sounded like a balloon slowly losing air, but whatever was in the syringe sucked all the pain right out of her. "Now," she said and closed her eyes.

"Is she okay?" Victoria asked Belle when she finally gave in to her request to visit her mother's room. "She looks awful."

"I like to think of detox as knocking a poorly built structure down right to the foundation. If you want to build something that'll last and be strong enough to endure the storm, it's very necessary." Belle spoke softly and her voice was soothing. "I promise the pain and discomfort she's in won't go on much longer, but the craving for whatever she was on will be a lifelong problem. We can teach her how to curb it once we get her clean, but the possibility of her backsliding is a harsh reality. It's the nature of addiction."

"Did she tell you what she was on?" How the hell had they gotten to this point? "There were so many pills, and she didn't care which ones she put in her mouth. Does it matter what the overdose itself was on?"

"Let's let her sleep, and we can talk downstairs."

They left Cassandra in the room, and she followed Belle to the kitchen where someone had left everything to make tea on the counter. "Do you think she can beat this?"

"How about you answer some stuff for me first, and then I'll answer your questions?" Belle filled the kettle and placed it on the stove. The sun was starting to set, and Victoria briefly wondered where Mason had disappeared to.

They'd taken another long drive after lunch and stopped at a roadside stand manned by an older guy in a wheelchair and bought two jars of honey. One of them sat on the counter next to the Earl Grey tea bags and cut-up lemon wedges. It was as if Mason had left the small comfort for what was going to be a hard conversation.

"What do you want to know?" The sad part was that she had no clue why her mother had turned to someone like Weston, when she had her. Granted, her mother had told her about her insecurities and a little about what brought them on, but did that really lead to total self-destruction?

"We'll get to that, but let's talk first." The kettle went off and Belle filled two mugs with hot water. "This is a scary time for you and Sophie, and you're probably thinking you're at least partly to blame for what happened to her. Nagging thoughts, that maybe there was something you missed, something you could've done, or someone you should have protected her from, things that allowed the demons that landed her in this position to flourish."

"It's true, though," she said, holding the honey with both hands while the tea steeped. "Weston kept giving her all that stuff, and I kept looking the other way because it was the easiest thing to do. She trusted me to be her manager as well as her daughter, and I didn't do anything about it."

"Oh, honey." Belle reached out and took the jar away from her so she could hold her hand. "You need to let that go. Sophie's up there because *Sophie* made bad choices, not you."

"Didn't you hear me? I should've gotten rid of that guy."

"Even if you'd managed that, there was another Weston waiting in the wings. That's what Sophie needed to survive because she needed that fix, and Weston knew how to fill it."

"I let him do this to her."

"Tell me who Weston is and what relationship he has with your mom." Belle listened as she told her what she knew about Weston. "Where'd she meet him?"

"We were at a show in Biloxi, and she got really mad at rehearsal and took off for about five hours." She wiped her face when she felt the tears falling on her hands. It didn't really hit her until then that she'd been numb from that moment on, and it'd spread like a cancer until she didn't feel anything. "Her rage had started to build over the months, but that day it was like an animal trying to claw its way out."

"How was she when she got back, or did you have to go looking for her?" Belle removed the tea bag for her and added honey and lemon. That was what her mom drank before every show, or what she used to drink before every show. She'd replaced the soothing drink with whiskey and more pills.

"What does that have to do with anything?" She was so tired, and the questions felt too close to the bone.

"I'm not trying to waste your time, honey, but we need to find the root of this problem. If we do that, there's a possibility we can help her stay sober."

Victoria relented. They were trying to help, and she had to remember that. "She came back, and she got even madder because one of the roadies had quit. It didn't make any sense to me, because she doesn't really care about that kind of thing, and she wasn't exactly on her game that night." For as much crap that she'd given Mason about social media, she'd read all the comments from that night, about how Sophie should maybe think about riding off into retirement. "We left for Baton Rouge, and that afternoon she introduced me to Weston Cagle and told me to make arrangements for him. He's been with us—or, should I say, with her—ever since."

Belle gazed at her empathetically. "What happened in Baton Rouge?"

"She and Weston had gone to her room after our introduction, and Bryce and I came to get her for the show." The memory of her mother crawling on the floor naked because she couldn't get up was tattooed on her brain. "She was totally out of it and so was he, and I had no choice but to cancel. That didn't go over well in an arena full of people who'd paid for a concert. There was so much blowback that it's also affected her ability to contract to record new music and book more shows."

"Part of our problem is that her dealer is so accessible. Hell, he lives with her, and that's something that has to change."

"She'll sever her relationship with me and everyone she knows before she sends Weston away." The truth hurt like someone hit her with a sledgehammer to the chest, but it was true nonetheless. "All I am, in her opinion, is a pain in her ass."

"Listen to me." Belle moved until she stood beside her. "You're her daughter, and you love her—that's plain. What's not so plain for you to see right now is that Sophie loves you too. On the other hand, Weston is a user, and he's found the one person who'll pay and pay to keep him fixed up. When the money dries up, or he kills Sophie, he'll move on in search of his next fix. Why do you think he called you when she was in real trouble? If the golden goose dies, there'll be no more drugs and fun."

"What can I do?" She knew she'd already lost her relationship with her mother, but maybe this woman had a way of getting her mom back, even if Sophie didn't want her in her life any longer.

"The one thing that's so much harder than what you've been doing." Belle squeezed her shoulders and looked her in the eye. "You need to stop fixing everything, and let go. That's not your responsibility or job. The most important job you have now is to let Sophie make the choice for Sophie, and you need to accept whatever that choice is. If you don't, then you'll both be right back here."

"What if she needs me?" Taking care of Sophie Roddy and her image was her identity. What did she have without it?

"It's going to be hard, but a pass now from you is the worst thing you can do. What she needs from you is tough love, not coddling." Belle lifted her mug and handed it to her. "Let's make a deal, you and me."

"You sound like Mason." The happiness of hot chicken was long ago.

"I seriously doubt it. I'm way cooler than Mason, and my deal comes a week at a time. My deal is this: let me and my team work week to week, and you find something to fill your days that *isn't* worrying about your mom."

"Like what?" Then she understood the implication. "Wait, you want me to leave?"

"If you want to stay because it makes you feel better to be close by, then stay. It's an obscenely big house, Victoria, and you'll know our schedule, which will guarantee you don't communicate with her. All I need from you is to keep clear of your mother until she's ready to see you again. Until we know she's ready to see you from a better headspace than the one she's in now." Belle held her hand out and waited. "Do we have a deal?"

"We'll talk again next week?" She took Belle's hand and held it.

"I'm not that antisocial. We'll talk every afternoon if it'll make you feel better, but I really need you to find that something to fill your time that in no way involves obsessing about what's happening upstairs. In that way, it's probably good if you stay here rather than going home, where you'll be besieged by Sophie's work life." They both stared out the window when they heard barking and saw Mason walking toward the house. "I could give you a few hints as to where to look for inspiration."

"Yeah, right. Mason Liner isn't going to spend her time babysitting me after doing all this."

"I was thinking more of you asking her for something to do. You're the manager of a successful artist, and Mason works for a recording company. I'm sure you have more than a few things in common, and I'm sure she'd appreciate the help."

"I don't think that's a good idea."

"Really? Why?" Belle didn't concentrate on her as she asked but kept her attention on Mason.

"This will be hard enough without being indebted to someone." She exhaled loudly. "More indebted than we already will be."

"Get to know her before you start judging too harshly." Belle picked up her mug and started out of the room.

"Do you know her? Know her well, I mean?"

"Mason and I are friends, and my impression of her is that she lives to make dreams come true without expecting anything in return." The smile Belle gave her made her think she really believed that. "What you need to figure out is what your dreams are."

The thought was overwhelming. "But what if I don't have any?"

"Then you have a beautiful and inspirational place to find some. That you've found someone who thinks you matter is a given. I can't know for sure, but I don't think Mason goes out of her way like this for just anyone. Take advantage of that and make a new friend."

"Oh, I don't think that's a given at all."

"That's a shame, then." Belle squeezed her shoulder on her way out of the kitchen. "Don't forget our deal."

Victoria stared out at Mason, as she threw a stick for the big Lab who was jumping around her, and thought about their afternoon together. "What's your game?" She tapped her nail against her cup and watched as she repeated the question she'd voiced earlier. Nothing came without strings. And the fact that Mason liked helping people didn't mean her help came without a price of some kind. While the idea of solitude and time to think about what she wanted from life was nice, she wasn't fool enough to believe it would all be fixed by a stay at Mason's place. Life simply wasn't that kind.

"In the end you'll probably be just like everyone else, demanding your pound of flesh."

❖

The next morning Victoria heard Mason's door open again, and she joined her for coffee downstairs. As if by mutual agreement neither of them spoke, not wanting to disturb the quiet that had finally come after another night of her mom's screaming and complaining.

"Want to go for a walk?" Mason finally said softly as she placed their cups in the sink.

Dawn had given way to a gorgeous pink sky, and she did have an urge to get out of this beautiful but depressing place. "Sure, thanks."

They headed to the fence line, and Mason handed her pieces of apple to give to the horses who hung their heads over, searching for a treat. It was the first time in her life she'd spent so much time with someone and didn't have the urge to speak, and it wasn't uncomfortable.

"Want to head to the river house for the day?" Mason asked as they headed in that direction.

"That'd be good." A morning of silence was okay, but she didn't know about a whole day of it.

Mason unlocked the door and let her go in first. "Make yourself at home and I'll come down for lunch."

"Am I keeping you from something?"

"Not at all." Mason stepped into the office and waved to the couch as she took the chair. "If I were in your place, I'd want some space and time to process what happened. You don't need me here if that's the case, so I'll work from the house, and come down later. The other option is to tell me I don't know what the hell I'm talking about."

"Lunch sounds nice if you really have the time."

"See you then."

She watched Mason walk up the hill and allowed herself the chance to cry. Her mother was close but untouchable, and she'd never felt this level of loneliness. No matter what the outcome of all this would be, the one reality was that she was alone.

The next two hours were spent memorizing every knot on the pine ceiling, but then she got tired of the self-pity and decided to use the piano. Music was not only comforting, but it helped her forget the acid-tinged chaos of life for a little while.

She'd finished playing and was reading, confident her eyes held no trace of her earlier crying bout, when Mason came back. The faded jeans, navy shirt, and cowboy boots made her stare longer than was probably wise, but shit. Mason and those damn dimples were hard *not* to stare at.

"Ready?" Mason asked.

"Where to?"

"I think it's better if you work up some anticipation with your appetite." It was the only hint Mason gave until they walked into Biscuit Love after a quick, quiet drive.

The place had a line out the door, but Mason took her hand and walked her to the back, where a cute girl opened the door after Mason knocked. They sat, and Mason ordered for her once she nodded when Mason'd asked if it was okay to do so.

"Two sweet teas and split a Southern Benny and a Wash Park, please."

"How the hell are you in such great shape when you eat like this?" she asked when the food came out.

"Tomorrow we'll get a salad, but for today, Miss Roddy, your assignment is to find happiness in that burger with pimento cheese and bacon jam."

"What am I supposed to do with the ham, egg, and sausage gravy biscuit taking up the other half of my plate?"

"I was upping my chances of making you happy." Mason cut a piece of biscuit and fed it to her. "Was I right?"

"That's delicious," she said with her hand over her mouth.

"You'd have to be a hardcore case if that didn't make you smile."

They followed the same schedule for the next three weeks, and the more time they spent together, the more the days changed. Their morning walks weren't silent any longer, but they didn't delve into any deep subjects, keeping things light and easy, and their lunches were the most fun Victoria had had in forever. Their meals together were a tour of Mason's favorite places, but they were also a peek into who Mason really was.

Mason wasn't demanding or intrusive, and Victoria started looking forward to every minute she gave her. Trusting those good moments could be her biggest mistake, but she wasn't scared enough to say no whenever there was something on offer.

"Where the hell will this lead?" she asked the empty room. The answer, unfortunately, ended at Sophie's door, and that didn't bring her anything like the same joy as Mason's daily lunch surprise.

Chapter Seven

Mason sat in the kitchen the next day and read the paper as she had her first cup of coffee. She'd gone running that morning since Victoria wasn't waiting as she usually was, and then she'd showered and dressed for the office before anyone else was up. She'd met Belle in the hallway when she was on her way down, and Belle filled her in on what was happening. She'd also reminded her of her promise to work with Victoria.

She didn't need any prompting for that, but today it was going to have to wait until she got back from the office and the scheduled meeting with her father and the management team. Not that her dad was going to change his mind after she'd asked for more time to resolve the Sophie matter, but there were some other issues that had to be sorted out and couldn't be put off any longer.

"Good morning," Victoria said when she joined her.

"Hey, did you sleep okay?" She got up and fixed Victoria's coffee for her. Victoria appeared so tired that she had an urge to hold her to make them both feel better. That thought made her blink a few times as she tried to figure out where all these out of character feelings were coming from. She wasn't a bitch, but mushy sentimentality wasn't her norm.

"I did, and I feel loads better this morning. Sorry I missed our walk."

"No problem, and if you're hungry give my housekeeper half an hour, and she'll make you a great breakfast."

Victoria looked lost in thought. "Are you going somewhere today?"

"I'll only be gone a few hours. I've got a couple of meetings I can't postpone, but I'm coming back this afternoon." She pointed to the keys. "Feel free to head down to the office and nap or read. Your other option is to go riding. We've always got horses in search of riders. Jeb will be happy to set you up and show you our trails."

"I've never been on a horse in my life."

"I thought Sophie was born on a farm?"

Victoria laughed at that. "She was, but the folklore I've been fed all my life is that I was born on the tour bus. My grandparents still owned the farm when I was growing up, but when I spent time with them, there were only chickens, and they didn't like me riding them. Not one horse to be found."

Mason laughed at the image of little Victoria trying to ride a chicken and got her phone out to call Jeb. "We need to remedy that."

Victoria shook her head as she joined her at the counter. "No, we don't." Victoria put her hand over Mason's to stop her from making the call. "I'm not cowgirl material."

"You never know until you try, and you absolutely need to try. How about we set something up this weekend, when I can go out with you?" She stood and placed her cup in the sink, trying to shake off the tingly feeling of Victoria's hand over hers. "There are spots on the property that are only accessible by horse, and I'd like to share them with you."

"Why?"

In their business, Mason had met some jaded, guarded, and cynical people, but none as wary as Victoria Roddy. The woman had some serious trust issues, and there had to be a way of working around them. The last three weeks obviously hadn't made a difference in that regard, though she seemed more relaxed in other ways. "Because I'd like to. That's the best answer I have. I know you think I'm trying to play you, but I'm not. All I want is to be your friend."

"I'm sorry," Victoria said softly, and she appeared ready to cry. "You've been nothing but nice, and I keep giving you shit."

"Major shit, but that's kind of your thing." Mason winked at her and smiled. "Cut yourself some slack, and go read a book or stare at the water." She didn't touch Victoria, thinking it wouldn't be appreciated, but she really wanted to. "And if you still feel bad, you can make it up to me by getting on a horse that's not a chicken."

Victoria laughed and impatiently swiped at the tears on her cheeks. "Okay, and thanks."

Mason nodded and grabbed her briefcase, wanting to get to the office early. She had Colt Kenny coming by the ranch later and didn't want to keep him waiting. The drive went by in a hurry, and when she saw the pile of paperwork on her desk, she wished there'd been more traffic. Her father didn't mind handing her assignments like sobering Sophie up, but that didn't mean she got a pass on the rest of her work.

"Sonny wants to talk to you about the Colt Kenny deal before the meeting," her assistant, Scarlet Devlin, said, "and there're a few songwriters in the studio today you really need to add to your schedule. You've already reviewed some of their work, and they're here to see if you're going to use any of their stuff." Scarlet had her iPad in front of her face, and if she didn't take a breath, she was going to pass out. "You also got a callback from a slew of daytime and late-night shows about Colt's appearances."

Scarlet had followed her back from LA and was the best assistant she'd ever had. Since they'd both learned some of the ropes together, she trusted Scarlet with almost everything. "You think they'd mind going out to the ranch? I don't want anything to make me late for Colt, and that way I won't have to rush them."

She smiled at Scarlet's brief expression of confusion, but she rallied, used to the way Mason would circle back to other topics. "The songwriters are green, so I'm sure they'll cream their jeans over you acknowledging their existence. They'd talk to you in a bathroom stall if you asked."

"Tell me they're not young enthusiastic boys with hay in their hair."

Scarlet laughed and shook her head. "They're young, really enthusiastic, and there's definite hay, but they're all the way female."

"Give them the address and have Jeb show them to the office. Colt should be at the ranch by two, which means I have to be back before then with good stuff to report. As for the different talk shows, check the concert schedule against whichever shows want him, coordinate the locations, and book them." She worked on the pile on her desk and signed a few things. The rest went in her bag for changes. "Let's hope he's not a diva on the road."

"He's kind of too pretty to be a cowboy, but Colt's cool. He'll do fine." Scarlet picked up the items she'd approved and went back to the iPad. "How's your other project going?"

"We've all slept for the last couple of nights, so that's progress, I guess. Victoria Roddy seems like the harder challenge, believe it or not." She glanced out at the Nashville skyline and sighed. Being conflicted was new, and Victoria made her feel that in spades. One minute she wanted to pick Victoria up and hold her until the pain subsided, and the next she wanted to fling her into the river from the deck of her home office for being so damn aggravating. The pull between the two things was starting to give her hives.

"Was Victoria Roddy part of what Sonny wanted?"

"It's a package deal whether we wanted it or not. Sophie's got some major problems, and they're contagious. If we can help both of them, then there's a better chance they'll come out of this with positive results."

"Your mother will be happy, then, and she'll get off my ass," Sonny said as he came in and sat as Scarlet went to deal with other things. "PCG signed, and your rock group just broke the top ten. Good call on that even if it's not my cup of coffee."

"If you were twelve to fourteen, you'd have their poster in your bedroom, and your mama would be screaming at you to turn the music down." She smiled when her dad laughed. "Can you do without me today? I have an afternoon session with Colt, and it's my last chance before he heads out."

"Go, Colt's all yours, but stay in touch with Woody. Sophie's left enough video out there to supply a full-length movie of all her shit. You need to stay ahead of that if we want to get results out of all of this. Woody put out a press release that she's getting help, but eventually we'll have to add to the story before someone does it for us." Sonny slapped his knees and stood. "You know how much I love a good drama."

"You know if she's sober but still pissed, she'll sign with someone else." Her father was a generous guy, but not too quick to forgive if crossed.

"I'm counting on it, no matter what kind of mood she surfaces with, but your mom will know we gave it our all. That's the most important thing to keep in mind here." Sonny pointed to her. "You're giving it your all, aren't you, Buckaroo?"

"You're the last of the romantics, Sonny," Scarlet said as she kissed his cheek. "Amelia is a lucky woman."

"She is, and I'm giving it my all, Papa. Don't worry so much, and thanks for letting me skip out." She grabbed everything she needed, and Scarlet followed her to the elevator. "Did our budding songwriters take you up on our invitation?"

"They're already on their way, and I'll email you if anything else comes up that needs your immediate attention."

"Thanks, Scarlet, and call no matter what. I'm not on vacation, so yell whenever you need me." The doors opened in the parking garage and her truck was close.

"What about Victoria Roddy?"

"What about her?" She dropped her bag in the back seat and faced Scarlet.

"Remember that broken things are best fixed with love and patience." She tilted her head. "It may not be a vacation, but you'll have your hands full trying to help her. Love and patience, don't forget either."

She laughed before waving Scarlet back into the building. "That's a good lyric, Scarlet, but Miss Roddy would rather chew her fingers off than accept any kind of love or patience from me."

"I'll remember you said that."

"You do that, and I won't say I told you so when the Roddy girls are Justin Sullivan's problem over at Brookline. Unlike you, both of them are dying to get away from me."

"Okay," Scarlet said, finally closing the iPad and smiling at her as if she had a secret she wasn't going to share.

"Okay what?" She was too forceful in her tone, but the aggravation came from the fact that she couldn't stop thinking about Victoria, and she didn't need that kind of complication in her life. Not to mention how angry Victoria always seemed. After a while she'd get tired of being unloaded on with both barrels for no reason other than she was the one standing there. "I'm not interested in anything except helping Victoria and Sophie, and I'm only doing my job, so stop making stuff up in your head. I can tell you are."

"Good to hear it," Scarlet said, patting her on the hand like she was mollifying an upset three-year-old. "And I'm not doing any such thing. Are you sure you're okay?"

"Good, and I'm fine." She could handle being around an attractive woman, especially one who wanted so little to do with her. Eye candy wasn't an issue unless you had a sweet tooth.

❖

Victoria was about to take a sip of tea when she heard footsteps on the porch of the river house. She'd started a book, a romance of all things, and she'd needed a break after a few hours of reading, but the door opening meant she wasn't alone any longer. Having Mason back was worth putting the book down, though.

A teenager who was very distinctly not Mason walked in. "Oh," he said, dropping his guitar case. "Sorry, I thought you were Mason, since the key was gone from the kitchen."

She shared his disappointment in Mason's absence, but when Mason left for work this morning she'd been reminded what all this was about. The rehab and getting her mom sober were a part of Mason's job and nothing more. She couldn't expect Mason to be there as her shoulder to cry on, every time she felt like breaking down. Which was a lot, right now.

"She left for the office, and I have no idea when she'll be back." She moved away from the kitchen trying to decide if she should go back to the house, or home to her apartment. The apartment suddenly seemed like the best option. "Were you supposed to meet her?"

"We have a standing date every week."

"Uh-huh." She stared at him and doubted he was even shaving yet. "Aren't you a little young for her?" Instead of leaving like she thought she should, she chose to sit at the piano bench.

"Mason is more like my buddy than a love interest." The kid had a great laugh and he picked a chair close to her. "I mean, seriously, have you seen her? She'd put me in some kind of death grip if I tried to make a pass at her."

"I'll give you that, which makes me curious about your standing date."

"She pays for music lessons for the types of music she wants me to learn, and I come play with her so she can monitor my progress." He tapped on the guitar case and smiled. "Once I'm good enough, she'll give me what I want."

"Which is?" The cover to the piano creaked as she opened it.

"To make a living on this baby and never make another doughnut in my life." He bent and opened the guitar case and took the instrument out. For a kid who made doughnuts he owned an uncommonly beautiful five thousand dollar Gibson acoustic guitar. "Unless it's a cinnamon twist for Mason or cranberry scones for Miss Amelia. Those I don't mind making."

"What are you learning to play?" She put her hands on the piano and thought about all those dreams she'd had when she was this kid's age. Granted, she'd never dreamed or imagined herself being the next big thing, but the dreams had been taken from her anyway, no matter how small they'd been.

"At the moment I've graduated from classical stuff to flamenco. Today was about malagueñas. You know, that Spanish stuff."

"How did that go?" She smiled at his eye rolling.

"I need more practice, but it was kind of fun. Why I need to know how to play that to get in a band, I don't understand, but Mason said it's not my job to understand, and to shut up about it. There's something she's planning, so I come to lessons every week here, and I don't complain—much."

There probably was some plan in place for him, and her instinct was to trust Mason that it was a good one. "Want to play for me? I'd love to hear what you learned today."

"Yeah, there's some spots I need to work on." He took the guitar and music out and got himself ready.

"What's your name?"

"Wilbur Corsot, sorry, I should've said. Are you who Mason wanted me to meet?"

"I'm Victoria, and I don't think so. Go ahead and start, Wilbur, and remember to keep your shoulders straight and feel the music."

Wilbur stared at the sheet he'd placed on the stand and took a deep breath before he closed his eyes. If he'd already memorized the music, she was impressed. She watched him as he worked through the intricate opening to the music that was needed for the passion that was flamenco. The genre was one of her favorites, and she turned to the keys and accompanied him. Wilbur was enough of a professional not to stop, and the kid was good, really good.

"Man, you're great," Wilbur said, resting his arm on the neck of his guitar when they were done.

"Thank you, and back at you, Wilbur. You play beautifully." She took a sip of her cooling tea, really enjoying Wilbur's company. She couldn't remember the last time she'd sat with someone who wanted nothing at all from her. "How'd you meet Mason?"

"I was playing on the street close to where Banu is, and she told me I really sucked. I mean really, really sucked." He laughed as if the insult was a badge of honor.

"That does sound like Mason. Not that I know her that well."

"Sounds like you do, and she was totally right—I sucked big-time." He laughed again and very carefully placed the guitar on an empty stand. "She took me to dinner and promised to trade me this guitar for mine, but it came with some stipulations." He pointed at the Gibson and treated it like a treasure he couldn't believe was his.

"You didn't sell your soul for a gold guitar like in that Charlie Daniels song, did you?" She played a few bars of "The Devil Went Down to Georgia."

"Nothing like that, unless guitar lessons to learn music I'm never going to play anywhere but in here means I made a soul-sucking deal."

Mason had given a street kid with passion a guitar and lessons, and she got nothing in return. Was that truly who she was? "What's your favorite non-Mason-approved song you like to play?"

"'Born to Be Wild,' I guess." He glanced at the guitar as if he wanted to play for her.

"Classic," she said, playing a little of that too. "Good choice, Wilbur, but which one is more technically difficult? They both should be played with passion, but one develops your craft more than the other."

"Want to try the flamenco again? With my luck Mason will play it perfectly, and there'll be six more months of lessons and doughnut making. That wouldn't totally suck, but I'm ready to start making a living."

"Sure, and don't be afraid to be bold and play big. You understand?"

"Mason says that all the time, so I totally get it. Thanks for playing with me."

She counted them off, then concentrated on the keys, wanting to give Wilbur a good experience. The addition of another guitar made her lift her head, and she figured it would be Mason, but instead she found a smiling Colt Kenny. That the biggest country star around played a perfect flamenco standard didn't surprise her as much as that he was there at all. Guys like Colt didn't make house calls, no matter how good their record label contract was.

"Jesus," Wilbur said when he opened his eyes and got the same shock she had. "You're Colt Kenny."

Colt laughed at the phrase he must've heard often. "That's what my mama keeps telling me, so I hope that's true, and Mason finally delivered on some great backup talent for our little work sessions. You guys sound awesome."

"We were just practicing, but I'd love to play with you," Wilbur said. "You need another guitar on your tour? I'm totally available."

"You'll have to talk to my manager about that. She keeps telling me she's the boss, so I try not to contradict her." Colt shook Wilbur's hand before taking hers. "And you are?"

"Victoria." She took his hand, and he held hers longer than necessary. She wasn't about to say her last name. Anonymity was nice for a change.

"And I'm Wilbur." The eager young man saved her from any awkward flirting. "Wilbur Corsot, but I'm thinking of changing it to something cooler."

"Is Corsot your father's name?" Colt asked.

"Yes, sir."

"Is he a good man?" Colt sat next to Wilbur and seated his guitar.

"Yes, sir, the best." Wilbur sounded resolute.

"Then keep his name and don't insult him. It's not a name that'll guarantee you success, Wilbur—it's your talent."

"Easy to say when your name's Colt Kenny." Wilbur made her and Colt laugh.

"Colt's the nickname my dad gave me, but the name on the contracts is Edgar Kenny, Jr., and that's what I answer to at home, especially when either of my parents is ticked with me." Colt lifted his guitar. "My manager put me through the same hellish lessons, so let's get to it, Willy."

Victoria had a feeling Willy would stick, and that Colt Kenny wasn't your average sucky bigheaded star who dashed all your belief in humanity when you met them. They played for half an hour until two young women arrived, and from the way they were working Colt, they must've been the entourage.

"Do you want to look at our stuff or wait for Mason?" the blonde asked, pressing close to Colt.

Victoria wanted to barf. This little haven of tea and reading and solitude had turned into a reality show.

"Let's take a look," Colt said, and Wilbur glanced at her as if not knowing what was going on.

The girls unzipped their bags and took out thick folders. The blonde said, "Mason's assistant said she'd narrowed it down to five she thought would fit, but one's a duet. You'll have to decide who you want, but we can do a run-through of the music. It's not a done deal until Mason hears it and you like it."

"Let's try that one first, since I requested it," Colt said, taking the sheet the brunette handed over. "I've got someone here now."

"I don't sing," Victoria said. How had she gotten in the middle of this?

"That's what everyone says, and most don't, but today's about a little work, a little fun, and a little about trying new things. What a coincidence—that's the name of the song." He placed the sheet music on the piano and stood next to her while Wilbur got ready to play. "Concentrate on the words and not on your voice and you'll be fine."

"Is that your secret?" She glanced at the music for the song "A Little Of." A flutter of excitement ran through her. It had been so long since she'd enjoyed music just for the sake of it.

"A wise woman told me that, and she said if I listened to her, she'd give me the world."

"And did she?" She peered at Colt and thought he was the most handsome man she'd ever met. She could certainly see his appeal to a huge audience.

"She has, but we're not done yet." He pointed to the music and made a circle with his finger, like it was time to get going. "Sometimes all it takes is having the courage to do something out of your norm."

"And you think that's singing a duet with you?" She laughed when he nodded and hit one of the keys on the piano.

"Go ahead and play," Colt said before turning to Wilbur. "You can keep up, right?"

"Yes, sir." Wilbur's enthusiasm convinced her to jump in.

Victoria counted them off and played the introduction, slowly upping her tempo when one of the songwriters started directing, nodding when she got it right. She glanced at Colt, and he was standing there rocking, as if he was trying to absorb the music. It was her singing that finally woke him from his concentration.

It'd been so very long since she'd used her voice for anything but trying to get her mother out of some jam or another, and the feeling of freedom it brought with it made her eyes water. They got to the refrain, and Colt joined her before taking the next verse. He had a beautiful voice, and she did her best to harmonize before she sang the next verse.

She lifted her hands slowly from the keys when they were done and gazed up at Colt before someone clapping made her turn toward the door, tears streaming down her cheeks. Mason stood there—she obviously liked it, and her applause seemed genuine. But while Victoria's own tears embarrassed her, the tears in Mason's eyes confused her, and she wasn't sticking around to ask why. "Excuse me," she said, before going back into the office and closing the door. The feeling of vulnerability was too much to take. Mason had seen her pain and had witnessed a private part of herself she treasured. She had to escape, and the office was the closest place to hide.

The door opening and the music starting back up didn't make her turn around, but she did inhale deeply when Mason's hands came to rest on her shoulders. "Why are you in here?"

"I don't ever do that." She didn't move when Mason moved close enough that she could feel her heat.

"You should. Your voice is as beautiful as you are."

She laughed so hard that she snorted. "Are you afraid of alienating my mother because of me?" This closeness, having Mason hear her play and sing, had left her exposed in a way that was riling her up and feeding her need to lash out. "Believe me, you don't have to try so hard to be my friend. I'm not stupid. All this comes down to is a job for you."

"Give me a break. Sophie's got nothing to do with this, and you're blind if you think I'm only blowing smoke up your—"

"I get it."

Mason didn't budge when Victoria turned around and looked up at her. That open expression in Mason's beautiful eyes held none of the deceit or pity she was used to seeing in others. It was Mason's gaze that made her feel like Mason had truly seen her and was left wanting more. It had been a common sight in their time together, but she hadn't wanted to try to understand it. She had to do a better job of accepting that perhaps Mason was telling the truth before she pushed her so far away that Mason would stay in the frozen tundra she kept sending her to. "I'm not good with compliments, and I—"

"Hey," Josette said, walking in without knocking. "I've missed you." Josette kissed Victoria on the lips.

Mason walked out before she could introduce her to Josette, and it bothered her for reasons she couldn't explain to herself. It was so bizarre that after a lifetime of trying not to feel too much, Mason Liner made her feel the gamut of emotions, but mostly aggravation with a healthy dose of desire. But what kind of desire she wasn't certain.

"I missed you too. Thanks for coming." She'd called Josette the night before and given her an update on how things were going, and how lonely she was.

"I don't know, girlfriend. You didn't seem like you were missing me too much when I walked in." Josette hugged her tightly before releasing her. "Was that the infamous Mason Liner?"

"More like the infuriating Mason Liner. She's so rude sometimes."

"Honey, not everyone is as friendly as we are, but her leaving might be because she was being nice and giving you and your girlfriend some space."

She stared at Josette and wondered if she'd recently experienced a head injury. "You're not my girlfriend."

"I know that, but I think your new girlfriend doesn't." Josette punched her gently on the arm and smiled. "I'm sorry about Sophie, but this is a sweet setup. It's not often that you have Colt Kenny in your den for a private show."

"He's nice in a non-narcissistic kind of way, but this isn't summer camp. I'm going out of my mind waiting to see Mom, and I'm trying not to think the world's coming to a damn end." She covered her face with her hands.

"Think of it this way. It must be nice having Mason Liner mooning over you. That's what it looked like when I walked in here."

"There's no way in hell that's happening." She raised her voice a little too loudly and Wilbur poked his head in, looking embarrassed.

"Sorry, but Colt was wondering if you'd come back and try that song one more time." He didn't wait for an answer and closed the door.

"Wow, get going, and do not screw up this chance."

Josette pointed her finger in a way that made Victoria think she'd poke her in the eye if she didn't go. "Don't get excited. Mason will pair him up with some big name for the recording, and the song will climb. It's really good, but I'm a background person, nothing more."

"You're so delusional sometimes, that it makes me insane. Why not think of this as an audition and try to kill it?"

"Because it's not an audition and I'm not crazy. It's a little rehearsal in a studio in a field." She shook her head. She was surrounded by optimists.

Mason was flipping through sheets of music when she and Josette left the office, and they locked eyes for a moment. The easy smile she was used to was missing, and Mason barely paid any attention to her. They went through the song again, and she could sense Mason's eyes burning into her, but only when she was playing. As soon as she looked up, Mason's attention was elsewhere.

"Let's go through it one more time, and then you can share it with your guys," Mason said once they finished. "Good work, ladies," Mason said to the songwriters. "This will be a winner, so I'm willing to try a few more of your songs." She looked at Colt next. "I want to get the last three tracks chosen before you guys start the tour. We can record on the road like we planned and have the new album out before you hit Vegas."

"Three's pushing it," Colt said, picking up his guitar. "Plus, the guys are going to bitch when they have to learn that much new music before a bunch of shows."

"Do they bitch when they hear all those screaming people that sell out all those arenas?"

He tilted his head and bit his lip. "Okay, I'll pass on the information. Let's try this other new one and we'll get together tonight."

Colt held the sheet and studied it while Mason grabbed a guitar and sat next to Wilbur. There was no way to be sure, but Victoria thought he appeared more excited to be playing with Mason than he had with Colt.

"I like this one too," Colt said when they were done working through it, and he asked to speak to Mason outside alone.

"Thanks, everyone," Mason said. "I appreciate all your help. My assistant is waiting with contracts if you have time to swing by tonight," she said to the songwriters. "I look forward to whatever you have to show me in the future."

Josette finally clapped her hands when Mason and Colt left, and she moved to sit at the piano with Victoria. "You need to consider a career with those hands and that voice of yours. Want to come by the bar one day this week? I'll buy you a drink and introduce you to the manager. Maybe he can fit you in the schedule some night."

"I'll be happy to buy you a drink, but I'm not trying out for anything. I can't commit to anything until Mom is in the clear." All Josette's shoving her out of her comfort zone was usually funny, but right now she wanted Josette to go. She wasn't in the mood to laugh while her mother was still in trouble, and while she'd wanted Josette there to lean on, she wasn't interested in getting pushed into doing anything she wasn't ready for. She shouldn't be doing any of this stuff while her mom was suffering. "I'll call you."

Wilbur moved closer, holding his guitar case. "If you want, I'll walk you back up the hill," he said to Josette.

"Thank you, and if you give me a minute, I'll take you up on your offer." Josette took her hand and led her back into the office, closing the door softly behind them. "Promise me something."

"At least you're not trying to cut a deal with me. That's getting old." She glanced out the window and watched the slow current of the river. Unlike the place upstream she'd stopped to throw a rock in, the water here barely moved, but it was just as mesmerizing.

"I don't care how much you want to do it, don't run scared. You have to stop living for your mother and putting yourself aside." Josette almost sounded like she was pleading.

"You've mentioned that more than once, and I tried." She sighed and blinked back her ever-present tears. "Sophie almost killed herself, though, and I'm right back to taking care of her. It's not like I can turn my back on her. She's my mother."

"I know you well enough to know that Sophie is important to you, but open your eyes and look at what's happening around you. You keep your head buried in the sand, and you're going to miss some wonderful things, and maybe even a wonderful someone." Josette kissed her cheek and squeezed her hand. "And don't forget to call me."

"Are you seriously going to talk like you're a fortune cookie writer, then leave?"

"I'd be great at that, but I'd tack *on the toilet* on the end of all my wonderful fortunes." They laughed, since Josette loved doing that whenever they went out for Chinese. "And you're smart enough to figure out all my hints. Besides, I have a cute escort up that hill, and I don't want to keep him waiting."

"Thanks for visiting, and I will call you." She watched Josette leave and was relieved for a moment alone. Maybe that was the problem, though. Maybe she'd been alone for too long, and now she didn't know how to really let anyone in. Maybe, somehow, she needed to change that.

Chapter Eight

Mason shook hands with Colt and Wilbur before facing the woman who was obviously involved with Victoria. She was a little pissed Victoria hadn't mentioned that little tidbit, but she had no right to be upset. It wasn't like they'd had some deep conversation about whether either of them was with anyone. "You can stay if you and Victoria need more time together. She's welcome to have any guest she wants." It was the last thing she wanted to say, but damn all those pesky manners her parents had insisted on. They sucked in moments like this.

"I have a shift later tonight, so I can't, but you're sweet to offer. I'm Josette Starling"—Josette held her hand out—"and I'm a *friend* of Victoria's. It's not at all what you're thinking, so you can take that dead fish out of your mouth."

"Mason Liner." She took her hand before putting it back in her pocket. "What do you think is on my mind? We'll discuss the fish comment after that."

"Victoria and I are friends, and I'm still looking for love." Josette laughed and it made Mason smile. "I listen to dozens of songs about that every night, but it's a bitch when you're the one who's waiting for Mr. Right."

"If I run across anyone also on the hunt, I'll let you know." Why this woman was telling her all this was a good question, but she was entertaining.

"I'd appreciate that, and while you're at it, could you keep an eye on my friend in there?"

Mason looked up at the house for a moment before turning back to Josette. "I'm not sure your friend would appreciate that, especially if it's coming from me. If everyone has a Patronus, hers is the offspring of a porcupine and a cactus. I've been pulling quills out of my ass since our first meeting."

"That sounds like her, and whoever decides to try to breach that quill zone needs to be someone who understands a few vital facts."

Mason nodded. Colt gave her a wave as he kept Wilbur entertained, signaling that she could finish this conversation. "What facts?" She amazed herself that she was still standing there, but it seemed important to Josette for her to play along. And if it helped Victoria…

"They'd need to understand how important Sophie is to Victoria, and what it is that Victoria wants more than anything." Josette stopped talking and smiled.

"Okay, I'll bite. What's she want more than anything? The Sophie part I've got in spades."

Josette laughed and shook her head. "There's only so many hints I'm willing to give. If you want it, you need to work for it."

"Thanks for the vagueness, and come back whenever you like."

"You have a beautiful place, and I love to ride, so I might take you up on your invitation if it comes with access to all the pretty horses."

"That you can do every day, so don't be shy." Mason noticed Victoria standing at the window now, and she was ready for the day to be over.

"Shy is the last thing I am. Thanks, Mason, and don't forget to work hard for that answer. Make us all proud."

She laughed as Josette joined the guys for the walk up the hill. The contracts and paperwork in her briefcase really needed her attention, but that was the last thing she wanted to spend time doing. Victoria wasn't in the window any longer, but there was no way she could have left without Mason seeing her escape.

"You've been holding out on me," she said when she found Victoria sitting on the back porch.

"Don't believe everything Josette tells you. I saw you out there with her." Victoria had made herself a cup of tea, but there was another cup on the small table between the deck chairs, and Victoria nodded at it when Mason sat down beside her. "She's got a vivid imagination, and she likes to involve others in those wild fantasies of hers."

"I don't need Josette or anyone else to tell me you have a beautiful voice, and that you play just as beautifully. Thank you for doing that today. Colt seemed appreciative, and it was good to pair him with another voice while he tried out those songs." She took a sip of her tea and gazed at the water. Everything she was saying was true, but Victoria seemed more comfortable when she wasn't being studied like a specimen.

"Why were you crying?" Victoria asked. She was staring at the water as well but turned in her seat when Mason didn't respond immediately. "You don't have to answer if you don't want to, but I saw you tearing up, and you don't strike me as the overemotional type."

Sometimes the simplest answer was the most honest one. "Your voice touched me, and you remind me of someone." In her life she'd met thousands of people, but very few of those were memorable enough to live in her heart after they'd moved on. Natalie Barnes was one of those people, and she was why Mason would've helped Sophie and Victoria even without her father's assignment. Love and loss went together in so many songs, but in real life, it sucked. The reality of that loss had stayed with her, and she still hadn't found the answer to drive the memory from her heart and mind. "And don't tell me you're not that good. I know better." She smiled when Victoria blushed at the compliment before going back to staring at the water.

"I'm passable, but I do love playing. Wilbur is wonderful." Victoria kept her face turned toward her and she sounded at ease. She was like a Siren and Mason had no choice but to turn back to her.

"You're good at changing the subject." She finished her tea and pointed in the direction of the main barn. "Want to take another walk with me, finish your book, or play some more?"

"Where are we walking to this time?" Victoria stood and grabbed both mugs. "The book will keep, and I'll be too self-conscious to play now, so a walk it is."

"I'm not that harsh an audience," she said, opening the door. It was getting late but there was still plenty of daylight left. "Am I?"

"Wilbur said you told him he sucked." Victoria laughed and it completely changed her face. She couldn't really say transformed because Victoria was beautiful, that never changed, but her laugh brought out something wonderful that made her hard to ignore.

"That was being honest, not harsh. Wilbur really did suck, but his heart was in it, and he loves working hard. I could see his passion and desire for more when he was playing on that sidewalk. Once he's as good on the guitar as he is at making a cinnamon twist, I'll put him with someone good. His dad's a little worried about the career path he wants to take, but I promised I'd look out for him."

She took a jacket out of the closet in the office and handed it over.

"Thanks," Victoria said, turning so Mason could help her on with it. "I don't think he minded the truth. He certainly seemed to love telling that story almost as much as he loved showing off his skill."

"He's a good kid." They headed out, and she led Victoria into the trees. Once the house was out of sight, she opened the gate and locked it behind them. Chasing horses out of her landscaping was a night of fun she never wanted to repeat.

"This place really is beautiful." Victoria closed the too big jacket, put her hands in the pockets, and faced the wind as if to keep her hair out of her face. The odd angle of her head made her miss a tree root, and she flew forward with a yelp of surprise.

Mason had good reflexes and caught her before she hit the ground, and they ended up in a pose as if she was dipping Victoria after a dance. "Are you okay?" Their faces were close together, and while she hoped Victoria wasn't hurt, she was enjoying this.

"Sorry, I didn't see that, but I'm glad you caught me."

She slowly came upright and kept her hands on Victoria's hips, wanting to keep some contact. "No need to apologize. My first week here I broke a bone in my ankle on one of the stupid things."

Victoria grimaced, and at first Mason thought it was in sympathy, but after a few seconds she realized Victoria wasn't just feeling her past pain and was standing on one foot. "I can sympathize. I don't think mine's broken, but it's definitely twisted."

"Let's get you to a doctor." She didn't hesitate and scooped Victoria into her arms. "We should've gone with the reading option."

"If you help me, I can walk." Victoria didn't seem to know what to do with her hands, and the uncomfortable prickly expression was back.

"It's not that far back to the river house." She gazed at Victoria with a small smile, wishing she'd simply go along.

"You're definitely getting your money's worth out of your shining armor." They started back to the fence, and Victoria moved her hand to hold on.

Mason tried not to shiver at the feel of Victoria's hand on the nape of her neck. It was warm, and soft, and most definitely a place she liked feeling a woman's hand under other circumstances. "Zeus would drop me on my head if I tried armor, and I'm sure you'd do the same if I referred to you as a damsel." She had to put Victoria down to unlock the gate, and Victoria held on more tightly when she picked her up again, even draping her arm over Mason's shoulders so it was easier to carry her. Jeb would have to lock the gate back up because she didn't want to let go of her.

"Is Zeus your horse?"

"The big menace surely is. I'll have to introduce you. Jeb's had him in the back pastures, or he would've hogged all your apples." She took her time going back, but not so slowly that Victoria would worry about making it. "Now that I have you at my mercy, when did you learn how to play?"

"You didn't plan this, did you?" The way Victoria teasingly pulled the hair at her collar came close to making her drop her, as the feeling shot straight to her clit.

"Yes," she said, laughing. "I had Jeb out there with a remote-controlled root. We've been practicing getting it right under your feet, and that awesome catch I made, since you got here. I figured you couldn't hate me forever and would be thrilled to fall into my arms."

"I don't hate you," Victoria said and laughed when she arched her eyebrow in response. "I marginally disliked you at first, but I admit that was wrong of me."

The house came into view and she was sorry. "And I admit you have a few things going on in your life that would've made anyone want to burn the world down around them. All that cursing was totally understandable, and I was a bit of an ass." She walked up the steps and bent so Victoria could open the door with her free hand.

"I could keep up the mutual admiration thing we have going and tell you that you weren't an ass."

"But you're not going to?" Mason laughed after the long pause.

"But I'm not, so put me down, Mason." Victoria pointed to the office. "You must be exhausted by now."

"Hold on." She knelt, carefully put Victoria on the couch, and quickly put a pillow under her foot. "Does it hurt a lot?"

"It's bearable. Give me a couple of days, and I'll be fine. I only have one problem." Victoria reached out and grabbed her hand when she went to move away to call for help. "I'm fine, but I'm hungry. Can you help me with that? And join me?"

"Tell me what you're in the mood for." She knelt next to the couch and placed her hand on the cushions.

"I bet that works all the time." Victoria surprised her by running her finger along Mason's jaw. "Doesn't it?"

"What's that?"

"That voice, and this face." Victoria caressed her cheek. "You must have women falling at your feet."

"I'll have to introduce you to my mother, and she'll explain otherwise." That Victoria noticed her in any way other than as the person helping her with Sophie made her happier than it should have.

There were lost causes that should never be attempted no matter how much you wanted to complete them, like climbing Everest in only your underwear, and then there was trying to romance Victoria Roddy. Both could end in the loss of vital parts, if not death, but life was more rewarding when you took chances rather than going the easy route. Her mother had taught her that as well.

"That doesn't come after the voice and the face have lowered everyone's defenses? Introductions to your mother, I mean."

Flirty Victoria was sexy, but some part of her brain was wary and treated it like a Bigfoot sighting. Those weren't common and were never in focus, which made sense because she couldn't really make sense of this. Victoria had gone from mistrustful to flirtatious, so maybe she hit her head as well as sprained her ankle.

"I've never introduced my mother to anyone who wasn't business related, but once you meet her, she'll be happy to explain her many lessons about using my voice or anything else to get one over on a woman. And if you meet my mother, it won't have to do with business." She moved slowly to wipe away the tears she didn't think Victoria realized were falling. "Do you want me to get you a doctor? Are you in pain?"

"No." Victoria allowed her to wipe her tears and smiled, but it only made her appear sadder. "Sorry. I don't know what's gotten into me."

"Stop apologizing already." She smiled and shifted her weight to her feet. "Would you excuse me for one second?" She stood and Victoria looked away. Sitting there on the couch, she looked small and alone, and it made Mason's heart ache. "Jeb, could you call the Golden Dragon and put in an order? When it arrives, please bring it down to the river house."

"Do you...I mean...would you be more comfortable back at the house? I don't want you to think I'm holding you hostage down here." Victoria didn't seem like the type of woman who stammered, but between the end of their afternoon with all their guests and their walk, something had changed, and it seemed like maybe a little piece of her fortified wall had crumbled. "It seems like I'm always apologizing to you, but I'm sorry."

"There you go again. I'm confused as to why you're sorry now." She moved a chair closer to the couch and sat down. "And I feel anything but trapped. Sometimes life gives you exactly what you want, and you need to learn to sit back and enjoy it."

Victoria laughed and pointed to her foot. "I'm apologizing because somehow your job now revolves around babysitting both me and my mother. I'm sick of us, so I can just about imagine how you must feel. But you're nice and polite not to admit it."

"You keep saying that too, which makes me curious."

"About what?" Victoria's nails sounded loud as she dragged them up her jeans, and the move seemed like a nervous gesture.

"Was there another option you think I should've gone with?" Victoria's expression bordered on panic now. "You don't need to answer that, and you can be sure that I'm here because I want to be. That part I wasn't exaggerating about."

"Why did you really sign up for this?" What Victoria appeared to want was an essay, complete with bullet points and graphs, that explained how everything came with a price. No short answers would appease her distrust of her and the world at large.

"Answer something for me first. What do you think I have to gain?"

"I really don't know, but it's got to be something. People don't usually go out of their way unless there's something in it for them." Victoria fiddled with her fingers and dropped her head as if she couldn't meet her gaze.

"I know exactly what you're feeling, and I blame it on the business we're in." She sat back and crossed her legs so she could tap on the heel of her boot. "People usually do want something from you if you're in a position to give it to them. It's a vicious cycle that puts you on a hamster wheel that makes you run faster and faster until you lose control, and the fall might just send you careening head over fluffy ass off the wheel."

"Tell me more." Victoria looked up at her, making Mason think she'd forgotten she was embarrassed.

"Once people achieve fame, the kind of fame Sophie has climbed to, you spend a lot of time wondering if people are with you because of you or the money." She shrugged because it was the same for her once people knew who her father was. "When people are chasing fame, they'll do anything to get it, and the people they walk over to get their fifteen minutes are left wondering if they cared or were just using them all along."

"That makes sense, but what does that have to do with all this?"

Mason inhaled and held it until her lungs burned. "Hopefully, Sophie will leave here sober and go on to even bigger things. She has so much more music to make, and with hard work she can do that while keeping everything she's accomplished." The nervous tapping was aggravating so she dropped her foot to the floor and took another deep breath. "All that's speculation on my part, but there is one certainty I'll swear to."

"Please tell me."

"Sophie will never record another thing for Banu." She put her hand up when Victoria seemed about to say something. "Not because we'll let her go, but because she'll never forgive me for this, much less my father."

"And you did it anyway?" The incredulity in Victoria's voice made Mason laugh.

"It's an old-fashioned notion, but there's such a thing as doing right by people. My father wanted to do this because he was set on showing Sophie his appreciation for all those years they worked together, and my mother wanted it done because she's a big fan."

Victoria smiled and held up a finger before pointing at her. "How about you? Why did you want it? We're at your house, after all, not your father's."

"Maybe it was because I want to spend time with you."

"Ha," Victoria said loudly. "That's the last thing I believe."

"Are you kidding? After all those great times we've shared when you cursed me out and slapped me around, there was no way I was passing up the chance to spend quality time with you." It felt like signing the hottest act in the world when Victoria laughed. The knock at the door made Victoria stop, so Mason hurried to get rid of whoever it was. Jeb handed over a bag and pointed to the utility vehicle. She shook her head, wanting no easy escape for either of them.

"If you help me up…" Victoria said, swiveling to put her feet down.

"Whoa." She put the food on the chair and took hold of Victoria and pressed her into the same position she'd been in. "I can put food on a plate and bring it in here. Now if I offer to cook for you, that's when you want to run, injury or no."

"That asshole persona is starting to crack under pressure." Victoria's smile was the widest she'd ever seen it, and it signaled that perhaps they'd crossed some boundary that had been in their way from the very beginning.

"And you're—" She stopped before the word *bitchy* got Victoria to brick up the wall again and shut her out. "Probably hungry. Give me a second, and I'll be right back. How about a beer?"

"Sure."

The time in the kitchen gave Mason a chance to give herself a pep talk. She needed to talk herself off the ledge. Women in no way scared her, but if she made a wrong move now, the fall might hurt, because Victoria was no casual relationship with no strings attached. She thought of her promise to Belle, and it finally made sense. Victoria wasn't a woman who was angry at the world because it didn't conform to her—she was angry because she was in a world she felt she had no place in.

"Here you go." She set a tray across Victoria's lap and went back for her own, as well as the ice pack she'd made up for the sprained ankle. "If I go slowly, would it be okay to take your shoe off?"

Victoria nodded. "It's not throbbing as bad as it was when it first happened."

"Good." She sat by Victoria's feet and slowly untied the athletic shoe, and just as slowly took it off. The sock made it hard to see how swollen her foot was, so Mason put the ice pack over it. "Tomorrow I'll take you to the doctor to make sure it's only a sprain."

"By tomorrow I'll be fine." Victoria speared a piece of chicken and held it out to her. "You don't need to waste time taking me to a doctor for no reason."

"Are you always this stubborn?"

"You're not used to anyone disagreeing with you, are you?" Victoria gave her another bite, staring at her as if she really wanted an answer.

"Miss Roddy, you have the wrong impression of me. People disagree with me all the time even when I'm totally right and it's in their best interest to listen to me." She moved to the chair but dragged it closer before she sat.

"How often are you right?"

"It's my curse, but every single time." She joined Victoria in laughing and started eating. They stopped talking while they enjoyed dinner, but eating together was something they were used to. Mason took the tray away when Victoria was finished and piled the dishes in the sink. The cleaning staff would take care of them, which only left her with the decision of what to do about Victoria tonight.

"Do you think someone can drive down and pick us up?" The ice was starting to melt, but Victoria's voice was steady. She didn't seem to be in a lot of pain. "I'm not going to let you carry me, so forget it."

"Actually, I was going to suggest something else. Give me a few minutes, and don't run off."

On the other side of the room with all the instruments were a bedroom and bathroom, in case she used the space as a guesthouse. Up to now only Colt had spent the night, after a work session that ran way late. It was still early but going up that hill and back to the house meant not only the end of their night but going back to work. Mason didn't want to do either one, so she turned the bed down and got it ready for Victoria.

"You aren't going to punch me, are you?" She knelt by the couch again and placed her hands close to Victoria's body.

"I haven't yet, have I?"

"You give me the impression that it's only because you have

incredible self-control." She smiled at Victoria's laugh and took advantage of her good humor to pick her up.

"I told you that I'm not going to let you carry me up that hill." Victoria put her arms around her and gazed into her eyes. "I'm too heavy for that."

"How about you stop exaggerating and hang on."

She walked to the back corner of the house. During the renovation she'd put in two walls of windows, giving the room an excellent view of the river. When there was a full moon, it was visible even at night, but tonight the view was a black void that was quiet and seemingly infinite.

"Ah, you have a casting bedroom instead of a couch, huh?"

Mason was about to protest but calmed when Victoria winked at her. "My only guest so far has been Colt Kenny, and I have no desire to see him naked."

"He's handsome enough," Victoria said as Mason put her down gently. "Why wouldn't you want to?"

If she'd mistaken any of their exchanges for flirting and the beginning of a different kind of relationship, the Colt Kenny haze quashed that fantasy. "Colt's not my type."

"What's your type?"

She lifted a blanket over Victoria's legs after putting her foot on another pillow. "The exact opposite of Colt, and I'll be in the other room if you need anything."

"No hints?" Victoria lay back and seemed to want to keep up their conversation.

"I thought I just dropped a big one." She turned off the overhead light and pointed to the nightstand. "The remote for the TV is in there, and I'm not leaving, so I'm only a yell away if you need anything. Get some rest, and we'll get you set up to be more mobile tomorrow."

"Thanks, Mason."

"You're welcome, and don't be shy about asking for help. You aren't a bother, and you're light as a feather." She had to admit strawberry-blond hair was even sexier when fanned out over a pillow.

"I'll remember that."

"I won't let you forget."

She stared a moment longer before forcing herself to walk away.

The truth was, she wanted Victoria there in her bed, needing her, and she'd never wanted anything remotely close to that. She shook her head at the thought as she went back to the office to get lost in work.

"Fuck me." She had to say it because there was no way in hell anything in her life was distracting enough to blow Victoria out of her head, no matter how hard she tried.

CHAPTER NINE

Mason had left the door open and Victoria lay with her eyes closed and listened to what she was doing. The quiet made it easy to hear the tapping of keys and the shuffle of papers, which meant Mason was working. She hadn't called anyone, and she hadn't come back to the bedroom for anything, either, but the smell of Mason's cologne still lingered on her clothes, reminding her of the beach.

She thought about what Josette had said, but she didn't have much experience with women, much less trying to entice someone like Mason Liner. She'd dated in college, but then Sophie had sucked the life out of her by being Sophie, and any chance she'd had at improving her dating skills had dried up. Performer Sophie and mother Sophie were two distinctly different people, but both sides of her mother's personality were incredibly demanding.

"Hey," she said when Josette answered her phone. The noise of the bar and the music blaring meant the place was packed, but she needed a sounding board.

"Hold on. Hey, Doug, I'm taking a break," Josette yelled at someone. It took a moment, but most of the noise bled away. "You coming by tonight? The band playing needs all the help it can get. There's not enough alcohol in the world—you know what I mean."

"No, not tonight." She told her what happened and everything Mason had done for her. "She was really sweet."

"Why in the hell are you talking to me, then? You need to pull out all the stops to get her back in there." Josette was so emphatic it made her laugh. "And don't play dumb. You know what I'm talking about, my friend. No one within a thousand miles of Nashville will ever call Mason Liner sweet. Hot, bitchy, or total badass, maybe, but not sweet."

Victoria heard a loud tapping noise as if Josette was beating her fingernail against the phone.

"You need to channel your best womanly wiles and capitalize. Do not disappoint me."

"My best womanly wiles? What is this, a Jane Austen novel? I'm not sure what to do with that." She was paying attention to Josette but also listening for any sound coming from Mason. She didn't need the embarrassment of Mason finding her talking about how to get her interested. "You're the expert wiler, not me."

"Do you like her?"

"Yes." There should've been more hesitation, and she'd mentally unpack later the fact that there wasn't, but it was the truth. She'd remained relatively unscathed and sane in life by isolating herself from as much pain as possible. Safety came from not inviting potential heartbreakers into it, and while Mason was sweet, there was some bad-boy behavior when it came to women, if the rumors were true.

"I'm glad you're finally being honest with yourself. I saw how you looked at her, and I'll be pissed if you let this opportunity pass you by. And it is an opportunity, honey. You weren't the only one with the lovesick expression." Josette sounded compassionate instead of her usual sarcastic but funny self.

"This is kind of scary." That was a total lie. This was *plenty* scary, and she hated the sensation of being terrified.

"Think of it as the first time you played piano with more than one other person in the room. You took the chance and loved it. This won't be any different, so make up some excuse and get her back in there. I expect a full report in the morning." Josette hung up, not leaving room for any more second-guessing.

Twenty minutes went by, and she couldn't think of any good excuse to lure Mason back in, and lure was really too strong a word. She heard Mason on the phone, but the conversation sounded like she was rattling off a to-do list to whoever was on the other end. It was time to admit she'd been wrong about Mason and any hidden motives, because she clearly didn't have any that concerned her or her mother.

Or if she did, she'd hidden them well, and Victoria could almost forgive whatever the hell they might be for the chance of being in

Mason's arms again. It had been so long since she'd felt the security she'd sensed when Mason picked her up and carried her back to the house and took care of her. Granted, she thought of herself as a strong capable woman, but it was nice to put all that down for a little while and have someone else hold her.

"Hey, you awake?" Mason spoke softly from the doorway, and Victoria turned her head and held her hand up to say hey.

"I am, but I have a dilemma." It was no made-up excuse, either.

"Need a lift somewhere?"

"To the bathroom, actually." She sat up and pulled the covers back. "If you get me in there, I'll be in your debt."

"In my debt? Hmm, that could be dangerous, but I promise it won't cost you too much." Mason picked her up again and carried her to the en suite bathroom. She stopped at the appropriate spot but didn't put her down right away.

"What's your price?" Victoria studied the slight laugh lines around Mason's incredible eyes and wondered what exactly in the hell was happening to her. There was no way she was regressing to a teenager with a crush. She hadn't even had that chance when she was actually a teenager. But, Jesus, she was so attractive.

"That you agree to go on a picnic with me tomorrow." Mason put her down but didn't let her go. "And I promise not to peek, so go ahead and sit. You can call me back when you're done."

"Okay." This wasn't what Josette probably had in mind when she ordered wiles, but it felt more real, if not embarrassing. She had to laugh at the image of giving Josette a report.

Did she get your pants off?

Why yes, and then I peed.

"You're being awful quiet in there. You're not embarrassed, are you?" Mason said from the other room.

Her new friend was either a good mind reader or she liked keeping her off balance. "I'm not usually a noisy bathroom goer, and yes. Needing help in this particular arena isn't exactly sexy. I mean—" Shit, she shouldn't have said that. "I mean, you shouldn't have to add this to your list of things to do…I'm ready." She smiled at the way Mason kept her eyes closed when she called her back in and held her steady while she washed her hands. "Are you finished working for tonight?"

"I'm trying to clear my desk so I can spend the day with you tomorrow, but I'm done for tonight." Mason sat on the bed when she put her back down. "And you're in no way a chore. I'm not glad this happened to you, but I am glad we're getting to spend more time together. Aren't you? Do you want some time alone? It's totally fine if that's what you want."

"No, that's not it at all."

"Do you need anything else?"

"Would you stay and talk to me?" That sounded needy, but she was proud of herself for asking. "You don't have to."

"Hold on a minute." Mason stood and took off her boots before moving to the other side of the bed. That she'd skipped the chair made Victoria happier than it should have. "Tell me when you're tired, so I don't overstay my welcome." Mason sat and hesitated. "Is this okay? I can sit over there if you need the space."

"Never mind about that." She leaned over and turned off the lamp, leaving only the bathroom light to cut through the darkness. "Lie back and get comfortable."

"Are you warm enough?"

Warm wasn't a problem. "I'm fine. If you don't mind me being a little nosy, can I ask if you like what you do?"

"I love my job." Mason rolled to her side and propped her head on her hand. "It's like a new landscape every day, but it's the same at its core."

"What do you mean?"

"The bands are different, but no matter what they play, it's all about the music. The country genre is changing, but what I want, in my capacity anyway, is to help it retain some of what people have always loved about it. I'm expanding what we record, but country is our bread and butter."

She enjoyed Mason's passion even if she didn't really have any experience with her job. "People must love having you on their side, huh? You seem like a great champion."

"I try my best, but it's not without the occasional nightmare scenario you couldn't dream up if you tried. You aren't happy with what you're doing?" Mason reached up and touched her cheek, moving her fingers to her jaw. "Remember, it's okay to tell me to mind my own business."

She shivered under Mason's gentle touch. It had been ages since someone had simply touched her. "I don't mind. Managing my mom wasn't my first career choice. I've tried my best, but she would've been better off with someone who wasn't so emotionally vested. Do you know what I mean?" She always hated admitting that, since it made her sound so ungrateful.

"I do know what you mean, and I have to confess that I don't like seeing you so unhappy. You deserve to have infinite joy and be in love with what you do. This business is hard enough without the baggage of not loving it."

"I have a feeling we're in the same boat when it comes to career choices. It's not like I can walk away from Sophie, and you can't walk away from Sonny."

"Forget about who our parents are, Vic," Mason said. It was a nickname she wasn't particularly fond of, but this wasn't the time to complain. "Tell me what it was you really wanted to do?"

"I wanted to play. Not be a star or sing, just play." She laughed a little, remembering their first meeting. They'd come a long way from that to her confessing her life goals.

"What?" Mason smiled and those damn dimples made her warm.

"I was thinking of the night we met."

"Ah, doesn't that seem a long time ago? I don't think I've ever pissed a woman off so fast in my entire life. You didn't like me very much, and I couldn't get enough."

"Yeah, right. I have to admit I didn't care for you at all, at first anyway, but I reserve the right to change my mind." She took Mason's hand and pressed it to her cheek. "I was so wrong about you. You're a good friend, and I'd like to return the favor."

"You're not offering to be my friend so I'll set you up with Colt Kenny, are you?" Mason tweaked her nose and chuckled.

"I actually want the complete opposite of Colt Kenny, and I think you can help me with that." She took Mason's hand back and locked eyes with her, not sure of the next step. "Would you? Help me out with that, I mean?"

Mason hesitated, her gaze searching. "Only if you're sure about what that implies. What I should say is, *I* want to be sure of what you're implying. I don't want to be wrong again." Mason threaded her fingers through hers and leaned in. "I don't want to scare you away."

"You make me feel all sorts of things, but I'm not scared of you."

She wanted to move ahead twenty steps, but then this would only be a hookup, and that wasn't what she wanted. "Just as long as you don't mind talking to me, and being honest."

"I'll talk to you all you want, and being honest is what usually makes you mad at me." Mason let her go, but only to poke her lip back in from her pout. "Don't deny it or try to distract me with this cute face."

"You're not interested in me only because of my mother, you listen to me, and you can carry me without breaking a sweat, so I'll do my best not to get aggravated with you." She sighed at the way Mason looked at her. That hopeful wanting expression mixed in with the pleasure of being in this particular spot with Mason amplified the loneliness she'd experienced up to now. She was tired of the loneliness.

"Hey." Mason shifted and put her arms around her. It was only then that she realized she was crying. Again. Mason didn't try to make it better by filling the silence with hollow words. She simply held her.

"You have to believe me when I say I'm not usually this weepy." She relaxed against Mason and enjoyed the way she ran her hand up and down her back. If this was what it was like to be romanced, she was going to enjoy it.

"Think of it as a release valve. It's good to let some of that go sometimes. If not, you might try to hide from it with unnatural stimulants." Mason kissed her forehead.

The kiss brought back memories of her grandmother and how she'd kiss Victoria's forehead whenever she was upset. That's where the similarities ended, though, considering Mason made her feel so much more in seriously better ways.

"I'd keep you locked in here with me to keep you from doing that."

"No one would come looking for me." The admission was true, but Mason didn't need to hear that.

"Will you believe me if I tell you something?" Mason held her tighter and kissed her forehead again.

"Okay." She totally meant the answer. She wanted to believe there was someone who truly cared about what happened to her and what she thought, and just her as a person.

"If you disappeared one day, I'd totally tear up this town until I found you. I told you you're not alone any longer, and I meant it."

"Thank you. It's been so long since I've felt like someone was on my side and had a shoulder I could literally cry on." She slowly put her arm around Mason and squeezed her eyes shut, hoping it would stop the tears. The last month had seemed like her tipping point, and she was fighting hard to get some sense of balance where her emotions weren't so out of control.

"You want some pajamas or something?" They were both fully clothed, and Mason didn't sound like she was using the offer as an excuse to flee. "I've got some big T-shirts in here if you want to get more comfortable."

"Are you trying to seduce me?" The dark cloud she'd imagined following her around for the last couple years blew away when Mason laughed hard enough to shake the bed.

"I'd be a bit smoother if I was trying that."

"I was getting ready to say that if that was your best shot, I might reconsider Colt Kenny."

"It's the hair, isn't it?" Mason was good at following her mood. "I can't quite get mine to flop over like that."

"It's that face and that voice. He could be dangerous on tour. You might want to warn him about STDs and getting a reputation." She moved her hand from Mason's abdomen to her shoulder. "Enough about Colt. If I asked you for something, would you think about it?"

"Whatever you need, I'll do my best."

Mason must've been some kind of scout and taken that oath of honor seriously. "First, I need you to believe that I'm not totally crazy."

Mason seemed to know she was being serious and didn't laugh. "If you're talking about any interaction we had when all this started, I think the complete opposite. Stress and panic do crazy shit to people, so forget about it. Unless you're asking me about something else. Are you asking me about something else?"

"At the risk of sounding, well, totally crazy, would you tell me? Why you think I'm not crazy, I mean."

"I think a lot of things when it comes to you," Mason said, stilling her hand on the small of her back. "When it comes to that particular subject, though, I think it's been a tough couple of years when it seemed like the person who should've chosen you picked the bottle instead. I could be wrong, but I bet that crossed your mind more than once. It seems logical and something I would've questioned if I'd been in your place."

"Kind of true, yeah. She was always like that." It wasn't that her mother had chosen a bottle over her, but the fact that she'd always been an afterthought in her mother's mind sliced through her like a hot poker to the gut.

"I'm not talking about Sophie right now—I'm talking about you. I could be wrong, but all that time you probably felt like you were alone in facing the demons that were dredged up by what you went through. No one, especially me, is going to blame you for how a few meetings went." Mason moved her hand lower but not onto her butt. "You were protecting Sophie and yourself, and no one blames you for being angry."

"I'm so sorry for all that stuff I said. God, I even hit you that second time." Looking back on her behavior left her mortified.

"That was then, and this is now. If you want me to dismiss you as some kind of unstable nut job, I can't do that."

"Why? You don't even really know me."

"You don't really know me that well either. Are you sure I'm the complete opposite to pretty boy Colt?"

"I want to find out." She pressed her forehead to Mason's and smiled when Mason didn't pull away. The kindness and understanding Mason had shown made a layer of her loneliness peel away.

"Me too, and I promise you won't be sorry."

"I'm going to hold you to that." She kissed Mason's cheek before lying back down. "And I'm glad you're my friend." Never had she imagined that Mason would fall into the friend category, and that lifted her spirits. Refreshingly, they'd put their cards on the table with no games or hesitation, and knowing where someone stood always made Victoria feel more secure. Now they just had to see where it led.

Chapter Ten

Mason read through some proposals the next morning as Victoria slept in the same spot she'd spent most of the night. She slept like the dead, considering Mason had gotten up, gone to the bathroom, gotten some stuff off her desk, and come back to bed. It'd been cute to watch Victoria inch back over until she was plastered to her side again. The last time she'd had a sleepover was in the first grade, but last night had been nice. Having Victoria next to her for the entire night was making her inexplicably happy, and she didn't want to stop and analyze why.

Being too analytical was a gateway to questions—questions she didn't have answers to.

She'd put her arm around Victoria and still managed to read through all the items Scarlet had edited and sent back. The stuff was ready for her father's approval, which opened up her day for the picnic she'd planned. A long breath from Victoria warmed her shoulder, and she wondered if this was the beginning of her waking-up ritual.

The stack of papers she'd finished didn't make a sound as she dropped them to the floor so she could concentrate on Victoria. "Good morning."

Victoria's eyes opened when Mason spoke, and there was a second when she thought Victoria would flee, but it didn't happen, and Victoria relaxed again. "Good morning. Thanks for staying with me last night."

"Slumber parties are my favorites."

"I'll just bet." Victoria sat up and finger-combed her hair. "Let's see if I can make it to the bathroom on my own steam." Mason rushed to the other side of the bed and waited, doubting a night would heal a sprained ankle. Victoria hissed after trying to put weight on it, and Mason lifted her into her arms.

"Give it a few days, or you're going to have to get used to me carrying you around for a while when you do some real damage."

"Why do I get the impression you're enjoying this?"

She stood Victoria up in the bathroom and studied her to see if she was kidding. "Because I totally am," she said hesitantly.

"Get out of here, so I can figure out a way to shower that doesn't involve you carrying me anywhere naked."

Mason groaned and leaned against the doorframe. "Great, put that image in my head, and exile me to the other room." She walked back to the kitchen to start the coffeepot and check for any urgent messages.

"Mason, I'm done."

She heard Victoria laugh when she walked back in with her eyes closed and her hands out in front of her. "Where would you like to go?"

"To the sink. Would you happen to have an extra toothbrush?"

"My staff stocked this place with about three hundred extra toothbrushes, and one in that drawer has your name on it." Her joke backfired when Victoria lost her smile. "It's a guesthouse, honey, not a revolving door of my conquests."

"Sor—"

"Don't apologize again." Mason pinched her lips closed. "Eventually, you'll figure out how totally awesome I am, and that I'm not an asshole. At least, not an asshole all the time. That big-hair tweet I read to your mother was over-the-top asshole behavior, but I promise to do better in the future."

"Do you have a blue one?" Victoria bunched her hand in Mason's shirt as she asked.

"I'm sure I do. Hang on to me." She sat Victoria on the counter and gave her everything she needed. They enjoyed their coffee on the couch in the office to avoid the morning chill, with Victoria's feet in her lap.

"Would you take my sock off and see what the damage is, please?" Victoria tensed her uninjured foot and pressed the heel more firmly against her thigh.

She was as gentle as she could manage and grimaced at the bruise that covered most of Victoria's foot. "I know you don't want to, but we really need to get this checked out."

"What about the picnic you promised me?"

"I'm not reneging, but I'll feel better if the doctor tells me there's nothing broken in there." She accepted Victoria's empty cup and placed her hand on her knee. "I can call my guy, and we can be back here before lunch."

"Okay, but I really do need to shower and change clothes." The shirt Victoria was wearing looked slept in, and her pants weren't that much better.

"Okay, what about I suggest something—and it's not a come-on."

"This should be good."

"How about a bath instead, if I can help you in and out of it."

"You're right," Victoria said pointing at her. "That's more of a blatant request to see me naked than a come-on."

"You have such a low opinion of me, Miss Roddy. Tell me what you want to wear, and I'll call up for it after I get you in the tub. Or I can have someone bring your bag down." The way Victoria was staring at her was putting the idea of begging for some naked time together into her head, so she shook it to knock that notion right out of it.

"Would it be okay to stay down here?" The question seemed to come out of Victoria's mouth without her permission, since she closed her eyes tightly and blushed.

"That's a great idea if you don't mind me staying with you." This would be a good way to get out of the office and get some work done, and it would give her the chance to get to know Victoria better, now that no subject seemed off-limits. "Let's see what the doctor says, but no matter what, you might need help getting around."

"Let's get going, then."

Victoria agreeing right off was like a minor miracle, and she carried her back to the bedroom before she changed her mind. "Relax for a minute, and I'll get your bath ready."

She started filling the tub and opened the blinds that overlooked the walled garden outside. The house was remote, but the privacy wall prevented any landscaper or any of the farmhands from getting a glimpse inside. All she needed now was one of the large bath sheets, which she placed on the bed next to Victoria.

"Ready?"

Victoria glanced from the towel to her and cocked an eyebrow.

"Take your time getting undressed, and then wrap that around you. You can get in the tub with it, and I'll leave another one for when you're finished."

"Mason, I don't—"

"I can call my housekeeper if it'll make you more comfortable." She started toward the phone, and Victoria almost fell off the bed grabbing her by the wrist.

"Stop interrupting me and sit down." Victoria kept hold of her wrist and tugged until she sat. "Do you have a robe down here?"

"There should be one in the closet." She started to stand up, and Victoria moved her hand to the back of her collar and held her in place.

"You're not some pervert, Mason, and the robe will be fine." Victoria let her go but only to put her hand on her shoulder. "You're not a pervert, are you?"

She shook her head and tried her best serious face. "Maybe a little, but nothing that'll freak you out when the moment's appropriate."

Victoria's laugh really was wonderful, and in a bizarre moment of conscious thought, she wanted to give her a lifetime of reasons to laugh, but she'd start with a day. "I'll get the robe and finish in the bathroom while you get ready."

Victoria started unbuttoning her shirt before she left the room, making it plain they'd gotten past the awkwardness of where they'd started. They didn't talk as she carried Victoria to the bathroom, and Mason closed her eyes again when the robe hit the ground. The sensation of all that skin tempted her to open her eyes, but she resisted.

"Do you need anything?" She turned her back on Victoria to dry her arms and heard the trickle of water as Victoria moved around.

"This feels heavenly." Victoria's voice was soft and oh-so feminine. It was that soft tone that wrapped around the part of your brain that wanted to experience all the pleasure a woman like Victoria could give you. "You won't go far, will you? I don't want to break my ankle for sure, trying to get out of here on my own." The room filled with the scent of lavender, meaning Victoria had found a bottle of something on the bath ledge.

"I'll sit on the bed and wait."

"I hate to ask." The hesitancy in Victoria's voice made Mason almost turn around. "Would you stay with me?"

"That sounds better than cooling my jets in the bedroom." She sat on the closed toilet seat with her back still turned, wanting to give Victoria as much privacy as she could while being in the same room. Victoria pulled the curtain so only her head was visible, and Mason was able to turn toward her.

"You're really sweet." Victoria leaned her head back and wet her hair. "You didn't come off like that at first, but you really are."

"It's a good thing you think so, but there's plenty of people out there who've had to negotiate with me who'd disagree." She watched Victoria rest her head back on the towel she'd placed on the edge as a pillow and fantasized about running her fingers through her hair. That she was thinking about that and not the million things she had to do for Colt's upcoming tour proved she needed an examination of her head as badly as Victoria needed one of her foot.

"That's business, and you said this didn't have anything to do with business." Victoria turned her head to the side and smiled lazily at her. She didn't think anyone could pull that off outside of a romance novel, but here was the proof. "Tell me why some eager young lady hasn't taken you off the market."

"You're not a fan of the gossip sheets, are you?"

"Tell me you're not a boldfaced name. Was I right about the voice and that face?"

She laughed at the fact that Victoria had a talent for making her self-conscious. No one had done that in a long time. "The trashiest one in the bunch named me the most eligible bachelor last year. It was a dig at my supposed talent with the ladies."

"Does that mean you don't have a talent with the ladies?" Victoria's smile widened. "I can't imagine you had grounds to sue for libel over that one."

"Granted, but it makes me sound…I don't know, animalistic. I'm not that shallow."

"No, you're not shallow at all, but there has to be someone in your life. You're sweet, a great friend, and there's that voice and face combination. Do you date a lot?" Victoria's gaze still had that lazy but sexy appearance, but Mason could sense it drilling all the way to the back of her skull as she dug for information.

The bath was a strange place to have this particular conversation, but it would be better to get shot down early than later, after she'd exposed her heart. "Believe it or not, I don't. I always have a date for events and that kind of thing, but my schedule is murder on my personal life."

"Sonny can't be that much of a taskmaster."

"He isn't, but considering I'm usually not tempted by or interested in dating a lot of people, I volunteer for more than my share. I'm a workaholic at heart." She put her hands up before Victoria said anything else. "And don't interject anything about your mother here. Neither one of you is something he railroaded me into."

"I wasn't going to say that," Victoria said with a small shake of her head. "All I was thinking is that you've taken quite a few days off since I've been here."

"How about that." She winked at Victoria and got her to blush again. "There's been only one serious girl, and the bad ending left me a little skittish."

"Someone left you?" Victoria sounded really surprised. "Was she not real bright?"

Mason grinned. "You're good for my ego, but no. Natalie was my high school sweetheart who followed me to college, and my plan back then was to graduate, work for my father, and marry Natalie." It'd been a long time since she'd said Natalie's name out loud. She thought about her every day, not obsessively, but briefly. The pain wasn't raw anymore, hadn't been in years, but it still lingered. "That's not how it worked out."

There was a heavy silence. Mason didn't want to go into detail, and Victoria obviously picked up on that. Victoria sat up and finished bathing, seeming in a hurry to be done. "Will you help me out?"

The earlier lightheartedness disappeared as they worked together to get Victoria out, dried, and back in the robe. Jeb brought the housekeeper down with Victoria's bag. Mason was lost in her own thoughts, and Victoria said she was okay to get dressed on her own, so Mason went out and talked to Jeb about the vet visits they had coming up throughout the week, and about the mares that were due to foal. When Victoria called out, Mason carried her to Jeb's truck and was touched at the way Victoria laid her head against Mason's shoulder. It was sweet and open, and it made Mason swallow hard against emotions she hadn't felt in a long while.

Jeb gave them a ride to Mason's truck, and they headed out to the medical center. Thankfully, while the doctor ordered Victoria to stay off her foot for a few days, nothing was broken. The only drawback was the boot and crutches the doctor provided eliminated the need for her to carry Victoria anywhere.

"Are you sure you don't need to be doing something else?" They'd taken one of the utility vehicles down the hill and back to the river house, because it was easier for Victoria to get in and out of it than Mason's truck. After the mention of Natalie, their conversation had been all business.

"I promised a picnic, and unless you're tired, it'll be nice to enjoy the day. With you, I mean." She didn't want Victoria to think she was an afterthought. Thoughts of Natalie had crowded her head this morning, but as the day progressed all she could see and feel was Victoria. Instead of freaking her out, though, it made her crave more, and she wanted Victoria to feel the same way.

"I'm not tired at all, but the incline to get near the water looks pretty steep." They were sitting in the Gator, and Mason had to smile at what Victoria was implying. "It'd be tough to navigate on crutches."

"I could help you with that, or we can keep it to the porch."

"Food on the porch is just lunch." Victoria placed her hand on her forearm and took a breath as if for courage. "I'd really like to spend the day with you, but I don't want you to neglect anything you have going on."

She lifted Victoria out of the vehicle and started down the incline to the spot she had in mind. The two tall pines created a level area close to the water but gave them some privacy from any boaters passing by. Jeb had spread a blanket and left the cooler of drinks she'd asked for, leaving her with only one more walk up the hill to get lunch ready.

"You make me feel special," Victoria said when she carefully put her down. Victoria ran her hand over the soft blanket and looked up at her with that smile that made her want things.

"I'm glad, because you are special." The breeze made it cool, but she took her boots off and sat next to Victoria.

"I sure haven't given you any reason to think that, but you have to believe those first times we met weren't me. I mean, obviously they were me, but not really."

"We've been over this already, and you need to bury it, with the knowledge that I'm not going to judge you forever based on those nights." Victoria didn't respond, and it made her sad. Not for whatever was going on between them, but because of the way Victoria obviously saw herself. "I'm not, just like I'm never only going to see Sophie Roddy's manager. You're so much more than a few bad nights and your job."

"Funny, you're the first person who's ever said that." Victoria bent her uninjured leg and rested her head on her knee.

"That's because I'm brilliant, and we have a lot in common."

Victoria laughed and leaned against her shoulder. "Is brilliant something we share or is that only you?"

"See, if I don't agree to the sharing, I doubt you'll go out with me again." Victoria laughed again and she loved it. "But you are brilliant, and you'll get all the slack you'll need from me because I probably understand you more than anyone in your life."

"I think you're right, even though we haven't known each other long." The way Victoria searched her face as if she'd find some answer to a hard question made her want to kiss her. "Why do you think that's true?"

"Because I know what it's like to be judged or measured against someone fate genetically linked you to." She took Victoria's hand. "It's a heavy load, and any perceived mistakes make it harder to carry. I know, probably like you do, how the world is always watching."

"You do understand."

"That I do, and hopefully that'll make you understand the truth of me cutting you slack."

They sat holding hands, having come to some mutual understanding. She leaned back against one of the pines, Victoria leaned against her, and there was really no need for any more words for a long stretch of time. Sometimes the best days were when you got to sit quietly with someone you cared about. You could just watch the hours go by, and the silence would tell you all you needed to know and more.

"Will you tell me about her?" Victoria finally asked. "The girl who broke your heart."

The question surprised her, but then she'd opened the door earlier. There was no reason to dredge up the now ancient history, but she would because Victoria wanted to know. "Are you sure you want to hear this? Believe me, she's not a factor in my life any longer."

"I realize that, and I do want to know. That way I won't repeat old mistakes."

"Oh, honey." She put her arm around Victoria, liking the closeness. "I don't think you could."

Mason closed her eyes and let herself be swept back to a time she'd tried to leave behind.

❖

University of Tennessee, Six Years Prior

"You need to talk your father into that Los Angeles job and tell him you want it to be permanent." Natalie Barnes stood swaying in her underwear in the living room of the condo she shared with Mason, talking a little too loud for Mason's comfort, considering their neighbors.

It was only eleven in the morning, and Natalie was already impaired. Mason sighed, already guessing what the next part of the day was going to be like. Natalie would escalate, if only to drive her insane or to get her to change her mind and go along with what she wanted. It was a crapshoot with no good payoff either way. "You know he's not going to do that, and that's not what I agreed to."

"Mason, for fuck's sake." Natalie's voice started to take on that shrill quality that started a painful beat over Mason's left eye. "You loved LA as much as I did, and it'll be boring as hell getting stuck back in Nashville. If he puts you in LA, you can grow the label the way you want to. Try to sell it like that."

She packed her tablet and laptop, ready to head to school early if only to get away from this conversation—again. They'd taken a trip to LA over their break to run some errands for her father, and Natalie had fallen in love with the fast pace and nightlife, and the excitement she kept insisting didn't exist at home. What had been her dad's way of treating them to a short vacation had turned into Natalie's obsession with moving to the city.

"What's wrong?" She shouldered her bag and saw Natalie grab the back of a chair for balance. "You were out late last night, but the hangover should've burned off by now."

"Nothing's wrong, and stop trying to change the subject." Natalie wiped her brow as if she was burning up, but the condo was cool and dark with all the blinds closed.

"You know what the plan is, it's not going to change, and you know why. It's time to accept it."

"I'm not staying with you if you're going to be this unreasonable."

Mason shrugged, tired of the game. "I'll talk to my father and see if there's something he can find you in LA if that's what you really want."

"Really? I swear you'll be so much happier with that than going home." Natalie started for her and Mason shook her head. "What, baby? I know what we had planned, but things can be so much better there. You know Sonny will give you whatever you want."

"I meant a position for you, not me. After graduation next month I'm going home and accepting my father's offer. What I want is for you to join me, but I won't stand in your way if that's not what you can live with."

"Are you being serious? I don't want that at all."

Mason smiled, stupidly thinking Natalie was changing her mind. Why that notion had formed in her brain was a mystery, but it was born out of the years they'd shared together. Natalie had been hers from the time they'd started sneaking off to kiss when they were sixteen, but something had changed. The woman she loved was gone, even though she was standing right in front of her, and she was at a loss as to how to reach her.

"I want you to come with me, but are you being serious?" Natalie asked.

"Am I serious about what exactly?" she countered, if only to see if they were on the same wavelength.

"You'd talk to Sonny for me?"

And that was that. Did Natalie realize the ramifications of her question? It didn't matter. It was done. "Sure, babe. Whatever you want."

CHAPTER ELEVEN

"I think that was the last time we were alone again," Mason said, as Victoria placed her hand on Mason's abdomen.

"You moved out?" Victoria wanted to go slowly because she sensed there was so much more to the story.

"No, she did, three days later. My dad offered her a job at my urging, and she left to get settled, not caring about graduation. It's like she couldn't run to the West Coast and away from me fast enough. Even if she'd wanted to graduate, she wouldn't have passed that last semester because of the partying and chemical enhancers."

It wasn't hard to miss the misery in Mason's voice, and she reached up and placed her hand on her cheek. "What happened? I don't think that was the whole story."

"Not by a long shot. I didn't see it, or I was too wrapped up in myself to admit I saw it and totally ignored it, but Natalie was hooked on E and she'd made the transition to heroin. There wasn't a gradual spiraling out of control but a rapid descent." She took a deep, shaky breath. "She was dead before she even started her new job." Mason smiled but her eyes were full of pain. "Too much of a good thing, I guess. When we took that first vacation to LA and I was busy doing some stuff for my dad, Natalie was making new friends and experiencing new things. I wasn't around."

"Mason, there was no way you could've known that's what she was doing." Victoria's heart ached for Mason's obvious pain.

"I'd been around my father's business long enough that I should've recognized her problem for what it was. It should've never come to her dying."

"What she did has nothing to do with you."

"You never believe *me* when I tell you that."

She smiled at Mason's accusation, which was right on point. "You're right, but I guess it's different when it's you." Mason closed her eyes when Victoria moved her hand to her cheek. "Is this why you did all you have for my mom?"

"It was part of the reason. I never understood how we went from sharing our first kiss right over there"—Mason pointed to a spot closer to shore—"to a funeral. Her mother blamed me for a long time, probably still does, and I'm totally guilty of missing all the signs. I thought it was simply a lot of partying combined with plenty of booze to burn off the boredom."

The similarities of their situations made some of the walls she'd built crumble just a little more. It wasn't lip service. Mason really did understand. "That's how Mom started. It was slow and picked up in the last year. The sad part is, I did know better. I saw it every day, and I still made every excuse for her to keep right on doing it. I wasn't strong enough to stand up to her and demand she stop."

"The funniest part of all this?" Mason held her tighter and it felt like she was using her as a lifeline. "The story of my first kiss is how I convinced Belle to come out of retirement to help your mom."

"You have to tell me now." She moved closer and loosely embraced Mason. The cool late afternoon breeze made her shiver, but Mason's warmth made it perfect.

"Natalie was the first girl I kissed, and your mom was on the radio. Talk about coming full circle."

"How'd you meet Belle?" Now was the time to sweep away any old business before they started whatever this was they were doing.

"The LA office called me to tell me Natalie had pushed her start date back and that she sounded out of it the few times they'd spoken to her. I thought she might need some counseling to deal with her newfound freedom, and someone recommended Belle."

"That's when she was still in private practice?"

"Yes, and I planned to fly out there with Belle and have her help me get Natalie into a program if that's what was warranted. But before we took off, Natalie was gone, and Belle ended up helping me grieve." Mason went back to stroking her back like she had the night before. "Life went on, and after a few years learning the business here, I left for LA to finish my job training. I lost touch with Belle until recently when I moved back."

"Socially, you mean? You mentioned she's retired." That Mason had gone from sad to squirming like a fidgety little kid was humorous.

"She has a show at Skull's Rainbow Room. I happened to see her there."

"What kind of show?" She was going to keep pulling teeth until Mason confessed. She remembered how Belle had gazed out at Mason the day they'd had tea. There was more than just an old friendship there.

"She and her girls do a burlesque show that I checked out."

"Along with Ms. Lenox? The checking out, I mean." She stilled her hand and bit her lip to keep from laughing. "I'm not stepping on any toes, am I?"

Mason shook her head and grinned down at her. "It's never been anything serious. That we both agreed on, and I wouldn't be here with you if it was."

"I know, and I believe you. You seem special to her, though." Victoria had seen how Belle's gaze in the kitchen was colored with blatant want. "It's amazing you're still single."

Mason chuckled as if she was on to her fishing expedition but didn't mind all that much. Mason's cell vibrated and they broke apart so Mason could get it out of her jacket pocket. "Hey, Mom."

Victoria took the opportunity to study Mason's profile while she listened to whatever Mrs. Liner was saying. Mason was the type of butch who had always captured her attention, but when you added the sweet and caring personality, she was irresistible.

"Do you mind if I bring someone?"

"No!" she whispered, and Mason simply smiled.

"Okay, we'll see you tonight."

"What was that about?"

"She invited me to dinner, and I wanted to make sure it was okay to bring Fred."

She started to get up, but Mason wouldn't let her go. "Who's Fred?"

"My dog."

She pinched Mason's stomach and started to pull away. This was moving too fast, and her experience had been that if something seemed too good to be true, it was. Gambling with her heart with all that was pending with her mother wasn't a smart move, and it was time to gain perspective, which would be so much easier away from Mason's warmth.

"Come on, I was kidding." Mason had both arms around her now, and she was pressed against her chest. "Miss Roddy, would you do me the honor going to dinner at my parents' place tonight? I'd like you to meet them."

"Why?" The whole tableau of meeting someone's parents wasn't something she'd ever done, but she knew what it signified. The entire universe knew what that meant. And they'd had exactly one picnic, a bunch of walks, and lots of lunches. They weren't in meeting-the-parents territory. Not yet. Maybe not ever.

"Because I want them to know you. You're important to me, and I want them to know that too. Whatever develops between us, that will stay true." Mason moved her head closer but stopped short of touching her. "And I don't want to leave you behind."

Those words were loaded with so much meaning, and she was afraid of believing them. It was just too soon, too crazy, and too out of her norm. But it was Mason saying them, and she wanted to believe as much as she wanted to kiss her. For once she was totally selfish and took what she desired in that one sweet moment. She pressed her lips to Mason's and smiled at the second of hesitancy.

Mason's lips were soft, and she tasted like mint, and once she accepted her invitation, she kissed her until she couldn't help the moan that escaped. She felt possessed, as if Mason had reached in and taken everything she had to give, and it was amazing. It wasn't what she expected, but she never wanted to stop.

"Thank you," Mason said softly into her ear. "I so wanted to do that last night but didn't want to get punched in the nose."

"You're not too bright, are you?" She traced Mason's lips with her finger and inhaled deeply when Mason bit the tip. Mason seemed at ease with the flirting, which left Victoria dubious about her whole I-don't-date-much protestation. "If a girl lets you sleep next to her, she might not mind getting kissed."

"I totally get that, but it's the *might* part of that disclaimer that gave me pause."

They kissed again before she put her head on Mason's shoulder and allowed her fear to creep through. "What happens now?"

"Right this second?" Mason was joking but Victoria wasn't laughing. "Listen to me." She lifted her head when Mason put her finger under her chin. "Tonight we have dinner at my parents', and then hopefully you'll agree to have dinner with just me. A date where you ask me stuff, and I ask you stuff, so we can decide if I'm wonderful or not. A date where we both know that it's actually a date and not a lunch where we tiptoe around each other."

That made her laugh. "What about Mom?"

"I don't want to date Sophie." She grunted when Victoria lightly punched her. "How we got here isn't as important as how we handle it."

"Do you promise?" It was juvenile to ask, but she needed this reassurance. Even if they ended up as friends and nothing more, she needed the reassurance.

"I do. Slow and steady until you're sure. Until we're both sure."

They decided to skip the picnic and head back to the main house since they were having dinner soon. As Victoria gathered her things, Belle texted. She wanted to give Victoria a progress report before she started her shift watching Sophie for the night.

The big Lab Mason had been playing with before came running up when they stopped at the back of the house.

"Is that Fred?"

Mason saved her from a tongue bath when the big guy jumped into the cab and strained against Mason to get to her. "This is Fred, and he's a goofball who likes to show his affection, so don't put your face anywhere near his mouth."

Belle came up to the truck to greet them. "You should've given me that heads-up," Belle said as Mason came around to help Victoria out. "How are you feeling?"

"A couple of days and I'll be fine." She sat next to Belle at the patio table and placed her hand on the chair next to her to encourage Mason to sit with her. "How's my mom?"

Belle glanced up at Mason, who threw a stick for Fred. "She's tired and drained, but we've come to the end of hard detox, and she's going to need some time to find the strength to begin the real hard work."

"I'll go and let you talk." Mason threw the stick again, and one of her field hands grabbed Fred and put a leash on him to lead him away.

"No," Victoria said, lifting her hand and holding it out to her. If

Mason really meant everything she'd said, then she wouldn't let her go through this alone.

"Are you sure?" It was funny that the question came from Belle and not Mason, who didn't hesitate to sit and take her hand. "I need to ask you some hard questions."

Mason had said their relationship was casual, but Victoria sensed Belle hadn't gotten that memo. At least, not completely.

"Could you wait for us in the kitchen?" Victoria asked Mason.

Mason nodded and didn't protest, but she didn't think it was from relief of escaping an awkward situation. Mason squeezed Victoria's hand and headed inside.

"Do you think that's a good idea?" Belle pointed in the direction Mason had gone.

"Did you think it was a good idea when you were with her?" She had to admit that the momentary shock on Belle's face brought her a sense of satisfaction. "Or is it that *your* good ideas with her have come to an end that's bothering you?"

"I have no hold on Mason." Belle frowned, looking thoughtful.

"Neither do I, but we're working up to that. If that's going to be a problem with you working with my mother, I'd appreciate your honesty." Why did everything in life have to be so fucking hard? And did the best person for this job have to be someone Mason had taken her pants off with? "Maybe whatever Mason and I have won't last, and maybe it started in a weird way, but she's a good friend. And I really need one right now."

"That she is, and I'm glad you have her to help you through this. You might not believe me, but I was only asking for your benefit, not because I have any doubts about Mason."

"Thank you, and I'd like to know if there's something I can do to help my mom with whatever comes next."

"For the most part she's clean, but I'd like some clue as to what got her here. Has she said anything that would help?"

"Would you mind if we went in?" She could see Mason in the kitchen looking at her phone as she stood next to the coffeemaker. "I want Mason with me. She's the one who got us this far."

They sat in Mason's home office downstairs, and Victoria held Mason's hand in her lap as she studied the room. The wood paneling and leather furniture gave it a formal feel, but really, it was anything but. It was a tribute to Mason and her obvious love of books and the pleasure she took in designing wonderful places to indulge her reading habit.

"The night of that fiasco at the Opry, my mom said something that really surprised me, and she admitted it, so I'd understand why she seemed so self-destructive."

Mason didn't let go of her hand but switched it so she could put her arm around her.

"She said she couldn't handle growing older, and she needed Weston and what he did for her to help her forget that she was getting old. She said she'd always been worried about not being enough, about being nothing. And now she's worried about dying as nothing. Considering what she's done, her worst fears might come true. No one is going to forget that performance that ended so disastrously."

"Did you believe her?" Belle asked.

"Not really. I thought it was an excuse so I'd sign her out of the hospital and back to that asshole. Sophie Roddy is a vain woman, that I won't deny, and I don't buy that her vanity made her an addict." Her chest felt tight over the fear that she might've been wrong.

"I've seen it before, but you're mostly right," Mason said. "The spotlight is an addiction all its own, and when it starts to dim, some people turn to other things to soften the blow. I doubt that's all of it, but you know your mother better than anyone."

"That's just it. I really don't know her at all. She insisted I travel with her, but it was never about being my mother or wanting me there. I know what most of the world knows about her. But the deeper stuff she kept to herself. All I wanted was to live with my grandparents, go to school, and make friends." She shut her mouth so hard her teeth clicked together painfully. "I'm sorry, this isn't about me."

"You're actually helping me a lot, and Sophie's going to need more time to process all that's happened to her. I think you're partly right about what she told you, that she was stringing you a line, but the whole truth is something we'll have to fight to get. Are you okay with another month if we give you updates?"

"Are you okay with that?" she asked Mason. "This is your house."

"How about you and I stay down the hill until your mom's rehab is done, and that way Belle and her team won't be confined to the rooms upstairs?"

She wanted to kiss Mason for the suggestion, but she didn't want to rub it in with Belle. "Great." It was a huge relief to let someone else take the wheel for however long they were willing. And the thought of having a whole month of respite, when she didn't have to live with her mother or even share the same space, was a massive relief.

"I think if Sophie has a bit more freedom, the process will be smoother. It's easier to dig a hole than to fill it in so that it doesn't form again. Sophie's been digging for a long time, and the crater she's formed is going to take time to fill back in. Having the run of the house will be good for her, and knowing she doesn't have you to use as a crutch will be good too. We'll get there." Belle smiled and excused herself.

"I know—"

"Please don't thank me or apologize again," Mason said. "My part of this deal is no sacrifice if I get to spend time with you." Victoria smiled when Mason brushed her hair back and kissed her. "And hopefully I can make this easier to bear."

"You do. Don't ever think otherwise, and I promised to make this as painless as possible." She framed Mason's face with her hands and tried her best to resist those dimples. "You're giving up more than you planned. Don't lie or sugarcoat it. If this becomes too much, do you promise you'll say something?"

"It's not like we're homeless, honey, and I'll have the crew get sheets for the couch. You and I are going to get to know each other better, and we'll give your mother the time she needs to heal."

"Why do we need to sleep on the couch to do that?"

"We don't, but my mother didn't raise me to be presumptuous. Speaking of…" Mason said before kissing her again.

"Are you sure you want me to go to dinner?" Being in the house and this close to her mother made the guilt of going on with her life and leaving the responsibility of all this to someone else crash down on her like a bucket of cold water.

"I don't want to push you, and I wouldn't have asked if I didn't mean it."

Mason's voice was so soothing. Her tone made it so easy to believe her, but Victoria had to remember to keep things in perspective. Good situations, good people, and good experiences weren't things she'd had in abundance for a long time. If she relaxed now and started buying in, it would be that much harder to recover later when this joy was all sucked into the vacuum that was her normal daily life.

"You know you can talk to me. Whatever you have rattling around in here"—Mason tapped her temple gently—"isn't going to scare me away."

"Maybe right now I need to concentrate on what I can do to help my mom get better." The confusion of what she wanted and what she needed to do was making her head ache.

"If I tell you something, will you try and accept that I'm not being harsh?"

She nodded, knowing she also owed Mason so much already. "Sure."

"Try to remember that you didn't push Sophie into what happened. She did that all on her own, and right now, she needs to find her way out alone. You do the hard work for her and give her another slew of excuses, and it won't be long before she's back in the same spot. No matter how much you want to, you can't fix this."

"She's my mom—shouldn't I care?" Unintentionally, some of her anger seeped into her answer, and she noticed Mason's slight flinch.

"Sometimes we have to let a person we love find their own way out of a complicated maze. It's the best way to show them they can work through the hard times without slipping into a bottle." Mason smiled, but she couldn't return it. "I think that's why they call it tough love. Not because you're turning your back on the person you love, but because it's the hardest thing in the world to make them stand and fight on their own."

She stared at Mason for a long, silent moment and thought about what she'd said. That was it exactly. Her mom needed to heal all those wounds herself and fight her way out of the situation herself. Victoria didn't have to like it, but she had to accept it. That she had Mason to lean on while that happened was a gift she perhaps didn't deserve but was lucky to have.

"Thank you." She pressed her hand to Mason's cheek and finally found the strength to smile.

"Keep reminding yourself that you're not alone, and that it's okay to lean on me. I'm not going to break, and I'm pretty awesome, as well as great looking."

"And your modesty is legendary, I'm sure." The ability to laugh lifted the oppressive weight of the dark cloud.

"Hey, you can ask my mother—she'll tell you the same thing."

"Let's go meet the people who are responsible for you. They need a stern talking to."

CHAPTER TWELVE

Don't be a stranger, Victoria," Amelia Liner said as she walked them to the door hours later.

Mason thought the dinner had gone well, and her parents had genuinely liked Victoria. "Thanks for dinner, Mom, and we'll be here Sunday."

"Good, but not so many doughnuts next time. Your father is watching his figure and his sugar intake."

"Does Dad know he's watching his figure and his sugar intake?"

"Let's keep it our little secret, and I still have the power to ground you if you tell him."

Mason lifted Victoria into the cab of her truck and put the crutches in the back seat. Dinner had been wonderful, but she was ready to have Victoria all to herself again. "Thank you for humoring them. Sometimes they're a little too much," she said as she slid into the driver's seat.

"They were fine, and they were so happy you finally got a girl to talk to you."

"You might be the one on the couch if you keep that up."

Victoria took her hand and pulled on her fingers. "Thank you for bringing me. Your parents are lovely, and it's easy to see why you turned out so wonderful." Victoria leaned over the console and kissed her. "Are we in agreement?"

"About what?" The way Victoria was looking at her made her hope it wasn't her bank account Victoria was after, because even if it was, she was ready to write a check.

"Start driving and we'll discuss it."

The drive was fast, and they stayed clear of the main house as they switched to a utility vehicle to get to the river house. Victoria made it in with her crutches and headed for the bedroom once she flipped on the light. Mason stood by the door, not sure what was going on. Hesitation was way out of character for her. And yet, here she stood.

"Mason," she heard Victoria call.

Heading into the bedroom was going to change everything and could jeopardize what they were doing to help Sophie. If things went south with Victoria, all the good she was trying to accomplish could blow up in her face, but right now her heart didn't care. She wanted to gamble for once and see where that got her.

"Mason, are you there?"

She locked the door and walked headlong into the unknown. "Do you need something?"

Victoria had her back to her and was sitting on the bed fully clothed. "Can you help me with this boot?"

It wasn't exactly the question she was hoping for, so maybe all her pondering was for nothing. She knelt in front of Victoria and started pulling all the straps open. "You want me to get you an ice pack?"

"Not right now." Mason closed her eyes when Victoria ran her hands through her hair. "What's wrong?" Victoria stopped her hand at the back of Mason's neck, prompting her to open her eyes. "Have you changed your mind?"

"About you?" For all her fight, Victoria really was just a lost soul who seemed convinced it was only a matter of time before another bruising hit would come. "No, and I know it's hard, but I want you to believe me. I'm going to be here until you tell me to go." Given the doubts that had just been floating through her mind, it felt like an untruth of some kind, but she pushed that thought away.

"You're really something." Victoria leaned forward and traced her lips with the tips of her fingers before she moved to her eyebrows and the slope of her cheeks. "That first night I saw you, I was so angry, but I was also so aware of you."

"What do you mean?" She took Victoria's shoe off and ran her hand up her leg.

"You're so damn good-looking." Victoria kissed her hard, and Mason dropped her hands to her hips and pulled her forward. "I thought about you for hours—you and these perfect dimples."

"Do you want to kiss me or smack a stick against my perfect dimples?" She laughed when Victoria scowled at her, but still put her legs around her. "Are you tired?"

"No."

She remembered her promise to go slow but she kissed Victoria again. "Want to change for bed? When you're done, we can talk if you want."

"I'm sure my pajamas are around here somewhere, but I'd rather talk to you than hunt for them." Victoria leaned back and started unbuttoning her shirt, and there was no way Mason could stop herself from staring.

There'd been plenty of women before Victoria, but none had completely captivated her like this. She now knew what captivated meant, but she was at a loss as to why it was *this* woman. She wasn't prone to romantic fairy tales, but she did want to sweep Victoria off her feet and make enough of an impression to make her want her. This had to be mutual, though, or it wouldn't have a future.

Victoria stopped when the shirt was completely open and the pretty pink lace bra was visible. "What's going on in here?" Victoria tapped her temple gently before kissing her.

"Are you sure this is what you want?" She didn't mean to be so blunt, but being sure was important.

"Am I not what you want?" Victoria leaned back, dropped her legs, and closed her shirt as if trying to protect herself from the hurt of rejection. "I'm sorry, I thought—"

"Vic, stop, okay?" She slid her hands up until she reached Victoria's skin. "I want to be sure you're okay because I don't want this to be a one-shot deal. I don't want you to feel like this has to happen in any way. I want you to want me."

"You're afraid the bitchy Victoria will make a comeback and kick you to the curb?" The teasing question seemed to relax Victoria and she came closer. "Believe me, Mason, you are the first person who actually sees me. You see me, and your first instinct isn't to criticize or to ask for anything. I'm sorry I was so distrustful and downright mean, but what I want comes from in here." Victoria put her hand over her heart and sighed. "I have absolutely no experience with this, and yes, the sky could fall, and I could get buried under the rubble before this is over, but I believe you when you say you want me here."

"I do, and this is more than about tonight." Mason placed a row of kisses from Victoria's chin down her neck and inhaled. The skin above Victoria's hips where her hands were resting started to warm as did the spots where she'd kissed.

"What do you think is going to happen tonight?" Victoria took her shirt off and lowered the straps of her bra. It seemed like a second later it was off her body and on the floor after Victoria reached behind her and unhooked it herself. "Isn't this about sleep and talking?"

Shit. Mason wanted to say the word out loud but thought it wouldn't be appropriate. What in the world was the protocol here? Was she allowed to look or was this a test? Would Victoria flick her in the head if she looked too long? Or would it be rude *not* to stare at the perfect breasts she'd only gotten a glimpse of? Even with the threat of a head flick, she couldn't help herself.

"I'll talk to you forever if you want." She smiled when Victoria put a finger at the center of her forehead and pushed back. "What?"

"My eyes are up here."

"True, but your nipples look really anxious to get acquainted, and if you wanted to just talk, you'd probably have kept at least your bra on."

Victoria smiled as she unbuttoned her jeans next.

"Is our conversation going to revolve around the naked truth?" Mason tucked her hands in her pockets so she didn't start using them with abandon.

"If you don't start getting ready for bed, it'll be hard for you to carry on any conversation from the couch."

There wasn't anything Mason wouldn't do at this point to stay, and Victoria appeared to realize that. The smile she gave her was anything but innocent.

"Will you help me off with these?" She tugged on the open jeans.

She helped Victoria stand and concentrated on keeping her upright, and not on all the naked skin under her hands. There'd been some great unplanned moments in her life, but Victoria tripping on a tree root ranked in the top two right this second. The sight of her bra hitting the ground was in the lead by a solid margin.

"You can put me down, Mason."

Victoria's voice broke through the adolescent Neanderthal part of her brain, and she steeled herself to look down. *And we have naked,* she thought when she eased Victoria back on the bed. It wasn't the time to break into song or a happy dance, so she stood there like an idiot instead.

"Aren't you joining me?" Victoria patted the spot next to her. "I really would like to talk to you."

"What would you like to talk about?" She considered taking her clothes off, but Victoria's shaking head made her drop her hands from the buttons of her own shirt. Maybe tonight was a good time to let Victoria take the lead. She'd gladly follow her anywhere.

"So many things." Mason sat down and Victoria turned back to her. "This foot is a pain. Will you help me move?"

"You need the bathroom or something?" She started to get up but stopped when Victoria grabbed the back of her shirt.

"Not the bathroom." Victoria got her to sit propped against the headboard. "I want to sit on your lap."

Mason exhaled so hard it made her nostrils flare. She wanted to rush, to put her hands on Victoria and ratchet up her want, but it seemed like a good time to quench her desire, to be a follower. Victoria had to take the lead and set the pace so she knew she had control, something she'd rarely been given before.

She was careful with the injured foot and smiled when Victoria put her arm around her once she was next to her against the headboard. There were so many words she wanted to say, but none came when Victoria started unbuttoning her shirt. She stopped after every button to touch the skin she was exposing, and Mason did her best to keep her breathing steady. There was no way she wanted to make any move that would scare Victoria into stopping. Wherever she touched, the slowness of Victoria's movements made her feel cherished.

"Is it okay to touch you?" The discipline of keeping her hands on Victoria's knees was making her sweat, but she didn't want to fuck this up. "Usually a good conversation is a give-and-take."

Victoria leaned in and kissed her like she wanted everything she could think of to offer. It was slow, thorough, and caring. Victoria said, "I have so much to say if you're willing to listen."

The smile on Victoria's face made Mason inordinately happy, and she caressed her cheek before kissing her again. She moved her hand up and cupped Victoria's breast, and Victoria moaned into her mouth. Her nipple hardened under her palm, and it made her want to lay Victoria down and touch her everywhere until she knew every inch of her. This wasn't about all the things only she wanted, but a dance they'd have to learn to do together.

Mason said, "I want to listen, and I will, even without this particular conversation." She slid her hand over the slight swell of Victoria's abdomen, and Victoria spread her legs slightly. The only conceivable way to resist that invitation was to get up and leave the room. And she wasn't about to do that. "Can I touch you?" She needed to be sure.

"I've wanted you to from the moment you picked me up and carried me back here when I hurt myself." Victoria tugged at the hair at the back of her head and kissed her. She opened her mouth slightly when Mason's fingers went over her clit.

"You're so wet."

"Uh-huh," Victoria said, laughing briefly. "I need you to do something about it instead of announcing it like you're a sports broadcaster."

She wet her fingers as she stroked from the opening of Victoria's sex to the base of her clit, not wanting to make her come too soon. Victoria's breathing changed, and she spread her legs wider. "Not a sports announcer, baby, just observant. You're wet, and your clit is as hard as stone."

"Maybe I am interested in what you have to say." Victoria smiled, and her words sounded strained. "I've been waiting for you to touch me."

Mason slipped her fingers inside her, as she wanted to possess Victoria and place her mark on her heart, one that she hoped would make it hard for Victoria to forget her if this didn't work out. "You feel amazing."

"*Oh*," Victoria said, her eyes closed. "Wait."

Mason stopped with her fingers inside and her thumb on Victoria's clit.

"I want to remember."

"Remember what, beautiful?"

"Having you like this." It sounded like Victoria thought their time would be fleeting.

"This means something to me. I promise I'm not going anywhere." She moved only her thumb and Victoria nodded.

"That's so good."

It seemed like any hesitation or fear had disappeared, and Mason took her fingers out a little and moved them back in. Her thumb, though, never stopped. "Look at me."

"Please, honey." Victoria squeezed her shoulders and parted her lips. "I want…oh, Jesus. I want you to make me come."

Mason increased her movements and moaned when Victoria kissed her. Mason was desperately turned on, but right now all she cared about was giving Victoria what she'd asked for.

"So good," Victoria said as Mason stroked deeper and faster. "So, so good." Her uninjured foot pressed into the bed, which allowed Victoria to lift her hips. "Holy shit, Mason, harder. Don't stop." The walls of Victoria's sex squeezed her fingers, and she threw her head back in obvious ecstasy. "Yes, yes, like that." Victoria kept talking until she grabbed Mason at the wrist.

"Do you want me to stop?" She was confused that Victoria would stop her now.

"Don't you dare." Victoria was so adamant, that she almost laughed. "I want you to slow down."

"I'll give you whatever you want." She bit down on Victoria's neck but was careful not to be too rough. "You just tell me what you need."

"I need you." Victoria released the pressure on her wrist but kept her fingers loosely wrapped around her as if needing the contact. "Slow and deep. *Fuck*." The word started low but ended up at a high pitch as Victoria stretched it out.

She glanced at Victoria's injured foot to make sure it was still okay before she gave Victoria everything she wanted. Victoria's desire soaked her hand, and she kept her eyes closed as if savoring the buildup again. Victoria's nipples hardened, and Mason wanted to suck them in, but she wasn't moving until Victoria came. All she could concentrate on was giving Victoria all the pleasure she could stand.

"Oh yes," Victoria said, strengthening her hold again, but Mason didn't think it meant stop.

Victoria tightened against her fingers, so she actually sped up. "Let go for me."

"Mason—oh God, Mason. Harder, baby, harder."

The way Victoria raised her hips and pulled her hair meant she was close, and Mason thrust as hard as the position allowed her.

"Oh yes, *please* yes, don't fucking stop." Victoria went rigid in her arms before completely relaxing against her. Then she started crying.

The tears didn't take long to turn to sobs, and Mason's heart hurt. It was such a physical pain that she worried there was something wrong with her. "It's okay. You're okay." She kept her fingers where they were, not wanting to move and make things worse. Somehow she'd hurt Victoria. It was the only reason she could think of for her tears. "I'm sorry, honey, but I promise I'll make it okay."

"Why are you apologizing?" Victoria's tears slowed, and she reached for her discarded shirt to wipe her face. "That was wonderful."

"Did I hurt you?"

"What? No." Victoria kissed her, and she tasted the salt of her tears. "You overwhelmed me, but you didn't hurt me. Please believe me—I wanted that as much as you seemed to want to give it to me."

"This isn't a one-shot deal, though." The way Victoria smiled at her made her wonder what was on her mind.

"Are you asking me or telling me?" Victoria's eyes were still puffy from the tears, but her smile was beautiful.

"It's a statement of fact, Miss Roddy." The way Victoria moaned when she pulled out made her want to taste every inch of her, but the tears had spooked her.

"Why don't you take your pants off and get more comfortable? We have so much more to talk about."

"Are you sure?"

"Do you want me not to be?" Victoria lowered her gaze as if she was suddenly shy, and Mason wanted to kick herself.

"Do you want me to tell you what I want?" She bent her head and kissed Victoria's throat.

"Yes."

"I want you, all of you, and when we're done, I want to wake up with you and do it all over again." She lifted Victoria off her lap and shucked her jeans and underwear so they could be skin to skin.

"I want that too, and I have to say"—Victoria stared at her naked body—"you're a great conversationalist."

Those were some of the last words they shared until Victoria laid her head on her shoulder and drifted off to sleep after driving Mason to the point of insanity and back. It took Mason a little while longer than usual, as she thought of the tears Victoria had shed. She could understand being overwhelmed, and hopefully that's all it was. But if the sobs meant that Victoria thought this had been a mistake, even fractionally, it would be hard to accept.

"Give me a chance," she whispered, and she almost cried from the truth of it. All she wanted was simply that. The chance to have what her parents had, because that's where true happiness lived.

CHAPTER THIRTEEN

The river was coming into view as dawn started to light the sky, and Victoria enjoyed the landscape as she lay in Mason's arms. The night had been equally intense and tender, leaving her exhausted. It was good exhaustion, not the tense kind she usually felt from dealing with her mother and the crazy life they led.

"You know what I learned just now?" Mason's whispered question made her smile, especially when she kissed her shoulder blade as she pressed closer behind her.

"What's that?" She rolled over but stayed close.

"It just hit me what *good* morning means." Mason kissed her and trailed her hand down her back. "Good morning."

"It is." She traced Mason's lips with her fingertip and smiled. It'd been a long time since she'd been intimate with anyone, and this was the first time she'd spent the entire night with someone.

Her nomadic upbringing had stunted the part of her heart that most people seemed to take for granted. That part that thrilled over finding someone to share herself with, followed by allowing them into her heart. Up to now she'd only shared her body, but never herself. It made for long nights, but it'd be unfair to lead someone to a place she wasn't willing to go.

The main responsibility she'd had to herself until this moment was to protect herself above all else. Not allowing anyone too close had kept her safe from more hurt than she had already, but it really was a lonely way to live. Loneliness wasn't pain, though, and there was Mason at the door, gazing at her like she really wanted to be let in. The problem was, her fingers were numb from holding the knob so tightly, unsure whether to turn it or not.

"You're really sweet." It was hard not to feel adored, the way Mason was looking at her. "Thank you for staying with me."

"Do you think it was a hardship?" Mason flattened her hand on the small of her back and pulled her closer. "If you need to hear me say it, last night was wonderful. *You* were wonderful."

"Mason Liner, are you a closet romantic?" She took Mason's hand. Mason's eyes seemed to focus on hers when she sucked her index finger to the knuckle.

"Romantic? I've never been accused of that, but I'm willing to expand my horizons. Maybe we both can."

She ran her tongue along the pad of Mason's finger before releasing it. "Can I admit something?" She buried her fingers in Mason's hair and sighed when Mason kissed her slowly and with so much tenderness it made her want to weep.

"Tell me. You can tell me anything." Mason started to move away but she resisted, held her close.

"I'm afraid." The admission was painful, but she wanted to be honest. "I don't know how to do this. Dating. Relationships. No clue." She'd never had a model of what a loving and committed long-term relationship was, with the exception of her grandparents, and even that relationship wasn't perfect.

"The truth is we're discovering new territory together. It may be new, and I can understand being afraid, but if you remember that I'm right here, it won't be so bad."

She took Mason's hand and brought it up to her breast. "I want to believe you."

"Remember the night we met?" Mason spoke softly and moved even closer.

"You know I do." The expanse of all that skin was making her forget anything but how fast Mason could make her crazy.

"Then remember that even when you didn't want to hear it, I told you the truth. I'll do my best now, even when it's something you don't want to hear." Mason moved her until she was lying on top and smoothed her hair back. "You're safe with me, Vic. We may not always agree, but—"

She put her hand over Mason's mouth and gave a quick order. "Stop talking." She was scared, but she was also turned-on and she wanted Mason again.

"Tell me." Mason's voice never rose, but it was commanding and sexy as hell. "Tell me what you want."

"You know—you know, and you'd better do something about it."

Mason was able to reach without moving away from her and entered her fast and hard. It was so good it made her suck in a breath and hold it.

"Good God."

It was starting to get embarrassing that she had no control over the orgasms Mason was able to urge her to with lightning speed. Mason filled her up and touched her clit and she was gone.

"You okay?"

"Eventually, I'd like to enjoy that for longer than a rider has to stay on a bull."

That made Mason laugh hard enough to shake the bed. "What an interesting thing to say. Should I start mooing? Or get a saddle?"

"Shut up." She moved and winced when pain shot through her foot.

"Let me get an ice pack." Mason carefully rolled her over and placed a pillow under her foot. "Try not to move until I get back."

"Wait, don't you want me to touch you?"

"I'll take any serious questions you might have when I get back, but right now I'm going to get you an ice pack for your foot. Do you need anything else?"

"It's not like I'm going jogging, so hurry back." The sun was starting to rise, and she felt a little guilty about waking Mason up so early.

They had coffee and toast in bed before Mason carried her to the bathroom for a shower. It was nice to stand under the rain head as she leaned against Mason for balance while she washed her hair. No one had taken care of her since she was a child, and she was enjoying it, but really, no one had taken this kind of time with her, ever. That simple truth usually made her sad, but not today.

"Do you have to go into the office today?" She'd gotten dressed with Mason's help and hadn't mentioned her crutches when Mason carried her to the office.

"I'm going to work from here for the rest of the week, unless you're trying to get rid of me." Mason sat her on the couch in her office and placed her crutches next to her. "Do you need some space?"

"No, but I don't want you to neglect your work, either." She combed her fingers through Mason's hair and liked that she could touch her without feeling awkward about it. "You're probably way behind because of me already."

"The world and all the problems in it aren't your fault, Vic. Learn to enjoy the good parts without any kind of guilt because you're having a good time."

"What do you mean?" It'd be interesting to see the world from Mason's perspective. She seemed so sure of herself, and that hadn't been a place Victoria had ever reached. It was tiring going from day to day waiting for the inevitable disaster that she would either have to clean up or take the blame for.

"This is new"—Mason lifted her hand and kissed her knuckles—"but it's nice. At least I think so, and I'm planning to enjoy whatever comes next. I'm not willing to stop because your mom is having a hard time—a hard time she chose, not you."

Could it be that easy to let go of the guilt? To accept that she played no part in her mother's downfall? Not likely. "I think it's nice too. It's a surprise, but a good one."

"It is, and it doesn't mean that we have to stop trying to help your mom. You can be happy, and we can help your mom. They're not mutually exclusive. And you're going to have to accept that I'm here for you. You and Sophie."

"You really are something, and I believe you."

"Good, go back to your book, and I'll run out and get some supplies so we don't starve." Mason kissed her and moved the phone closer. "I won't be long, but if you need anything, call. Will you be okay on the crutches?"

"I'll be fine, so take your time."

She decided to move to the back deck with her book but spent most of her time staring out at the water. There wasn't any experience in her life that she could gauge Mason against, and their night had been so much more than sex. If it had been simply that, there wouldn't be all these emotions to work through.

The sad truth was, her relationship with her mother was the

longest and most constant connection she had, and the scars of all her war wounds would prevent her from trusting a future that revolved around sharing herself completely, even if that was what someone expected from her. Mason hadn't spelled it out, but it was easy to see that she wasn't going to accept anything less than a true partnership. It's what Mason had grown up witnessing in her parents, and it made sense she'd want the same. But what Victoria had witnessed in her own life was altogether different. And it wasn't like she and Mason were already declaring undying love for one another. Thoughts of a future together were misplaced, but she couldn't help herself. Spending time with Mason's family showed her just how out of kilter her own life was.

She jumped when she heard someone clear their throat behind her. With her hand on her chest she turned to find Colt Kenny standing there like a denim-clad god.

"I hope I'm not interrupting." Colt wasn't someone she'd expected to see again, but she returned his smile when he sat next to her. "Sorry for scaring you."

"That's okay. I have a bad habit of getting lost in my thoughts." She placed the book on her lap and tried to think of some small talk to keep him entertained until Mason got back. "Mason shouldn't be long if you want to wait for her. She's running an errand and coming right back."

"I'm actually here to see you." Colt removed his black Stetson and held it between his legs. "I'm glad I caught you alone. I wanted to talk to you about something."

"Sure, if I can help." All the relaxed feelings from the morning bled right out of her, and she hoped this wasn't going to be something that'd come between her and Mason if her big star tried something stupid.

"The studio sent a list of names over for the duet we did together, but I don't think I could do better than you. You have a beautiful voice, Victoria, and I'd like it if you recorded the song with me."

She opened and closed her mouth a few times but had to stop and think of what to say. "Are the people the studio wants on the charts now?" Opening your heart to someone enough to trust them with whatever load you had in life was one thing, but having them try to give you outright charity was another animal. If this was Mason's idea, and she'd run it by Colt before talking to her about it, they'd have to have a long, uncomfortable conversation later to review boundaries.

If Mason had indeed done that, Victoria was back to thinking it stemmed from wanting something. That was the way of the industry, and she was an idiot for thinking otherwise. One night with someone wasn't going to change their true nature.

"That's usually how management works, but maybe that's not how it should be." Colt was extremely handsome, especially when he hit you with that full-wattage smile.

She wasn't naive to the business end of things. People schmoozed you to get what they wanted, and then they discarded you like an empty Starbucks coffee cup. It was a trait her mother and most of the people like her had in common, and it was so ingrained, there was no changing it.

"I appreciate the offer, but you can tell Mason I'm not up for charity." She was proud of herself for not answering through gritted teeth. If this was what Mason had in mind, she should've had the decency to say it. If getting blindsided by Colt was supposed to impress her, it'd had the opposite effect.

He looked surprised and held up his hands. "This isn't coming from Mason. It's coming from me, and that's because I'm in love with your voice. I'm not sure where you've been hiding, but you should be onstage somewhere." Colt reached out but stopped before he touched her. "Will you at least think about it? I don't have a lot of time left in the studio, and I want this one cut before we leave."

Her thoughts spun, and she tried to find his angle. "You expect me to believe you're only recording one track and leaving the rest for when you come back?"

"We're touring and recording along the way. The album's called *Highway*, and I pitched the idea to Mason to record as we travel, and she went along with it. We'll be debuting each new song in the cities where we record them. You probably think it's gimmicky, but we're giving it a try. I liked the spontaneous feel of it." Colt lifted his hands as in defeat. "I'm not sure where all this is coming from, but what I want is to pull together the best people I can find to finish this project. For the song you debuted with me, that's you, but I won't bully you about it. How about you think about it, and I'll call you tomorrow and the day after that and so on until you say yes?"

She shook her head, but it was in self-admonishment. She was so desperately jaded, and once again, she'd judged Mason for something that had nothing to do with her. "Colt, wait. I'm sorry, and I'll think about it. It's been a rough few months, and I didn't mean to jump down your throat."

"Happens to the best of us, and you really do have it all. You have the chops, and that's all that should matter, but you have a beautiful face, so it's definitely a winning combination."

The comment smacked of misogyny, but unfortunately that was also part of the business, and another reason she didn't want to swim in the pool that was the music industry. Still, the compliment about her voice made her smile. "Thank you, and I'll be in touch. You might want to review that list again and review your options. A better-known artist will help you out more than me, and you're at the top of your game now. No sense taking any chances."

"Think about it, but be prepared for persistence. The only chance I'll be taking is going with someone else if you say no."

Colt left and she closed her eyes, enjoying the sun on her face and the quiet surrounding her. The offer was a surprise, and she didn't fully believe the great opportunity didn't have something to do with Mason. No matter what the truth was, she had to start taking a breath before she lashed out in response to people's kindness. All the anger she'd pent up through the years wasn't anything Mason or anyone else deserved from her.

Mason came back with bags of groceries two hours later, as well as a stack of work. The nicest part of the morning was that Mason searched her out and took her time kissing her hello before anything else. Having someone in her life who seemed to put her first made her want to hold on and take risks. She didn't mention Colt's visit right away. She was still pondering his offer and wasn't sure how she felt about it.

"How about a piggyback ride down the hill for a picnic since our first one got ruined?" Mason spoke loudly from the small kitchen, and it made her wonder what Mason was doing. Up to now Mason hadn't cooked anything.

She balanced on her crutches and headed inside. "I'd love to. Do you need any help?" She smiled at the not so complicated ham sandwiches Mason was putting together.

"How about you carry this, and I carry you?"

"I have a feeling I'll be completely healed, and you're still going to be carrying me down that hill."

"Don't tell me that you're complaining about that. I think you secretly like it, and I make no secret that I like having you in my arms. It's an all-around winner, so don't ruin my fun."

Mason packed everything and moved to put her arms around her. The solidness of Mason was more comforting than anything in her life, and the feel of her made her want to stay there.

"You okay, sweetheart? You've been kind of quiet."

"Colt was here." She stopped talking, wanting—no, needing—to hear what Mason had to say. Anger was the one thing she had to let go of, but wariness had kept her safe all these years.

Wariness had made her vigilant around some of Sophie's boyfriends, and some of the slimy venue managers who were quick to take advantage if you gave them the opportunity. It was a tough thing to overcome, but Mason wasn't the enemy in any scenario she could fathom.

Mason frowned and leaned against the counter. "Did he bother you about anything?"

"Do you know why he was here?"

"The last place he should've been was here. He should be in the studio finishing the tracks he has slated. He and the band will be gone for a long while." The way Mason leaned against the counter with her arms folded didn't give a hint as to how she was feeling except maybe a little peeved.

"So you don't know why he was here?"

"Do I want to know why he was here?"

She couldn't be sure, considering how long they'd known each other, but Mason actually sounded jealous. "Are you okay?" The question only got her silence, and she didn't know what the problem was. "Do you happen to remember what we talked about last night?"

"Every detail of it."

"I'm not looking to share my conversational skills with anyone else, so lose the frown, baby, and take me on a picnic." She balanced on one foot to pry Mason's arms down and put them around her waist. "If you kiss me, I'll tell you what Colt wanted."

"He didn't hit on you, did he?" Mason certainly sounded both peeved and jealous, and she wasn't doing a very good job of hiding it.

She felt Mason's hands tighten on her hips, and she tried not to smile. "You aren't going to go all ape-man on me, are you?"

"No, but I also don't want someone bothering you if that's not what you want."

"Why do I get the impression some small part of you thinks I might've wanted that?" It was almost humorous to see Mason's eyes drop like a chastised little boy's. "You're such an idiot. He wants me to record the duet with him, which is totally odd since you didn't put my name on the list of possibles. You *didn't* put my name on that list he talked about, did you?"

"I would've if I'd thought you were seriously interested. Are you seriously interested?" Mason's hands moved down and cupped her ass briefly before she lifted her onto the counter. The granite's chill seeped through her jeans, but the way Mason was staring at her made her decisively warm. "You have a beautiful voice, and it might pave a new way for you that has nothing to do with your mom."

"Would that be completely true, though?"

"What do you mean?" Mason leaned in and kissed the spot where her neck met her shoulder. "You need to start seeing yourself for the amazing woman you are. Give yourself the chance to live your dreams. You deserve only good things."

"You think I should do it, then?"

"I think you should do whatever will make you comfortable in your own skin. You should chase the dreams that make you happy." Mason kissed the same spot but on the other side. "In the end that's all that's paramount, and it's not something that comes right away sometimes."

"Are you? Happy with yourself, I mean." Victoria knew it was a question with layers, but she felt safe asking it. After a life spent uncomfortably adrift, being with Mason was like finding a buoy in a raging storm.

"It took leaving here to prove myself and duck out of my father's shadow to start seeing what I could be, not what was expected of me."

Mason didn't say anything else and she kissed her for being so honest. "But you came back."

"I did, because I had to face that there was no getting around my dad and his accomplishments. And what I could be was enough."

"So you settled?"

"I'd like to see it as adapting. There's no denying Sonny Liner, but there is a way to survive in his shadow. And surviving doesn't mean you can't thrive. It doesn't mean you can't do great things too, things people appreciate and acknowledge, not because of your relatives, but because you've done them." Mason cupped her face, and her hands felt warm and wonderful, and she wanted to stay in and enjoy the feeling all over her body.

"You make me crazy."

"In a good way?" Mason moved her hands down until they landed on her ass so she could pull her closer.

She had to laugh at that. "In the best way. Want to have a picnic inside?"

"I'd love to if you're okay with the fact that I'm starved."

The thought of keeping Mason hungry for a long time was appealing. Thoughts about the future, as usual, could wait. "Let's do something about satisfying every appetite."

❖

The trip from the kitchen to the bedroom was short, but having Victoria wrapped around her made it seem like they were headed to another state, it was taking so long. Whatever their feelings were in the beginning didn't matter as a hunger Mason had never experienced before consumed her. Victoria was a beautiful sexy woman who inspired that part of her core that lived to prove herself and fight off anyone or anything that wanted what she craved.

"Take your jeans off," Victoria said when Mason put her down. Victoria was unbuttoning hers but they weren't coming off over the boot, so Mason removed it for her.

"You're so beautiful, you make me insane."

"Beat your chest later, baby, and put your hands on me."

There was nothing sexier in life than a woman who wasn't shy about what she wanted, especially when all that need was directed at her. Victoria certainly wasn't shy, and she kissed Mason like she really wanted *her*. Mason leaned back to slow them down, wanting to enjoy their time together.

"Are you thinking about what to do?" Victoria leaned back as well, resting her weight on her palms. "Or do you need a hint?" She spread her legs and put her hand on her sex. "If you need a hint, I need your mouth right here."

"Jesus Christ, seeing you like this is like a blessing." She sat on her heels and didn't want to move.

"Don't make me beg, baby." Victoria's hand slipped lower, and she appeared almost embarrassed, but Mason could understand considering she was so turned-on it was getting painful.

Mason lowered her head, flattened her tongue on Victoria's hard clit, and froze again when she felt how wet Victoria was. She almost laughed when Victoria slapped the side of her head softly with her uninjured foot. "Stop Sunday driving, Liner, before I force you off the road and take the wheel."

"No one appreciates a back-seat driver."

Victoria inhaled deeply, appearing ready to comment, so Mason sucked her in and Victoria threw her head back. "Fuck…oh, fuck."

She increased the pressure and slowly put two fingers into her, never lifting her mouth.

"Yes, like that. It's so good." Victoria got demanding as her hips came off the bed. "Harder, baby, harder." The order came breathlessly as Victoria's movements became almost frantic. "Come up here."

The way Victoria clung to her as her body went rigid made it impossible for her to move her hand, so she simply held her as best she could as the orgasm swept through her. "I'm here—let go."

"Jesus," Victoria said before finally relaxing. "You're amazing."

She kissed Victoria's temple and smiled. "I am, aren't I?" The way Victoria laughed made her widen her smile. "But it's easy to achieve amazing when you can only take half the credit."

"Does being with me freak you out at all?"

Victoria held on to her tighter, and in that moment she realized Victoria was scared and asking if she was too. "I haven't been in a relationship in a long time, but I think we should figure out how to let go of the fear and make this work. You're the first person I've wanted to try with since Natalie." She held Victoria and waited to see if she'd say anything else, but she stayed quiet. "All we need to do is be honest with each other about what we want and, more importantly, what we don't want."

"Does that mean you want me to take Colt up on his offer?"

"That means you and I are good together, but you're the only person who can best answer what it is you want to do." She rolled them over so that she could see Victoria's face. "What'll make you happy?"

"The answer's what freaks me out." Victoria took a deep breath before speaking. "You have to know that I haven't had anyone I could trust to help me do anything for a long time. Letting you in scares me. What happens if it doesn't work out?"

"What happens if it does?" She wasn't going to let Victoria quit so easily, and she wasn't going to stop caring even if this part of their relationship didn't work out. "Letting me in isn't something you're ever going to regret, sweetheart. Start wrapping your brain around the fact that you aren't alone any longer, and you won't be, no matter what. Even if we decide the relationship thing doesn't work, I'll always be here as your friend." Making those kinds of promises actually did freak her out more than a little, but it wasn't the time to admit that.

Some wise person once said courage was being afraid but doing whatever scared the piss out of you anyway. Now was the time for courage, time to let someone into the parts of her that would bleed to death if they cut her, but eventually would wither and die if she didn't let them in.

"You don't understand. My fear isn't you, Mason. I'm scared because of me and all the baggage I come with. Eventually you're going to get tired of dealing with my shit." Victoria squeezed her shoulders hard, and she appeared upset. "And when you do, you'll leave."

"Give me a chance, and you won't be sorry." She lay back down and was content to hold her.

"Are you sure?" The fear mixed with hope in Victoria's tone made her hurt.

"I'm positive, and all you need to remember is you're safe with me."

Victoria flattened her hand on Mason's abdomen and sat up slightly. "Are you turned-on by me? I think you are," Victoria said as she moved her hand lower.

"I think you're...*fuck*."

Chapter Fourteen

Why won't you let me see my daughter?" Sophie said, sounding hoarse and tired. It had been the hardest four weeks of her life, and the fun wasn't over yet. That's what this damn woman kept telling her, along with the fact that the cravings wouldn't ever subside completely. If that was the case, what the fuck was all this about?

All she wanted was her life back the way it was before that night at the Opry. She wanted to perform, have Weston in her bed, and enjoy everything she'd worked her ass off to get, in whatever way she wanted to enjoy it. Now all she had to look forward to was this tag team of Belle and Cassandra giving her shit about her lifestyle choices. People needed to face the fact that's what life was and what made it so great. You made choices, good or bad, and they added up to who you were.

"It's a good thing, you giving up the booze and the pills," Belle said as they sat outside in the nice patio area. "And I've answered that question enough times that you should have it memorized by now."

This place they'd brought her to was gorgeous, but she had no clue where exactly it was. "I'm not forgetful, and I don't give a shit what you think—I simply don't see the harm." She ran her hands through her hair, and it felt flat, disgusting her all the more. Her career was so much more than her voice, and a lot of it was wrapped up in her image. Right now, she was a tired old woman with flat hair who people stared at with pity. She needed to get the hell out of here and fast.

"How about I explain it another way? The best thing right now is for you and Victoria to take a break from each other." Belle seldom glanced up when they spoke, as if she was writing a novel of notes. "Stop worrying about Victoria, and worry about you. Only you."

"She needs me," she screamed, but it was more from the frustration of not having her pills and a drink than from not getting to see anyone, including Victoria.

"For what, exactly?" That question finally got Belle to make eye contact.

"What are you talking about?" She reached for her cigarettes, but her hands shook so badly she couldn't light one, and she wasn't going to ask for help. "I'm her mother, and I'm also all she has."

"Why do you think she *needs* you, though?" Belle put her notebook to the side and gave her what seemed to be her full attention. "From what I can see, she's doing everything for you, including saving your life. Weston Cagle was there—he gave you the drugs, but he called Victoria when everything went south. You put your trust in him, yet it's your daughter you have to thank for being here."

"I'm her mother, so of course she saved me. That's her responsibility."

Belle shook her head. "Tell me one thing you've done for Victoria, and I'll make the call myself. I'll get her here, and we can decide together what's the best next step."

"I gave her a job." Her answer was quick and would settle the issue. Her job as a parent wasn't up for discussion with someone who probably had no children.

"I see. Was it a job she wanted?" Belle asked with a fair amount of skepticism. "And I think you misunderstood my question. I'm talking about something you, as a mother, have done for your child."

"Victoria knows I love her."

"Sophie, I'm sure Victoria knows that on some deep level, but you need to face the truth about how you've treated the people who love you most. Forget about yourself for a moment, and really think about how your actions have affected them." Belle held her hand up. "We're going to be at this until you drop the poor, poor, pitiful me routine and start really talking to me."

"Talk about what?" She scratched the tops of her arms, wanting to get rid of the unpleasant sensation under her skin. "Everyone needs a little something to help them through the day, especially when you're someone like me. You have no idea what it's like to have everyone pawing at you and pulling you in a million different directions."

"So almost overdosing twice was you indulging in your little something to cope?" Belle shook her head and Sophie wanted to punch her. "You should be proud of the career you built, and of the family you have. The band guys love you as much as Victoria does, but eventually everyone gets tired of caring."

"Ain't that the truth?"

Belle shook her head again. "You didn't let me finish. They stopped caring because you don't care about them, or yourself, at all. You've allowed a man into your life who's sucking everything good out of you, and you've pushed everyone else away."

"I'm not that hideous. Weston wants to be with me, and he's not after my money." She needed him and was tired of defending her choices. Why the hell didn't anyone realize it wasn't their business? "He loves me."

"I don't know Mr. Cagle, and I don't know his true feelings for you." Belle opened a folder and handed over a sheet of paper. "I do know Mr. Cagle withdrew close to forty thousand dollars from your account the moment you were taken to the hospital, and he hasn't been seen or heard from since that night. If Victoria hadn't locked down your accounts, that might not be the only thing he got away with."

"Where did you get this?" Sophie's hand shook as she held the bank statement. Victoria was going to pay for this humiliation.

"I asked Victoria to check, and she's taken care of locking up the house as well as your money until you're ready to go back."

She laughed at how pathetic Victoria really was. The kid hadn't been planned and had been a burden from day one, but your career went nowhere if you were a woman who abandoned your child, at least by the time she'd had her. She'd done Victoria a favor with the job, but Victoria's problem was that she'd never overcome her lapdog ways. Everyone, starting with her clueless kid, thought Sophie was some blind idiot who didn't realize who Weston was and what he wanted. "You can stop looking at me with all that pity. You don't understand anything about me or my life."

"Okay, explain it to me."

"You think I'm letting some young guy get one over on me because I'm *that* desperate, but Weston isn't getting anything more out of me than I'm willing to give." Okay, she hadn't known about the forty grand, but she knew he'd explain it once this shit show was over. She picked up the cup of coffee Belle had made and took a big enough gulp that she burned her tongue.

"I didn't ask you about Mr. Cagle. I asked about Victoria. She's your child, and because she is, maybe she deserves something from you. Children aren't something that are foisted on you."

"Like I said, she should know how I feel about her. I might sound harsh, but a kid was never in my plans. But it fucking happened, and my mother wouldn't let me get rid of it." Sophie closed her hands into fists, reliving the frustration from that loss of control.

Back then men did as they pleased, took what they wanted, then walked away free as the wind. It was still that way, but they were more careful about their images. But back then, her mistake had been hers to deal with. Her lover never looked back or acknowledged his part in the life they'd created. No, it had been her, and she'd put up with the snide comments and rumors of who she'd slept with and whether she even knew who the father was.

"Why did you keep her so close, then? From what I understand, your parents would've gladly taken Victoria in while you were touring."

"Oh yeah, right. Like that wouldn't have ruined my career. Having her and being branded a slut almost did that, so we were stuck together, and I took on the role of doting single mom. Underdog of the fucking century. So fucking no one was happy, and that's the hard truth. The alternative was going home and ending up with nothing but a screaming brat and parents happy to have dirt under their nails."

She turned away from Belle and thought back to her mother's disapproving expression as she'd endured the worst months of her life. The morning sickness lasted her entire pregnancy. That alone should've made labor easy if life was fair, but easy had been the last thing it was. It had been hours of misery, pain, and fear before Victoria finally made her appearance. She arrived only to teach her that the work had only just begun.

"I understand what you're saying even if you think I don't." Belle's soft tone was soothing, but only drugs and alcohol had ever dulled the fury over the things in her life she couldn't change. "Being coerced into having a child must've been bad enough, but going through that alone had to have been hard."

"Does that buy me a ticket out of here?" She drank the coffee and stared at Belle sullenly.

"The truth is, you can leave whenever you want." Belle pointed to the door and smiled, probably at her surprise.

"You want to help me pack?"

Belle shook her head, and her smile faltered some. "We saved you from yourself when you were incapable of making smart choices. If you leave before you're ready, you have to understand the consequences. Victoria understands and agrees, even though it will crush her if you decide to throw everything away."

Her anger rose faster than bile in her throat after a bad night. "I can take care of myself. I always have. You keep talking about what could've happened, but it didn't, did it?"

"Do you honestly think you're here because you took care of yourself?" Belle shook her head. "I know that you're responsible for you, and so does everyone who loves you, but believe me, life isn't easy to navigate without a safety net. And you've had one for too long. If you leave, there will be consequences."

"Just lay it out straight, and stop trying to stretch this out any more than you have to."

"Victoria will give you what you want. You'll no longer have to answer to her or anyone else. If your goal is to kill yourself, that'll be your right."

Belle spoke so matter-of-factly that Sophie blinked, not quite believing her. This asshole was talking about her demise like she was ordering a latte in one of those ridiculously overpriced coffee places.

"Victoria is no longer your responsibility, and in turn, you are no longer hers. That's what you've wanted, isn't it?"

"Victoria's my daughter, and she works for me." She stood, still shocked this woman was addressing her like this, and all her bullshit had obviously turned Victoria against her. She might not have any respect for Victoria, but dammit, her brat owed her. "She'll have to deal with me one way or the other because that's her job."

"She told me she wasn't your manager any longer, and you were fine with it. That was before you ended up in the hospital for the second time. When she found you within moments of death." Belle stood as well and picked up all her notes. "That frees you to handle your life how you see fit with your candy man, until you eventually kill yourself because no one is around to care anymore." Belle cocked her head to the side and smiled, making Sophie hate her that much more. "Or you can stay and put all this shit you've carried for so long down and leave it here when you're ready to move on. Aren't you tired?"

"Why the hell should I move on?" She leaned over the table and slammed her hand down. "After this, who's going to want to have anything to do with me?" The thought of being alone in that big house with only Weston and their fun made her nauseous. She'd worked all her life to achieve fame, but it had disappeared in a second, and she had nowhere to go after this. That realization almost made her wish that Victoria hadn't arrived in time, so she could have surrendered to oblivion.

"Are you kidding? Open your eyes, Ms. Roddy, before it's too late. You have people who love you and are rooting for you. Victoria wants everything to do with you, and I bet the guys who've played with you for a very long time do as well. Grab on to all that, but also know that's not enough."

"What's your suggestion, then?" She wanted a drink so bad she could taste the whiskey in her coffee cup. But what Belle said about being tired…yeah. Maybe that was true.

Belle held her hand out but didn't come closer. "Before you can appreciate how others love you, you need to learn to love yourself. You need to be enough for you, and that only comes with being comfortable and happy with who you are."

"That's the most ridiculous mumbo-jumbo I've ever heard."

"Sounds like it, doesn't it," Belle said and laughed. "But trust me, it works. Do you need help packing?"

In truth, Victoria was a pain in her ass, but the thought of her giving up on her depressed the hell out of her. A future without her daughter would certainly stop the constant nagging, but it would also be empty. Weston knew what it took to give her a good time, but he didn't really care about the triumphs, so she'd never shared them with him. She had Victoria for that. At least if she stayed, she had a chance of keeping the only relationship that mattered.

"I think I'll keep you around if only to spend some of Sonny Liner's money. That, and I don't want you to think I totally hate

Victoria. I don't think I ever learned to love her, but I don't hate her." She took Belle's hand and followed her back inside. "Thank you, Belle, especially for kicking my ass."

"Don't thank me yet. I'm not done."

"I'm sure, but not to worry—I can hit back."

Mason stepped out of the bathroom buttoning a denim shirt, and her hair was slicked back with what looked like copious amounts of gel. It certainly was a new look, but she was gorgeous no matter what. Victoria was still sitting on the bed in her panties, not ready to get dressed. An afternoon of great sex, cuddling, and talking had left her with a need to be close to Mason, and she really didn't want to go out.

"Are you going somewhere?" She watched as Mason tucked her shirt in before threading a black belt with a large Western-style buckle with bull horns on it through the loops on her jeans. All that was missing was a horse and a cowboy hat to complete the outfit. "Or are you rounding up some little dogies?"

"*We're* going somewhere tonight." Mason pointed between them then tilted her head back as if she was studying the ceiling. "Do me a favor and get dressed before I forget my name or go blind from staring at you."

Black alligator boots completed the outfit, and Victoria had to run her tongue along her bottom lip as she considered how delicious Mason looked.

"You're not helping, darlin'. Put that back in your mouth and think of what you want to wear."

"Where are we going? And do I need to channel a cowgirl to fit in?"

"Wear something that'll be comfortable to play in." She was about to ask what that meant when Mason picked her up and carried her to the closet. "What's your pleasure, Mistress?"

"Staying in and breaking you like a wild bronco, but I guess that's not in the cards right now, so I'll go with the white sundress."

"You are trying to kill me."

She smiled when Mason put her down so she could slip the dress on over her head.

"I need you to behave and agree to be part of Incognito tonight."

"You're in the band Incognito?" Now all the instruments in the studio made sense. She'd assumed they had to do with Mason bringing talent over and working with them, but clearly that wasn't the only reason.

"You know it?" Mason sounded surprised.

"Babe, everyone in town knows it, and I'm lucky enough to have Josette as a friend, who gives me a heads-up whenever the band is coming to her place. She called me the last time Incognito played there and saved me a seat at the bar. You guys were fantastic, but I don't remember seeing you."

"The girl singing that night was Claire Murphy, which usually guarantees fantastic."

Claire Murphy had been the hottest female act in country music for the last three years. "Your lead singer looked nothing like Claire Murphy."

"She was dressed down and blending in. Incognito is more of a lab than a band. It's a good way to test new music with an audience who's only paying for drinks. We try stuff out, and if it works, it's the music you hear on the radio or in concert. If it's a flop or only so-so, we drop it and try something else." Mason sat her on the bed and helped with her boot, and she decided on a cowboy one for the other foot. "We're filling in at Josette's place tonight."

"Exactly who's trying new music?" Victoria crossed her arms, remembering what Mason said about wearing something she could play in.

"Colt, and he needs a duet partner. You don't have to, but it might help make up your mind on recording with him or not."

Mason was speaking loudly from the bathroom, and she was trying to remember why she had no memory of Mason with this band. Even if they'd never met, Mason was noticeable. She did remember the guy with the ponytail and a full beard who'd walked out of the bathroom.

She started laughing. "You take that incognito thing seriously, don't you? I don't have to put on a beard, do I?" She put her hands on Mason's face and stroked the facial hair. The only thing familiar were those beautiful blue eyes.

"Once people recognize you, you'll have to go undercover, but you should be fine for tonight."

She stared at Mason all the way into town and couldn't help but reach up and touch the beard every so often, making Mason smile. This was the part of being a couple that made her curious when she'd witnessed it in other people. Being free to touch or kiss the person you were with without it being awkward wasn't something she was familiar with, but it was nice. It was maybe a stepping-stone to having Mason belong to her because it would be mutual.

The trees flew by on the country road, giving her time to think about what she was getting ready to do. Granted, Mason had given her an out, but she was also gently prodding her to at least try to sing, and in that, she wasn't going to disappoint her. Once she started singing, that might be where the disappointment started, but there was no denying the nervous excitement making her stomach queasy and her palms sweaty.

Singing with Colt Kenny in front of more than a handful of people was comparable to being dropped on Mars and convincing yourself it was normal. It was far from that, but this was one of those opportunities that came along once in a lifetime, and only if you were really lucky. If she took the chance and succeeded, it would change her view of the world. Seeing that she could build the courage to do something that seemed insurmountable would help slay whatever windmill stood in her way.

"What are you thinking so hard about?" Mason asked as she turned toward Nashville.

"Dreaming impossible dreams."

"Those are the best kind, darlin', because you have the chops to make them come true."

The place was full, as usual, and the second scheduled band of the night was still playing when they arrived. Mason left her at the bar while she went to finalize some stuff with the manager. Josette opened a bottle of wine and poured her a glass, leaning over the bar to kiss her cheek before she delivered it.

"I thought you'd have come with Mason," Josette said close to her ear. "I haven't heard from you, and I was hoping it was because things were going well. You look relaxed enough to make me think you've been having lots of sex. Are you?"

"All I'm admitting to is that things are fine, and she's meeting me later."

"Does that mean I can buy the pretty lady a drink?" The tall blond guy wearing the tackiest Western shirt she'd ever seen on a man sat close to her and spoke into her other ear. It was necessary to get that close to be heard. What the current band lacked in talent, they made up for in volume.

"No, thank you." She leaned away from him and rolled her eyes so only Josette could see her, and she spotted the gold teeth when he smiled. What possessed people to put their initials on their teeth? It was like tattooing your own name on your body. Was there a chance you'd ever forget it? Could you ever be drunk enough to have to refer to your arm or chest to remember who you were? "I'm here with someone."

"Just one drink, and maybe a song later." The guy was persistent, but he kept his distance. That made her take a better look at him. "Hey, Victoria," he said quietly, winking.

She laughed at Colt's disguise. He looked ridiculous, but he probably enjoying going into a public place and not getting mobbed. "Hello, TJ." She went with the initials on his teeth. "Thanks for the invite."

"Did you think about my offer?"

In the quiet moments, between bouts of sex and food and reading, she'd done some soul-searching. Taking a deep breath, she nodded. "I did, and I talked it over with Mason. If you're sure, I'll be happy to."

His face lit up. "Great, and you'll see tonight why I'm so sure about you. These people are going to fall in love with you."

Josette glanced between them, seeming totally confused, and that expression only deepened when Mason came over and kissed her when Colt started for the stage. "Did you have some kind of sexual epiphany I should know about? Mason couldn't have been so bad in bed that you've jumped into the world of tacky testosterone."

She laughed and pushed Josette away. "As if." She tugged lightly on Mason's beard. "You really need to shave this off, baby. I'm not a fan."

"You can wield a razor later, but now it's time to work."

Josette laughed, shaking her head, and waved them away.

Wilbur was setting up close to the piano, and he shyly kissed her cheek when Mason helped her up the stairs and to the piano bench before picking up her guitar. The other bearded guys were probably with Colt, but all that flew from her mind as she started playing. This was the largest crowd she'd ever played for, and it was empowering. It erased some of her self-doubt and cemented her decision that saying yes to Colt's offer had been the right thing to do.

The first two songs were from the new album, and the growing crowd loved it. His voice was beautiful and made it hard to concentrate on the music. It was clear the crowd was enjoying it too, and she smiled at Mason's wink.

She'd been here often but never on a night when the place was this packed and buzzing with energy, and she'd certainly never seen it from this vantage point. "This is crazy," she mouthed to Mason as more people crowded in. The sidewalk was full of people who couldn't get inside.

People had their phones out and were recording and taking pictures as Colt sang some music that wasn't his, and she had to think that Incognito wasn't such a secret, especially tonight when Colt's distinctive voice was singing lead. This was certainly a new experience, and she couldn't help but think of her mother. Having this many people so into what you were doing was certainly thrilling, and it had to be even more intense when it was a venue fifty times this size.

"You guys are in for a special treat tonight," Colt said as he started toward her. They'd had another short conversation before they'd begun, and she'd made a rash decision about a question that probably needed more than a split-second reaction answer. It would be hard to undo. "It's my honor to introduce you to"—he smiled at her—"Everly."

Mason's eyebrows went up, but tonight she didn't want to be Victoria Roddy, hot mess and daughter of even messier Sophie Roddy. Tonight was a tribute to her grandparents' belief in her, and Everly was her grandmother's name. It was also her middle name, and a memory of happier times.

She glanced at Mason before she started to play and wished it was Mason standing next to her at the microphone and not Colt. The song was beautiful, but also incredibly intimate. It was sure to become one of those pieces people would play at special occasions like weddings when expressing love and devotion was paramount. If tonight was her opening and closing act, and she never got a chance to sing anything else in public, she was incredibly lucky to have it be this song.

Mason's eyes never left hers as she sang her part, and while it was way too early to express the forever kind of love the song spoke of, she had no problem singing the words to this woman who'd come into her life and swept away so many horrible things so quickly. She finally glanced away when they finished, and she saw Sonny and Amelia Liner sitting at the bar.

The sight of them shocked her, but the rational part of her brain understood. Mason's parents seemed to be the involved type, and like it or not, they knew what Mason bringing her for dinner meant. Even if Sonny didn't, Amelia sure as hell did, and it was comforting to see that she wasn't upset.

"We're going to take a little break, so grab a drink and get ready for some more music in fifteen. Don't forget to be generous to your waitstaff and the bartenders." Colt unstrapped his guitar and turned the mic off. "Told you," he said when he leaned toward her. "You're not only a natural, but you're fantastic."

"Thanks, Colt, and thanks for taking a gamble on me."

"Easiest decision I've made yet."

"You invited your parents?" she asked Mason as she held her hand down the stairs.

"It's more Sonny and Amelia assessing music than Mom and Dad coming to a recital. Colt's been a big investment, and Pop likes to reassure himself every so often. On the nights it doesn't go this well, Mom is here to talk him off the ledge."

"Thank you for not saying anything ahead of time. I would've been nervous enough to make my voice crack."

"The only thing you have to worry about is getting my father not to force you into a contract before you finish your first drink. You really were excellent, and the four hundred people in here agree." Mason stopped her in the dark spot next to the stage and put her arms around her. "Just remember one thing."

"What?" As thrilling as the night had been, she was ready to spend the rest of it with Mason.

"Only do what'll make *you* happy. You have the talent, but it's yours—no one else's."

"I think you're biased, bearded man." She tugged on Mason's chin hair, laughing at how it made her mouth pop open with each pull.

"I'm certainly guilty of that, but it doesn't make it any less true. The only thing you need is to believe it."

The dream of playing, or more accurately being part of the band, had been her daydream for a long time now. It was what kept her afloat all those days when she wanted nothing more than to give up, or at least walk away from her mother. Adding her voice and being out front hadn't factored into that, but tonight gave her plenty to think about.

The other thing it brought into focus was how addictive this could be, and she understood better why her mother had driven herself so hard. Once you heard the applause and had the adulation of the crowd, it could drive you to keep going to hear it again and again. Was that the life she really wanted?

She glanced at Mason, and that adoring expression was her permission to believe she could have anything as long as she had someone not only to share it with, but to lean on. If she wanted to step out of her daydreams and make this a reality, all she had to say was one word, and it fell from her lips as easily as falling into Mason's arms.

"Yes."

Chapter Fifteen

There was still a crowd outside the bar by the time they were done, making Mason glad she'd parked behind the place. Her parents had treated them to drinks and complimented Victoria on her performance before getting them both to promise to come to lunch again on Sunday. The night had been magical, and she was happy to see the excitement in Victoria's eyes that hadn't been there before when it came to music.

She'd listened intently to the songs Colt had chosen when Victoria performed with him, and she was amazed at all she'd missed the first time she'd heard her sing. Victoria's voice had much more depth than her mother's, and her range was so much better. With a little more training, Victoria could have a successful career, if that's what she really wanted.

"What'd you think about tonight?" Victoria held her hand and had her head back with her eyes closed. It seemed like she'd had a good time with her parents, but Mason didn't want to guess about the rest. "You really have a beautiful voice." It was a good opening to gauge where Victoria's head was at when it came to performing anything beyond what Colt was asking of her.

"This is kind of funny." Victoria turned her head and slowly opened her eyes.

"What's funny?"

"I'm sure there are a lot of acts and singers out there who'd line up to have your baby if you gave them five minutes to hear how wonderful they are."

Victoria lifted her hand and kissed her palm before biting her finger, which made her hard. It was ridiculous in a great way, since she felt like a teenager with a crush, but there was no way she was questioning anything.

"I wasn't asking, and I wasn't looking, yet here we are."

"It might shock you, but I give a lot of five-minute timeslots without the baby option. Not that I don't want kids for my parents to spoil, but I don't want them in exchange for a contract with Banu." She tried pouting, but the damn fake mustache made her face itch. "Sometimes, though, talent falls on your head like a rock from the sky, and you have to act before someone else figures out what a treasure they have on their hands."

"You're good at the compliments, baby, but I doubt I'm the next big thing."

How could she break through Victoria's self-doubt? "You'd be surprised what I think."

"Honey, you don't have to offer me anything. I'm not expecting that at all."

"How about you listen to me and stop guessing what's on my mind," she said and smiled to take any sting from her words. "When I joined the company, my dad knew I wanted to expand out of the country genre. The country scene is what he's concentrated on, but I've moved us beyond that. It's a market with a lot of fans, but there isn't a lot that gets me excited about it, nothing new anyway, until tonight." She turned into her driveway and pulled off at the line of trees so she could face Victoria. "You're right, though, you didn't ask, and you weren't looking, yet here we are. I'm in love with your voice, and I'm excited to hear more."

"You aren't disappointed, are you? Would you like me to be more aggressive?" Victoria moved away slightly, but Mason quickly filled the gap by moving closer.

"Sweetheart, I want a lot of things, and I'm aggressive enough for the both of us, but that you aren't with me to improve your chances of getting a contract is a wonderful thing." The admission prompted Victoria to kiss her. "To answer your question, though, I meant what I've said more than once. You have to do whatever you think is right for you."

"I'm asking your opinion, Mason. Not as a woman you're seeing and sleeping with, but in your official capacity at Banu. I just want to make the right decision. Contract or no, though, it won't change my mind about you, well, unless you toss me out."

She wanted to be direct, but she also didn't want to sway Victoria toward one decision or another. It had to be totally her choice. "If I'm totally honest," she said, staring into Victoria's green eyes, "I'm enjoying having you all to myself. Once you record with Colt, I'm going to have to share you. That's how confident I am in your voice."

"Enough crazy talk for tonight." Victoria held her hand between hers and pulled Mason closer. "You know this song will probably be my one claim to studio fame, and then I'll go back to playing in whatever band will have me that'll keep me in town. There's no way I'm going anywhere and giving some other woman the opportunity to trip over a root, fall into your arms, and need to be carried around." She pulled on the beard next before moving her hand down to her neck. "Can you shave this off or whatever you need to do? I'm ready to get your face back."

"That nixes my idea of making out in the truck."

"But raises your chances of making out in bed. Come on, I'm through with sharing you for the night as well."

Mason started the truck and got back on the drive toward the garage where she'd left the utility vehicle. The kitchen door opened when she shut the motor off, and the sight of Belle stepping out didn't bode well for the rest of her night. Belle spoke to Victoria almost daily to assure her Sophie was okay, so a face-to-face after midnight meant nothing good.

"Hey, that's a different look for you," Belle said when she got out and walked around to help Victoria down.

"My hormones are way off."

Victoria laughed at that as she put her arms around her neck and held on.

"Did you overcaffeinate today and can't sleep?" Mason asked. "I feel like I'm late for curfew and my mother's waiting to bust me."

"I'm in no way old enough to be your mother, but I want to talk to Victoria now that Sophie's asleep. Could you give us a few minutes?" Belle waited until Victoria had her crutches before heading for the study.

"Sure," Mason said.

"Come with me…unless you don't want to." Victoria grabbed Mason's forearm before she could walk away. "Did something happen?" Victoria asked once they were seated, and from her grip, Mason could tell she was anxious. "Is Mom okay?"

"She's fine—actually, better than fine." Belle lifted her hands and made a slowing down motion. "We had a session today, and I gave her the option of leaving. She turned me down."

"I'm curious," Mason said, not moving as Victoria held her arm with enough pressure to leave bruises. "What would've happened if she had taken you up on that offer?"

"It'd have been followed by a long lecture about making better choices, but we have to give her the chance to make them." Belle sighed and rubbed her hands on her jeans. "No one does well in therapy if they don't have some freedom to choose some things for themselves. We can't keep her locked up forever, but she has to realize how her behavior affects others and take responsibility for it. If she feels like she's made the choice to stay, she'll start to open up some more."

Victoria nodded and let up on her forearm a bit. "That's good, but I doubt you waited up for us to tell me that. What's the *but* in this equation? I know her well enough to realize that with Mom, there always is one."

"I need to tell you some of what we discussed, because I think it's important to your journey too. Sophie has given me permission to do so."

Words were only words, but what Belle was saying clearly sliced into Victoria with the ease of an ax through rotten wood. Victoria didn't have to say a thing for her to know that—the way she sucked in quick breaths and released them in small spurts was proof enough. It was equally clear that Sophie Roddy was a total bitch.

"I believe some of that rage has to do with her anger at being here, but we need to work on the very real residual resentment she's feeling about a life-changing event she felt stripped her of her choices. You have to understand that this isn't about you," Belle said, and Mason was amazed she could keep a straight face saying that. "I believe her true anger lies with your conservative grandparents and the man who fathered you."

"Oh, I'm sure she's angry at me too." Victoria's tears fell steadily but she didn't lift her hand to wipe them away. It was like her exhaustion over this whole thing was too much to bear a second longer. "I didn't ask to be born, but she's mad I'm here. Trust me, I understood that when I was four, and time hasn't blunted it. But after everything I've done. Everything I've given up…"

"It's more like she's mad that she put herself in that position, and believe me, I would've rather skipped this conversation with you. The problem is, you're going to have to start therapy with her, sooner rather than later. It's probably the last thing you want to do considering the situation, but it's also a starting place to wherever you two are going to end up. You have to understand that it might be on permanently separate paths."

Belle really was the best person for this job, but at the moment Mason wanted to order her to shut up and get off her property. She hated seeing Victoria in so much pain.

"What exactly does that mean?" Victoria asked.

"The basic truth is that your mom has hit rock bottom, and she wants someone else to take the blame for every mistake she's made. It hurts like hell, but it's not an uncommon behavior. No one wants to admit that they are the only reason they've fallen this far. Once you air all that out together, she might feel she'd be stronger without you in her life, and you might come to the conclusion that things will never change, and you'd be better off getting out of the vicious cycle you're stuck in. Or it could go another direction, one that keeps you in each other's lives. But you have to be prepared for both possibilities."

"Thanks for telling me, I guess," Victoria said, falling against Mason and sounding defeated.

Mason was at a loss about what exactly she could do to help Victoria, but she'd be there and stay no matter how many bad days they'd have to face. The rest she'd figure out, considering she was way out of her comfort zone on this. Whatever came next, she was sure her mother's advice would be to stay strong and present.

"I'm really sorry, Victoria, but I didn't want you to get blindsided in a session. Our goal is to—"

"*My* goal is to make it better so she can live her life without killing herself," Victoria said, seeming to have found her footing. "I won't have that on my conscience, but I'd like my own life as well."

Belle smiled. "I told her that, and she says she understands, but when that time comes, and you're no longer there to clean up after her,

I think she won't, and we'll have another setback. But my professional advice is that it's time to drop the employment part of your relationship for a while. Take your life back, and learn to be the person you want to be without her around. That's only my opinion, though. Whatever relationship you have with your mother going forward is up to you."

"Is that all?" Victoria asked.

"Do you have any questions?" Belle stood and waited.

"I think this is enough to handle for the night," Mason said, hoping Belle took the dismissal hint.

Belle nodded and squeezed Victoria's shoulder on her way out of the room. "We'll set up a session time another day."

"Oh my God," Victoria said when they were alone. "I shouldn't't"—she buried her face in Mason's chest and released a ragged breath laced with tears—"be surprised."

"Listen to me." She held Victoria by the shoulders and pulled her back a little so she could see her face. "None of this is your fault. The one thing I agree with Belle on is that your mother has a skewed sense of what her role in all this should be, but you"—she cupped Victoria's cheek—"are a treasure. Don't ever think that you're lacking in any way. You can't believe that how she feels and thinks has anything to do with you."

"It has everything to do with me," Victoria said through her tears.

"Is that what your grandparents thought?"

"No."

"It's not what I think, either. Sophie might be inducted into the Country Music Hall of Fame for the music she's recorded, but the best thing she's ever created is you." She put her arms around Victoria and held her as she cried.

"Thank you."

She could feel Victoria's breath against her neck, and it made her want to be the one Victoria turned to for comfort no matter the hurt. That she couldn't take away the pain on Victoria's face bothered her more than anything ever had.

"I'm not sure what I'd do without your friendship."

"I don't think that's something you should worry about." She moved so she could pick Victoria up and stood. "How about we go to bed and sleep in tomorrow?"

"I'm sorry our night got ruined, but I'd love that." Victoria's face was wet, and she looked tired. "I want to do that song with Colt, but only if you represent me."

It was like Victoria had to plant her flag and claim something that was hers and not anything to do with Sophie to prove she had worth on her own. She'd had a taste of getting her own life going, and she clearly wasn't going to just walk away from it now. "Honey, every professional in this town will warn you away from having your label be your manager."

"Are you planning to rip me off?" Victoria's mouth curled into a smile for the first time in the last hour.

"You can't believe that."

"Then say yes."

She smiled back and headed outside. "I promise I'll consider it if you do one thing for me."

"Tell me, so we can get that out of the way."

"Meet with an agent first and understand what they can do for you. That way you'll understand what having me represent you should entail." She settled Victoria in the utility vehicle and kissed her. "There should never be any doubt between us, and the more you know, the less likely that'll be." She kissed her again. "How about it?"

"You're hard to say no to, Mason, but I'll do it if that's what you want."

"That's what I want, but eventually we'll both get what we want."

"Which is?" Victoria took her hand when she sat in the driver's seat.

"We have to leave a few surprises out there. If not, what's to look forward to?"

"Right now, I'm looking forward to a bed with you in it."

Chapter Sixteen

A week went by with Victoria going into Banu with Mason daily. She was avoiding Belle and her request that she join her mother for therapy. Now that she knew the absolute hard truths of what her mother thought of her, it was impossible to consider sitting with her and discussing what a huge mistake she was, at least right now. Everything Belle had told her only magnified all the mistakes she'd made along the way, and all for someone who was never going to love her anyway.

To Sophie Roddy she was an error, a huge screw-up, but she'd given up her dreams and her childhood for whatever sick need Sophie had to have her around. Victoria doubted it was *all* for show, but maybe it was also a way to punish her grandmother, who actually wanted her. That kind of selfishness was a foreign concept to her, but it was the blade her mother had used to cut her so deep, the wound would never really heal.

That was what she was planning to tell her mother when they finally did sit and talk, but she had to find a backbone before that meeting. There was no going back, but she did want to leave her mother in a place where she could survive the addiction on her own. Trying to keep all that swirling emotion inside was nearly impossible, but she didn't want to frighten Mason away, even though she'd been nothing but a great friend up to now. What they were building was becoming something special, but everyone had their breaking point, and she didn't want to reach Mason's limit.

"You want to take it from the top?" the recording guy said. "You were off tempo on that last run."

"Sorry." She put the headphones back on and listened to the song's opening. Colt had already recorded his part and was on his way to New York for the first stops on his tour.

This always looked easy when she'd watched her mother do it, but having only the voice and the music in your head while you stood alone in a studio made it hard to conjure up any feeling. That afternoon singing with Colt while Mason was listening had freed something in her that hadn't been there before, and all that emotion had come from singing to Mason.

She started singing again and stopped when she spotted Mason in the booth smiling at her. That Mason had stayed away while they were at the office for the entire week had surprised her, but she'd given her space after they'd signed the contract that would pay her new manager half a percent going forward. They'd argued about it, but that's all she'd been able to talk Mason into taking. This song would most probably be the only thing she'd ever do that would make money, so she guessed she should be grateful for the extra income.

"You doing okay?" Mason asked into the intercom and she shook her head. The others in the booth took a break when Mason said something to them before joining her. "You change your mind? Your manager will take care of it if you have."

"No, it's not that. Surprisingly, this is so foreign." She put her arms around Mason's shoulders and stood between her legs when she sat on one of the stools scattered throughout the studio, bringing her to eye level. "And I'm lonely."

"You don't have to be, especially when I'm in the building trying not to plan ways to sneak down here to see you." Mason kissed her like she had all the time in the world and the guys waiting on them didn't cost a small fortune. "You want to try something different? If it works, we can get out of here and do something fun."

"Will you stay? Maybe if I sing this to you and not the twelve-year-old you have mixing it, it'll help me out."

Mason smiled and nodded. "Whenever you want to sing me a love song, feel free."

She took some deep breaths while Mason got everyone ready. The guys waited for Mason to put on headphones and sit back down with a microphone over her head. It was different this time when the music started, and she looked into Mason's eyes and felt her blood ignite at what she saw in their depths. There was no denying the desire and perhaps something more that was plain and strong.

They hadn't put words to their feelings out of caution, maybe fear, but there it was in Mason's eyes. They hadn't known each other long, but Mason's face was so open, and she couldn't hide much from her when they were this close, and that truth was like a soothing balm on a horrible cut. Mason gazed at her like a woman who wanted more from her than a casual fling, and she wholeheartedly returned the sentiment. She tried to convey that through the words she was singing, letting emotion flow through the music.

Caring was what made every touch, every kiss, and every look from Mason special. Mason had been passionate but tender with her, and she made the process of falling for her so easy she'd willingly opened her heart, barely thinking of all the things that could go wrong. That had always been her habit no matter what she was contemplating doing, but she'd gone into this not only with her eyes open, but with an enthusiasm she'd never experienced for anything else. She sang as she stretched her hand out to Mason and closed her eyes when she took it.

This time, though, the voice in her head wasn't Colt's, but Mason's. She opened her eyes to find Mason singing along with her. She'd heard her play, but this was the first time she'd heard her voice, and she was ready to cry at how beautiful it was. They made it through the whole song holding hands until the booth guys interrupted.

"Great job, Vic. We'll drop the boss's voice out and finish mixing yours with Colt's. It's a wrap unless you want to try it again. I can't imagine you could be more perfect than that last one, but it's your call."

She shook her head, never breaking eye contact with Mason. "We're done, but could I have a copy with the boss on it? She sounds better than Colt."

"I won't tell pretty boy you said that, but there's a reason Mason's the voice of the company. The boss has some great pipes as well as awesome brains."

Mason laughed and shook her head. "Kiss ass."

He grinned and turned off the mic as he started talking to the rest of the crew.

"Thanks, honey." She squeezed Mason's fingers and waited for their audience to leave so she could kiss her the way she wanted to.

"You're welcome, and *you* are great."

Mason walked her outside and led her to her office. She knew the way because she met Mason every afternoon when she was finished with rehearsals, but today, she wasn't ready to go home.

"Will you go out on a date with me tonight?" Mason asked as if reading her mind.

"Anytime, anyplace." She stood between Mason's legs again when she sat on the edge of her desk. Her foot had healed enough to walk without the crutches and boot, but heels were still a few days away. "And this," she said, kissing Mason slowly until she felt the tightening of her hands on her ass, "is for helping me today."

"Believe me, darlin', you don't need any help, but I'll be happy to inspire you whenever you like. Right now, how about dinner at Rolf and Daughters? I won't even make you sing for it." Mason finished her tease by kissing the slight cleavage visible at the top of her shirt.

"I'd love to, but I doubt I'm dressed for that." Victoria glanced down at herself and grimaced.

"Stop making that face, and you're fine. If they don't let us in, we'll go out for doughnuts that I'm planning to eat in my pajamas." Mason packed her bag and put her jacket back on.

"Did you run out today and buy pajamas?" Waking up with Mason every morning, pressed to her skin to skin, was something that put her in a great mood for the rest of the day.

"I did not, so I'll have to go with the naked option. It makes it easier to clean off any unfortunate jelly spills."

Mason held her hand as her assistant Scarlet followed them to the truck, finalizing things as they walked. She enjoyed the teasing relationship between Scarlet and Mason because Scarlet didn't leave her out.

"Stop talking, Scarlet—I've got a date."

"What crazy woman agreed to be seen with you in public?"

Victoria laughed and raised her hand. "You can sign me up for a mental health assessment tomorrow, but I'll take my chances tonight."

"Have fun and try everything." Scarlet waved and turned to go back inside.

"At the restaurant, you mean?" she called before Scarlet made it through the door.

"There too, but not at all what I was talking about."

"Good advice," she said as Mason opened her door. "Can we talk about what comes next?" She waited for Scarlet to disappear before asking.

Mason closed the door and moved quickly to get in. "What do you mean?" She didn't put the truck in gear and placed her fingers under Victoria's chin. "What are you thinking?"

The inside of the truck still had that new car smell, and it reminded Victoria of the newness of their relationship. Hopefully they'd get to a point where she could simply say what was scaring her or bothering her without fear of laying it out there.

"For the first time in my life, I'm not sure of who I am. I can't go back to being my mom's manager, but that's all I've ever done. I'm recording this track, but it's just one little thing, and…what do I do next? Who am I?"

The rapid-fire words sounded almost panicked and Mason wasn't sure where they were coming from. It's like Victoria had finished the one thing she'd decided to do, and now all that was left was the abyss of the unknown that was clearly scaring the hell out of her.

"You've already done so much for both of us, but there's no way I expect you to keep my mother in your house indefinitely, and that's how long it will probably take to make her a decent human again."

"And you think I'm tossing you out when your mom goes?" She got no answer and it clued her in to how Victoria thought. Doom and gloom were the first things that crossed her mind no matter what the situation was, and it would take time to change that mindset. "If I ask you to do something with me, would you?"

"I'll try my best."

"I know what your life has been, and the conversation with Belle last week confirmed it for me." She brushed Victoria's hair away from her face and wiped her tears away with her thumb. "There's nothing I can do to change the past, but I'd like you to give me the chance to be a part of your future. I want that more than anything, but you don't have to believe me or even trust what I'm saying. The proof will come in time when we wake up together every day and I'm there through everything—the good and the bad."

"I'm not sure how I lucked out, but thank you."

"I simply want you, and Sophie's free to go whenever she's ready. You, though, are free to stay, and to be honest, I'd really like you to.

If that's too fast for you, though, keep your place, or better yet, keep the river house until you're ready to take the next step." She leaned over and kissed Victoria lightly on the lips, not wanting to mess up her lipstick. "No matter what you decide, I'm going to be here. Nothing about this scares me enough to want to lose you."

"That I believe with all my heart." Victoria wiped Mason's lips clean of the bit of color that transferred from her lips, then pressed her hand to her cheek. "You are by far the best thing that's come into my life, and I do want you. There's certain things every woman should be sure of, and for me, that's you."

"Good, don't forget it." She chanced more lipstick before she started the truck, wanting to get to the reservation Scarlet had made for them. "I do have an idea about what comes next, though, if you're interested."

"If it has something to do with being your love slave, we might have to negotiate."

She had to laugh and shake her head at Victoria's quick wit as she turned into traffic. She might get insecure and panicky, but she was always quick to recover. It was sweet, but Mason hoped it wasn't a way to mask her true feelings. "Maybe later we'll iron out my lifelong servitude to you, but I was thinking more about your music career."

"Honey, you're kind, but I don't have a music career."

Victoria ran her fingers along her forearm, and she thought about how much she'd generally disliked being touched this much in the past. Victoria had broken through so many barriers that it should've scared her, but so far she hadn't wasted brain power on this truth.

"Now that I've finished with Colt's project, I thought maybe you could make me an intern or something. I can start small, but with a little experience I could eventually be useful to you." Victoria looked hesitant, but it was good she was taking a chance and voicing something she was interested in.

"I do want you to work for me, but I had something else in mind." She stopped at the valet stand and glanced at the guy walking to Victoria's door. He opened it and wasn't exactly covert in checking Victoria out. "Do you think you'll be more attractive with a black eye and missing teeth?"

Victoria snorted at the question when the valet handed over a ticket, shaking his head vigorously.

"No," the guy said hesitantly.

"Honey, the faster we eat, the faster we get home and talk about that sex slave thing." Victoria spoke loud enough for the valet to hear, and Mason had a hard time keeping a straight face when he swallowed hard and went pale. "I don't want to waste the night out here on stuff that's not ever going to be a problem, or in any way a possibility."

"Sorry, guys like that make me nuts." Mason put her hand at the base of Victoria's back as they went inside. The possessive side of her was new, but Victoria didn't seem to mind.

"It's flattering that you're pissed on my behalf, but trust me, it's not necessary. You're the one I want to be with." It didn't take long to get a table, and the secluded spot gave them the privacy to finish their talk. "There's also the fact that things like that rarely happen."

"Were you surrounded by fools all your life?" Mason tapped her fingers on the table enough that Victoria finally covered her hand with hers to get her to stop. "I don't mean to get all possessive on you, but open staring makes me want to punch people. Not that I can blame them, but I'm the only one that I want openly staring at you."

"I don't care about any of that." The way Victoria smiled at her made her relax. "Besides, I want to talk about something else. I'm done with Colt's project, so I can't put Belle off much longer. My mother is going to need assistance getting through therapy, and Belle seems to think I'd be good to help with that."

"Are you worried about talking to your mom?" The waiter took a wine order from Mason and left quickly when she motioned him away. "There's no rule that makes you have to do this."

"I do want to, but I want to be sure of myself and what I want to say before I do. This last week has shown me I can stand on my own, and when I can't, you'll be there to hold me up."

"Damn right." Mason took a sip of the wine she'd poured. It was delicious, and she'd enjoyed having a glass with Victoria every night as they shared a chair on the deck.

That sense of domesticity was something she'd often dreamed about, but she had always wondered if it would eventually suck the excitement out of any relationship. So far that was something she couldn't imagine happening with Victoria, and she was loving their take on domesticity.

"I'm serious. Only do this if it's what you want. Don't let Belle talk you into something you aren't comfortable with. I know you love your mother, but Sophie's a big girl who got herself in this position. Maybe it's time for her to work on getting herself out of it."

"Trust me, there's nothing Belle could tell me that'd surprise me about my mother. Well, hearing that I was an unwanted mistake wasn't pleasant, but there won't be anything worse, I don't think. I'm sure you've dealt with difficult artistic personalities, so you know what I'm talking about." Victoria twirled her glass by the stem as she stroked her fingers with the other hand. "The truth is, I have to make peace with my mom, and once I do, we can move forward without that hanging over us. This isn't your responsibility."

"I want it to be my responsibility because it's you. Whatever you need from me, all you need to do is ask. There's no reason for us to suffer in silence any longer. Whatever is bothering either of us, I want to be able to talk about it without fear of what the other person will think." She signaled the waiter when she saw him hovering nearby and ordered, after Victoria asked her to do the same for her. "Once you start taking those steps, there are some more I'd like you to consider."

"Take your own advice, Liner, and just spit it out."

Victoria threaded their fingers together and smiled at her in a way that made her feel that in this one moment Victoria was truly happy.

"There's this song I think will be the cornerstone of a new album, and I'd like you to consider it." The great smile was replaced with confusion, but she wasn't stopping her pitch. "If we lead with the song I'm talking about, we can release it close to the duet with Colt, and the marketing from that will help it get where I think it will go."

Victoria was quiet and had slumped back, but she hadn't let go of her hand. "Could you explain that again, because I don't think I quite understand?"

"I wrote a song for you. To lead off an album all your own." She let Victoria go, reached into her pocket, and handed her an envelope.

Her job revolved around the music business, but her heart and her head agreed that no one could do any job effectively unless they understood, and loved, every aspect of it. Her father had grown their family business with her mother's help because he understood the nuts and bolts of what sold, and her mother understood the music. She'd learned all of it from both her parents' perspectives, and while she knew her best talents were from her father's side of the equation, there was no denying her mom's influence.

"*You* wrote a song for me?" The way Victoria glanced from the papers to her in constant motion almost made her laugh.

"I did. It doesn't happen often, but when I feel strongly about something, I've been known to try to capture it."

Victorian nodded slowly. "When did you do this?"

"A week of missing you did the trick, but I wanted to give you the freedom to do your thing in the studio without me hovering." She stood and opened her arms when Victoria got up and walked into them.

"You're too much, and I'm so lucky you're with me." Victoria kissed the side of her neck and hugged her tightly.

"There's never going to be too much between us. You're going to fly because of you, and I'll be happy to watch. All I can give you is the chance to do what you obviously love, but the rest is up to you." There was no way to erase every heartbreak, but she could give Victoria everything she needed to live her dreams. Even if, in the long run, those dreams didn't include Mason. "All you need to do is say yes."

"Nothing is going to change if I say yes—between us, I mean."

It most certainly would, but as long as Victoria was happy, that's all that would matter. "You're going to set the world on fire, and I'm going to be there for all of it."

"You're damn right. I won't do it unless you're there every step of the way. Thank you for this. Even if all I ever get to do is sing it to you while I'm cooking dinner, it'll be special because you wrote it." Victoria sat and lowered her gaze to the pages. "Talk to Me" was a song about their first night together and the very intimate conversation they'd had.

That night, all those unspoken words that encapsulated devotion, love, promise, and commitment were the ones that resonated the loudest. It had taken one night to fill her heart with everything Victoria meant to her, and maybe she was an idiot for allowing it to happen, but she wanted this woman forever. The song in Victoria's hands represented her ticket to a new life, far different from the one she was living now. It also represented freedom. Mason wasn't about to bind Victoria to something she didn't want if she wanted no reminders of that old life.

She didn't say anything as Victoria read, and she shrugged when Victoria looked up at her with an expression of wonder.

"There are moments in your life that you have no idea of their impact, for good or bad, until they play out." Victoria placed the papers back in the envelope and slid her hands to the center of the table. "You get thrown in my path at what seemed like the worst moment of my life, and you've done everything to make me fall in love with you. You've been the biggest and best impact on my heart, and I love you because of it."

"You're the woman I've been waiting for, and I have no intention of letting go, but I won't hold you back, either."

"Shut up," Victoria said. She squeezed her hands, and Mason could see the candlelight dancing in her eyes. "I never wasted time waiting or hoping because I didn't think anyone like you existed, but here you are. The best part of being with you isn't this." Victoria cocked her head toward the envelope. "It's being with you, doing all those things people think are boring, but they're not because you're right there. I love you, and I'm not letting go either."

"I love you too." It was good to finally say it out loud. "It's probably way too early to say it, and it's probably crazy, but I love you."

"Think they could pack everything we ordered to go?"

"Waiter!"

Chapter Seventeen

Victoria smiled against Mason's shoulder as the house creaked around them in the quiet of the night. So this was what it was like to be happy and in love, and to have a home to enjoy it all in. The location didn't matter, only the woman in the bed who held her protectively even in her sleep. A couple of months ago she would've been content to find a piano job and work in a dive, living in solitude, but now nothing made sense without Mason.

The song Mason had given her was beautiful, but there'd been no time for that after they got home and made love, stopping only to eat when her stomach growled so loud it made Mason laugh. The eating had been fast, though. If Mason had been passionate before, admitting their feelings had brought them to new heights. Their fun should've exhausted her, but she was too giddy to sleep, and she'd never used the word *giddy* in her life.

Mason's steady breathing didn't change when Victoria rolled away and got up. It was two in the morning, so she didn't bother with clothes as she closed the door to their bedroom and sat at the piano. The small light over the music stand was all she needed to play the slow ballad that only she and Mason would truly understand.

She made it through the whole thing and started over, planning to sing this time. Mason's words were hauntingly beautiful, and they would've given away her feelings if she hadn't already confessed them. The introduction would be only the piano, and she got through it, anticipating what the rest would sound like with accompaniment.

"Talk to me. Tell me all I want to know through your kiss. Those are the words of lovers that only you and I understand. Those are the

words that fill my heart with how much you love me.

"You are mine and I am yours. The truth of that is the love song of our lives, and I want nothing more than for you to talk to me.

"Talk to me. Tell me about forever in the way you hold my hand and walk by my side into all my tomorrows. I know you won't let go even when there are no more days to share, because—

"You are mine and I'm yours. The truth of that is the love song of our lives, and I want nothing more than for you to talk to me."

She played, having difficulty seeing the music through her tears. Who knew Mason was such a romantic? She finally stopped before it was done, needing to take a few deep breaths so she could try again. Composure was impossible when Mason, completely naked, sat next to her and started playing where she left off.

"Talk to me. Tell me how much you love me in the way you hold me. Your touch is all the poetry I'll ever need, and your eyes hold every song we'll dance to until our time is done."

She pressed closer to Mason as she sang the chorus.

"Talk to me. In your silence I can hear your promise that your love is mine alone. Those are the words written on my soul and they give me courage to face whatever life brings.

"You are mine, and I am yours. It's the love song of our lives, and I want nothing more than for you to talk to me."

Mason lifted her hands from the keys and turned to smile at her with those perfect dimples. She straddled Mason's lap, smiling herself when Mason's hands immediately landed on her ass. It was amazing to go from a long period of celibacy to being this ravenous for Mason's hands on her.

"Baby, please." She locked her feet at the small of Mason's back and moved when Mason leaned her against the keys, sucked her nipple in, and bit it gently. She felt it all the way to her clit, and she pulled Mason's hair to get her to suck the other one. "You make me want you so much."

Mason lifted her head and kissed her hard enough to make her lips feel bruised, and it wasn't enough. She needed Mason inside her, loving her, reminding her she'd found her home. It was like Mason had read her thoughts. She squeezed her hand between them and then into her, fast and hard, but then didn't move at all.

"You want me, baby?"

"Oh my God, yes." She pumped her hips, desperate for the stimulation against her clit. The damn thing was so hard she thought she'd die from need. "I don't want to wait…I'm so ready."

"Tell me what you want." Mason's deep voice wrapped around her like a spell that left her craving an orgasm. "Tell me or I'm going to stop." The sensation of Mason pulling out and slamming back in would make her come too soon, so she concentrated on her breathing and on hanging on.

"I need you to make me come," she said, biting down on Mason's shoulder. "And when you do, I'm going to suck you until you come in my mouth."

She almost laughed at how fast Mason went back to her nipple as she moved her hand in time with the thrust of her hips. It was clear Mason could play her as well as the piano, and the way she made love to her made her want to keep her inside, but she couldn't hold back any longer.

"Oh yes…yes, holy fuck, yes." She squeezed Mason's shoulders, and she tried her best to take Mason deep by tipping her hips forward. "Oh…" She felt the orgasm rush through her, and she jolted forward to kiss Mason. There wasn't a tense bone in her body, and she was ready to go back to bed, but she had a promise to keep.

"You okay?" Mason asked when they came apart.

"I'm perfect, but you need to turn around." She slowly stood and exhaled when Mason pulled out. "Go on, move."

Mason swung her legs around and put one hand in Victoria's hair and the other behind her head when Victoria knelt and sucked Mason's hard clit in until it was pressed against her tongue. She wanted to make it last and show Mason how she felt about her, but Mason was wound too tight to hold on.

"Fuck," Mason said and tightened her grip on her hair. "So good, baby." It was all Mason could manage before the muscles in her thighs tightened and she let out a string of curses.

She kissed Mason's sex one more time before coming up to kiss her on the lips. "You're a sexy beast, Liner, and we need to clean this bench before we play out here again."

"It's playing that makes it necessary to clean it." Mason picked her up and carried her back into the bedroom.

"Play music, honey, not house."

"Live a little, sweetheart, and all those memories will hopefully inspire your playing if I'm not around." Mason spooned behind her and flattened her hand on her stomach. "Right now, go to sleep."

"Thank you for yesterday." The last twenty-four hours had been like finding a lucky penny that actually worked, and all her wishes had come true. "You're like my own personal Santa."

"I love doing things for you because I love you." Mason yawned so she rolled over and pushed Mason onto her back. She draped her arm and leg over Mason's body and rubbed small circles on her abdomen.

"It's that simple?"

"When it comes to you, yes, it is." Mason kissed her forehead and put her arm around her so she could pat her on the butt. "Loving you is the easiest thing I've ever done, and I always want you to know how special you are."

They fell asleep and the phone woke them up at eight the next morning. It was Colt, and it sounded involved, so Victoria went to the bathroom. This morning her reflection didn't appear haunted by the ghosts of the past. She looked…happy. It was time to let go and rebuild something she and her mom could live with.

"Hey, Belle." She answered her own phone, and smiled at the sound of Mason's voice still coming from the bedroom.

"Hey, I'm surprised you answered. I thought you were avoiding me."

"I was," she admitted, and Belle laughed.

"I don't really blame you. It's not like I'm asking you out for a fun night. Are you ready? It's okay if you're not."

She dropped her head back and stared at the ceiling. How easy it would be to say no, she wasn't ready, would never be ready. But she had her own life to live, and it was time to do what had to be done. "It's time, and I'd like to do it this morning if Mama's okay with that."

"If you can be here in an hour, we'll be ready."

That was that. It was like pulling the trigger and waiting to bleed, only the wound wouldn't be fatal. All she had to do was keep reminding herself that her fear always stemmed from the fear of being alone, and wishing she mattered to someone. That had started when her grandparents died and all she'd been left with was a relationship with her mother. She'd twisted herself into knots trying to please her, but she'd never come close. Now she knew why.

The great Sophie Roddy had seen her as lacking, and that had sealed the fate of their relationship. It wasn't her mother's fault, though, that she'd been weak and had tried so hard, even into adulthood, for her mother's approval. That was on her and her need to have someone in her life no matter how they treated her. Now she was ready to reclaim her pride, and Mason's love was like a talisman that reminded her that she was worthy.

"This must be my lucky day."

Victoria put the phone down and turned to face Mason.

"Did Colt make you a gazillion dollars?" The sensation she always got from Mason's embrace was wonderful, but it doubled when they were naked.

"A gazillion might be a reach, but that's not it." Mason's arms came around her, and her feet came off the floor. "I'm lucky because I wandered in here and found a beautiful naked woman in my bathroom."

"You are lucky, not to mention flattering, but that's as lucky as you're getting. I'm meeting Belle and my mother in an hour." She rested her head against Mason's and sighed. "Are you going into the office?"

"I think the office can come to us this morning." Mason led her back to the bed and sat. "You are the woman I love, and you need to remember a few things before you go up there. The most important is if you need me for anything, I'm a call away. I'll be here when you're done. If you need to talk, or if you just need space and silence, whatever, I'm here. The other things to keep in mind are that I love you, and you have a place. You have a place and it's one where you're wanted, so don't let Sophie make you think otherwise."

"I know." They kissed like they had all morning, before they went and shared a shower. She dressed casually, not bothering with her hair except to pull it into a ponytail.

"You want a ride?" Mason offered.

"I have time to walk, but I might need one back." There were horses at the fence in the distance, and they added to the beauty of the area, but the best part was Mason stepping behind her and holding her.

"I love you, darlin', and I'll be waiting right here."

"Knowing that gives me the strength to do anything." It was time to claim her future and all it had to offer. "I love you too, and I'll be back."

❖

Victoria took her time walking to the main house and waved at the ranch hands she saw along the way. She spotted Belle sitting with her mom outside, and she stopped in shock at how pale and exhausted her mother appeared. She hadn't seen her since they'd arrived here nearly six weeks ago, and she looked nothing like the country superstar of Victoria's chaotic life. She looked worn down and old. It drove home the reality of how close she'd come to losing her, and it would've hurt despite their differences. Perhaps Sophie wasn't a great mother, but she was the only one she had.

"Thank you for coming, Victoria," Belle said when she was near the patio. It had taken a few minutes to get her feet moving again.

She nodded and went to kiss her mom's cheek, but Sophie put her hand up to stop her. This wasn't going to be a joyous reunion, and her stomach dropped with the well-known dread of being a disappointment.

"Just sit and stop pretending you give a shit about me," Sophie said.

"Sophie, we talked about this." Belle tapped her pen on the notebook and shook her head.

"Don't you mean *you* talked about this? I've listened and done all this crap until I'm sick, and where the hell has *she* been?" Sophie sliced the air with a rigid finger in her direction. "You fucking abandoned me here, but not before you took everything that was important to me. Weston is gone, my tour is over, and the band has probably moved on as well."

"You're seriously going to lead with that?" She spoke so softly that her mother had to stop her rant to hear her. "I agreed to get you help, and no one, especially me, told Weston to go anywhere. He left of his own accord, along with a lot of your money, I might add. The only thing I've done was to try to protect your assets while you got better."

"Didn't she tell you the truth?" Sophie's tone was back at full throttle as she pointed at Belle. "You and me have been stuck together, and we need to face that. I might've given birth to you, but nothing can make me happy about that."

"Wow. You're right." She stood up and ignored Belle's motions for her to sit. "Neither one of us got what we wanted or deserved in each other, and I'm sorry for my part in that. You didn't have a choice in the beginning, and I totally understand that, but you have a choice now. Just be honest and tell me what you want."

"I want my freedom."

"From me, you mean?" She refused to cry, not anymore. "Of course, from me," she said, and her mother stayed quiet. "You got it. I'm never going to tell you that I don't care what happens to you, because I do, but you're not obligated to me any longer for anything. All I wanted was to get you help before you killed yourself, but that's it. You don't owe me anything. And I most certainly no longer owe you anything, either."

"Don't be so dramatic. That's always been your problem."

Sophie's voice was harsh, and she almost wanted to laugh. When her mom didn't get her way, her instinct to fight was overly emotional, as if trying her best to get you to back down.

"What exactly was supposed to be the correct response, Mama? I'm not being dramatic—I'm giving you what you want." She stood with her head slightly cocked, breathing in the jasmine-scented air, and found some comfort in the peaceful surroundings. The warmth of the wrought iron armchair she was standing behind made her realize she was squeezing too hard, but she repeated the question despite not wanting to be there or hear the answer. "What would you like me to say?"

"You could say that you give a shit about what happens to me. You should've been here helping me through this."

"Make up your mind." She wanted to shake her mother until she stopped this stupidity. "Either you want me, or you don't, but you were never alone. I was frantic at the hospital after Weston called. You were this close to death"—she held up pinched fingers—"and I was praying you'd survive. That's all I cared about, and I did whatever I could to keep you alive. You say I don't care, that I wasn't there for you and I should have been. But I've been there, and it wasn't enough. What do you want?"

"Let's take a minute," Belle said when it appeared like her mother was about to start again. "This isn't about playing the blame game. It never helps and does nothing to solve any problem."

"Fine," Victoria said and tried her best not to telegraph how pissed she was. "What can I do to help get her to a safe place where she's not going to overdose?"

"You—"

"All you need to do," Sophie said, talking right over Belle, "is put things back the way they were. I didn't ask to be saved, and I didn't need it."

"Victoria," Belle said, cutting off any response she had. "Can I talk to you?" They stepped into the kitchen, and Belle kept her eyes on Sophie. "This might've been too soon, and for that I apologize."

"If you think I'm surprised, I'm not."

"Actually, the one who's surprised is me," Belle said, shaking her head. "You might not believe me, but in our private sessions Sophie never displayed any of this hostility. I'm a little baffled, to be honest. It's my mistake in bringing you two together too soon, since it's clear she can't let her guard down around you yet. It's often hardest to be vulnerable around the people who know us best."

"Maybe what you just saw *was* her being totally honest. Did that ever occur to you? You and I see an addict out of control, but Sophie didn't have a problem with her life. That's the truth of it, so maybe it's us who have to accept it."

"I refuse to believe that, but I do understand where you're coming from. We need to give it more time, and hopefully I'll find out where this hostility is coming from before we try again."

Victoria tried to stop the shaking in her hands. Even after several weeks, she was still her mother's scapegoat, and she still wasn't good enough in any way. "No need to apologize—believe me, I'm familiar with her temper. Can you legally keep her here? I'm all for trying some more, but that's not what she wants, obviously."

"I've logged her as a danger to herself with the local mental health agency and made this a treatment center, which means I can keep her for a while yet. A few more weeks, then it's going to take a lot of convincing. Are you sure you and Mason don't mind being displaced?"

"The river house isn't exactly slumming it. We'll be fine, and I'm sorry if I lost my temper."

Belle laughed and rubbed her back. "Sophie is what I see as a carrier of misery, and she loves to share. None of us are immune, and if that was you losing your temper, I think we're all safe. I think I'd have said far more."

"I'll go out the front so I don't upset her any more than I have. Thank you for all that you're doing."

She stopped when Belle took her hand. "Go out the back and tell her good-bye. She might not be nice or remotely agreeable, but it'll give her peace of mind that you haven't forgotten her."

The five deep breaths she took before stepping outside didn't help clear her head, so she decided simply to deal with whatever her mom threw at her without yelling or hitting something. There was no way her mom would change her mind about her, but she was strong enough to handle it. She could feel that now, deep in her bones. She could see her mom's hands shaking as she combed her hair back repeatedly as if in a trance, and it was sad how far she'd fallen from that superstar she'd grown up with.

"Mama, I'll be back, but if you need anything, Belle will let me know." Sophie stiffened when she kissed her cheek and hugged her. "I love you, and I want you to be okay, no matter how you feel about me."

She left before her mom could inject any further cruelty. The hill was steeper than she remembered, and she made her way slowly down, careful not to put too much pressure on her still healing foot. As hard as she tried to ignore them, her mom's words kept hitting her like spiked hammers to her heart. She knew her mom was being illogical and had a long way to go in her journey. But that didn't mean the words didn't hurt, that knowing she was such a deep disappointment to her didn't make her heart ache. She was halfway down when she spotted Mason coming from the opposite direction. Her horrible mood vanished as Mason sped up to reach her.

"Have you been pacing down here?"

"It was more like I was anticipating you. I didn't want to get too close, but Sophie's voice really carries."

"Well, who can blame her? I ruined her life by surviving birth, by getting rid of Weston, and by ruining her career." She pressed against Mason and snuggled in once Mason put her arms around her.

"She can blame me for part of that. I remembered you talking about him, so I had someone go over to convince him it was time to move on." Mason shifted so they could walk back to the river house. "Sophie isn't the first one to indulge his love of illegal substances, and hopefully he can find someone else to share that particular hobby if she's out of the picture."

"That might be true, but he's going to come running back the first chance she can get him on the phone." They sat on the front porch, and even after hours of sleep, she was tired. "Belle's going to keep trying, and in a couple of weeks we might have a problem if she wants to leave before she's ready."

"I'm sure that's not what you wanted to hear, but we'll try our best to get her what she needs." Mason kissed her palm. "How about a few days away from here to get a taste of things to come?"

"We still have some spots in the house we haven't tried, so you don't need to bring me anywhere if you want to get more adventurous." She loved the way Mason sounded when she truly laughed. It seemed to come from her soul, and hearing it lightened her mood no matter how down she was.

"I love you, and I love the way your mind works, but I was thinking more career related."

It was hard at times to accept how happy Mason's loving her made her, and that it was real, but Mason proved it to her with every kiss. Mason always held her and poured out a little of the magic she'd created with the song she'd written for her every time she pressed her lips to hers. The wonder of it assured her that Mason's feelings were true. Her mother might not think she was worthy, but Mason did. And that meant everything.

"This may sound sappy, but I'll follow you wherever you take me." She stroked Mason's hand with her thumb. That's when she heard the laughing close by.

"You look like some old couple ready for rocking chairs," Josette said. She was getting out of the utility vehicle Jeb was driving. He got out as well and placed a bag on the porch. "What's happened to you?"

"This one happened to me." She kissed Mason again before going to hug Josette. "Not that I'm not thrilled to see you, but what are you doing here?"

"When someone invites you to a concert in New York, you don't turn that down."

"We're going to a concert in New York?" Victoria looked back at Mason.

"Overnight trip," Mason said. "This is the first concert release of one of Colt's new songs, and I want to see how it goes. If we're going to go with this model for the rest, it might need some tweaking if Colt's idea doesn't go over like he hopes it will."

"It's not the duet, is it? I don't think I'm ready for that." Victoria's heart pounded at the thought of standing in front of a crowd like that.

"Not yet." Mason opened the door and pointed to the bedroom. "You get to enjoy it as a spectator this time, but soon you're going to have a legion of fans. Just don't forget who the president of your fan club is." She shook her head when Josette followed them and sat on the bed. "Like I said, a taste of things to come."

"So pack for one night?"

"This time around. When we get back, we'll start working on your concert tour."

"I'm sure I'm not anywhere near doing that."

"Faith, my love, faith."

Faith was a word she'd only heard in songs, and it held no meaning. Being with Mason brought her comfort, but there was that nagging fear in her that nothing seemed to kill, and it belonged exclusively to Sophie. Her fear was that the day her mom found out what Victoria had planned for her own future, she'd see it as the biggest betrayal of all.

She was happy, but the anchor that tethered her to her past would take time to cut loose, and for once she wondered if even having Mason and a new career would be enough to cast off those bowlines. A month ago fear would've kept her from even thinking it was possible to have a new life, but here was Mason looking at her like she was the only person in the room, and faith made perfect sense.

Mason's faith in her, and her faith in what they had together, would be the foundation she'd build her new life on.

"I believe you." And more importantly, she believed in herself. She was enough, and she'd never allow Sophie or anyone else to convince her otherwise. Never again.

CHAPTER EIGHTEEN

Mason stood in the booth of the recording studio at Banu listening to the conversation going on inside. It had been two weeks since their overnight trip to see Colt, and he was working his way back to Nashville before heading to the West Coast. These practices with the musicians she'd put together for Victoria were to get her ready to record, and to hit the stage with Colt.

The musicians were already in love with Victoria, but she hadn't doubted that would happen. Despite Victoria's talent, she'd tried to ease her in as gently as possible. To make things familiar, Mason finally gave Wilbur the job he'd always wanted. He was Victoria's new lead guitar and was thrilled to leave the doughnuts behind.

"We'd better behave." Victoria's voice broke through her day-dreaming and she smiled. "The boss is checking up on us."

Mason stepped into the light and crossed her arms. "How's it going?"

"So good we're taking a break."

Victoria met her in the booth and walked outside with her. Mason was careful not to show too much affection in the office, to keep people from giving Victoria any crap because of their relationship.

"Have I done something wrong?" Victoria asked.

They stopped at the edge of the garden Mason's mother had commissioned for anyone who needed to decompress during a day of recording. "No, and I wasn't checking up on you." She sat when Victoria chose a bench and took her hand.

"Is there some reason you act like I have some contagious disease whenever we turn into the parking lot here?" Victoria lifted Mason's arm and put it around her shoulders, making her feel like an idiot because she hadn't done that without prompting. "Do we need to take a break from being us from nine to five?"

"You know that's not true, but I don't want anyone saying anything hurtful to you because of me." She smiled against Victoria's lips when she turned and kissed her.

"You're a clueless but sexy idiot sometimes. Are you doing all this just because you love me?" Victoria kissed her again and pinched her cheeks. "Unless you don't want people to know."

"Don't drive yourself crazy about stuff that's in no way remotely true. And you know why I'm doing this. Granted, I love you, and I'd do anything for you, but this is your decision. What you do with it is on you." A few people came out of the building carrying lunch bags, but she didn't move, trying to redeem her clueless idiot status.

"One of the reasons I'm enjoying myself is because I'm doing it with you. You've given me the courage to try."

Their time after their concert trip had been spent mostly working, and spending time together as they planned an album. The women writing with Colt had also started working with Victoria, and they'd narrowed down five more songs that were possibilities. The writing partners had been at the river house every afternoon, and they seemed to have a better rapport with Victoria than with Colt. Wilbur and Josette were there every day as well, since she wanted Josette to consider coming to work for Victoria. She'd need a good and loyal friend once they launched her music, and Josette would do anything to watch Victoria's back because she loved her.

"Is there anything you need? Am I falling down on the job as your manager?"

"You need to work a little on the hand-holding job, but you're doing great otherwise. Actually, the music is starting to come together, which of course means I heard from Belle this morning. Can't have all good news, can we?" A few Banu employees smiled from nearby benches when Victoria put her feet up and leaned against her. "She wants to give the family meeting another shot."

"That much has changed in a few weeks?" When they were working or alone it was easy to forget that Sophie and her shitload of problems were a short mile away from them. But really, Sophie was like a time bomb ready to blow everyone's life to hell. Or to try to, anyway.

"Considering what she said, I doubt it, but we're getting to the point where we have to give her some freedom." Victoria played with her fingers and sounded more subdued than she had in a while. "I'm not sure how she'll deal with leaving here and going back to Weston, but everyone deserves their life back, including Belle and Cassandra."

"Let's see what we're facing before you start worrying. If it's necessary, I'll have someone go by again and have another conversation with Weston. I have some friends who are good at explaining things to people who have trouble understanding anything." She rested her head on Victoria's and sighed. "If he's a tough case, I'll talk to him myself."

"You'd beat someone up for me?" Victoria reached up and rested her hand on the side of her neck.

She chuckled at Victoria's teasing. "Anyone you want, baby. The time Sophie's spent with Belle has hopefully given her some tools to work with when the cravings hit. Maybe she won't go back to him after all."

"Let's hope, but I feel bad I haven't helped more. Mama has a point when she says I've abandoned her." Victoria plucked at a loose thread on her shirt.

"Don't do that to yourself. Remember that you saved her life, and you've done everything that's been asked of you." She lowered her hand to Victoria's waist. "You love her, and she's going to have to accept all this was for her own good. And if she can't, well, that's on her. You're learning to live your life, and she'll come to terms with that or she won't. But it doesn't mean you gave up on her. You just moved onto your own path."

Victoria was silent for a while, and Mason let her process. Victoria tilted her head back. "Want to come play with me?"

Mason grinned and raised her eyebrow. "You want to try the office?"

"Maybe when your father's not in the building, and you know that's not what I was talking about. But thanks for putting that in my head. Time will slow to a crawl now."

"Anytime." She kissed Victoria's cheek before they got up. "Now let me go tell the band I'm madly in love with you, while I hold your hand in case they have any funny ideas."

❖

Belle was waiting on the deck when Victoria walked up the last part of the hill. Mason had driven her more than halfway, but she wanted to keep her out of Sophie's line of fire. She'd stayed away the last two weeks as well, and she couldn't deny how happy, how light, she felt without the weight of her mother's decisions dragging her down.

The sun was close to setting, but Mason was on her way to check on some horses before returning to give her a ride back to the house. Most of her nervousness disappeared against Mason's lips when she kissed her before she got out.

"No matter what, remember—you belong somewhere, and I love you." Mason had hugged her tightly before Victoria started walking the rest of the way.

"Are you ready?" Belle asked. "She's been really quiet, and she's expressed how sorry she is about what happened before."

She nodded, but hope wasn't something she could afford. Her mother had practiced a certain behavior over and over, so it was hard to believe she'd changed over a two-week span. "Has she done okay otherwise?"

"She has, and she's waiting in the kitchen."

Her mom stood when she entered and seemed to really think about it before opening her arms. "Vic, thank you for coming." She was dressed, and her hair was done, which made a huge difference from the last time she'd seen her.

"You look good, Mama."

"It's been some long weeks, but it was time to pull myself together."

She didn't release her mom's hand as they sat at the table. "You scared me," she admitted. The tears came when she relived the night she saw the paramedics bringing her mom out, so close to death. In that one moment she'd never felt more alone, but also so angry. "It's like you didn't care any longer."

Her mom took a deep breath and kept her eyes on their hands. "I know I'm lucky you never gave up on me, no matter how horribly I treated you." She sounded contrite, and it was the first decent conversation they'd had in a long time. "I'm sorry, and I want to try to start over with you."

The words sounded too good to be true, which made her think they *were* too good to be true. Belle might have spent lots of time with her mother, but there was no way she knew her as well as Victoria did. Sophie Roddy was a music legend and a great con artist when it came to saying or doing anything that would assure she got her way. The right words would unlock the door to the prison she saw herself in and free her to go back to the life she wanted.

That meant Weston, the pills, the booze, and the freedom to enjoy them until she was dead. The truth of what Victoria knew to her core hurt almost as much as the hurtful words, because it was like all of this was for nothing.

"I'd like that, and like someone told me recently, we all deserve to be happy. That's been missing from our lives for way too long."

Her mom's hands were cold but sweaty, and she was squeezing her a little too hard. It was like she was trying to get through her lines and was trying not to forget any.

"I appreciate you bringing me here. It's a beautiful place."

It was almost unnerving how nice her mom was being. Maybe Belle and her team had helped her work through a lot, and it'd made a real difference. That was a big maybe, though, and she wasn't willing to believe so readily.

"Please tell Mason thank you. I didn't mean to put her out."

She glanced at Belle, surprised she'd told her mother exactly where she was, but Belle only shrugged. "She was happy to help, and she didn't mind as long as it made you better."

"Sounds like she helped you too."

They should've been talking about everything that had happened between them, but she'd indulge her mom if only to keep her talking. "She's become very special to me."

"Wait." Sophie's face changed dramatically with a big smile. "You're *with* Mason?"

"I am," she answered slowly, suddenly wary of where this was headed.

"In a sexual relationship?"

"We're in a relationship, and that's all I'm comfortable saying. Does that bother you?"

Her mom laughed like that was the biggest joke she'd ever heard. "I didn't realize you were so desperate for company. Mason Liner…I'll be damned."

"So it bothers you?" She regretted the question as soon as it came out of her mouth. Would she ever be free of the desire for her mother's approval?

"Does Sonny know?"

"Yes." These weren't the responses she expected, but it wasn't exactly negative. "Mason and her family have been really nice, and I'll always be grateful for what they've done for both of us."

"You're right, and I'll thank them the first chance I get." Her mom let go of her hand when she finished speaking, then yawned. "Thank you again for coming, but I'm exhausted."

She kissed her mom on the cheek, and Sophie only slightly tensed. "Okay, can we talk again tomorrow?" If her mom had buried her feelings, she'd have faith in Belle to navigate them through it. She just didn't want to do it by talking about herself and Mason. Her mom nodded, but Victoria didn't miss the thoughtful look in her eyes. "Good night, then."

"That was interesting," Belle said when Sophie was well out of earshot. "I don't think we can trust it, but hopefully it's a starting point. She sounded rehearsed to me, and that makes me wary. Until Sophie can be truly honest, I can't believe we've made any real progress. Although I know for certain we've made at least a dent. I think she's seeing a lot of things about herself she doesn't like. But whether her words will match her actions, I don't know."

"I thought the same thing."

"If anything, this might be a correction from what happened last time. She lashed out and it delayed her leaving, so she's pulling back and biding her time."

"Has she mentioned leaving?" The false contrition in her mom's tone had been easy to make out. She'd apologize if she was wrong, but she doubted her mom was happy for her about Mason, and she definitely wasn't thrilled she was still here. But she was making all the right noises, and Victoria knew her well enough to know she probably had some endgame in mind.

"No, but we'll sit and talk about it tomorrow. Before you got here, the whole day was about complaining how she was wasting time with me." She shrugged. "That said, she's talking. She's opened up about things, and I do believe she's accepting some of her culpability in this mess. Whether she thinks she's *responsible*, though, I can't say yet. I'm going to be direct tomorrow and see where we stand."

"I'd like to be here for some of that. Maybe my presence will get her to show her real colors. This seems like it's taking forever, but I want her to be okay." She rubbed her hands on her jeans, trying to get rid of the sticky feeling from her mom's clammy hand. "Did you tell her this is Mason's place?"

"No, I think she was fishing, and you gave her what she wanted. And she may have seen Mason out and about on the property." Belle shook her head and smiled. "Don't worry about it, and I'll call you if something comes up. If not, same time tomorrow?" Belle hesitated and Victoria waited to see what she wanted to add. "The other thing I want you to consider is maybe some one-on-one therapy sessions for you. If you're not comfortable with me, I can recommend someone, but I think you'd benefit from sorting out your feelings about all this."

"Tomorrow sounds good, and I'll think about the counseling." She stepped outside and the darkness was welcoming. Their meeting had left her more discomfited than the one they'd had two weeks before.

She had no reason to doubt Belle's competence to help people like her mother, but the last hour of her life had been total bullshit. It was Sophie Roddy at her best fake self. If she was right, then all this, all the sacrifices they'd all made, were for nothing. It was her mother biding her time to get back to the chaos of the life she'd left behind, that Victoria didn't fit into. Most likely, she was just trying to figure out how and when to do what she wanted to do.

It was like being stuck on a hamster wheel of her mother's construction, and she was tired of running in a circle. But what if she got off the wheel and something horrible happened? There was no way she could live with herself, but the running and the waiting to crash were draining her to the point that she'd eventually be empty for anything but her mother's drama. That wasn't fair to Mason or to her.

"This must make me lucky twice in one day, Fred."

Mason's voice warmed her, and Victoria laughed when Fred ran to her and licked from her hand to her elbow.

"We're out here looking for squirrels, and you found this beautiful woman we get to take home. Good boy."

"Do you have any idea how glad I am to see you?" Relief flooded her when she saw Mason's smile.

"We had to come looking for you. Fred missed you." Mason hugged her and didn't say much else as she simply held her. This was the main thing she was afraid of losing. She'd found her place, and it was with Mason, but she still had a responsibility to her mother.

"Can we go home?"

"Want to talk about it while we walk?" Mason took her hand as Fred tried to press a stick into the other one.

"It really wasn't horrible." She threw the stick in the direction they were headed. "Mom was actually nice, and that worries me more than if she'd been her usual self. When she's horrible, I know what to expect. But nice…that throws me. Does that make sense?"

"You probably know Sophie better than Sophie, so I believe you. Are you worried about anything?" Mason threw the stick next, and Victoria wanted to forget everything on her mind and enjoy the rest of their night. "Does she want to leave?"

"She didn't talk about that. She mentioned how grateful she is that I helped her, and she thanked you for giving up your house. She's really enjoying Blue Heaven, and she was interested that you'd become important to me. But she cut the conversation short, and I admit that I'm glad." They stopped when her phone rang and it was Belle. "Hello." She put it on speaker so Mason could listen in.

"Are you sure you're okay?" Belle must've figured there was something off.

"I'm fine, and I'd like to believe my mother is as well. But I don't."

Mason distracted Fred with the stick again, and it was like having a foot in two vastly different worlds, but only one would eventually win out for all her attention. Whichever one that was, the loss of the other would leave a gaping wound.

Belle hesitated. "It does seem like an about-face, but maybe we've really turned the corner. What she says in our sessions isn't always what you get to hear, but I'll find out if today was an act or the beginning of something good. Try not to worry, though. That's our job. You concentrate on the great things you have going on right now."

"Thanks, but call if something changes."

She put her phone in her pocket and faced Mason. "I want you to remember one thing."

"Sure." Mason smoothed her hair back and smiled down at her.

"No matter what, I love you, and this has been the greatest time of my life."

Mason's smile faded. "Are you going somewhere?"

"No, but I didn't want to leave that unsaid." No one went out of their way to get sucked into what they didn't want, but sometimes you couldn't fight it. "I love you, and I want you to always know it."

Mason stood in the booth as Victoria and her band went through a song for the sixth time. They'd been at it for a few hours, and Victoria was a little off, and she'd been off in everything for the last five days. Five days of spending hours doing this in the morning, and every afternoon talking to Belle and Sophie, then being quiet for the rest of the night. Mason knew she wasn't sleeping well, but she wouldn't talk about what was bothering her no matter how often she asked. It was affecting her work as well as their time together at night.

"Take thirty, everyone," she said when Victoria's head fell forward when they finished again.

"Sorry," Victoria said when she joined her in the studio.

"Nothing to be sorry about." She sat next to Victoria and kissed her cheek. "As a matter of fact, we could call it a day and start again whenever you're ready."

Victoria gave a humorless laugh. "Honey, go ahead and admit I'm screwing this up. If you want to, we can call it quits. This has to be costing you a fortune."

"I'm sorry, have we met? You know I'm not going to tell you that." Mason waited, but she'd learned Victoria sometimes needed a nudge. In this case perhaps a hard shove would do the trick, since gentle prodding during the week hadn't worked. "What you can do is tell me what's wrong. It can't be that you're nervous, since this isn't your first rodeo. You killed that duet, so what's the problem?"

"I'm not sure. Believe me, I'd fix it if I could."

"Want to take a break with me? If we go for a walk, I can help you get in the right frame of mind." She held her hand out palm up and waited. "Dr. Liner is here and ready to help."

"Let's go, Dr. Liner." Victoria accepted her hand and laughed. "Is this a private session you offer everyone?"

"Private session for only one patient." They headed back to the booth where she let Victoria enter first. "Lou, tell everyone to take a few hours, and have lunch brought in. We'll be back and ready to go by then."

"You got it, boss."

"I'm not hungry," Victoria said when they entered the elevator to the top floor.

"Okay, I wasn't planning to eat just yet." They headed for her office and waved to the assistants as they went. Scarlet didn't get up but smiled as they stepped inside. "I thought we could spend some time kissing. It might not relax you, but it's something we both like doing."

"I like your thinking, Doc." Victoria fell into her lap when she sat on her couch.

"But if you need to, you can talk to me."

"You're the best thing in my life. You know that, right?" The way Victoria traced her eyebrows with her fingertips made her close her eyes and enjoy it. "I love the way you love me."

"Are you trying to change the subject?" Mason tried opening her eyes, realizing this wasn't about her.

Victoria covered them, though and hummed for a minute.

"Believe me, baby, whatever's bothering you, you can tell me. Is it about your mom? Did she tell you something? You haven't told me much about your sessions this week."

"Really all we talk about is you and me." Victoria kissed her after dropping her hands. It felt like Victoria was trying to hide from her, and all she wanted was for her to find strength in what they were building together.

"Is she upset it's me?"

"I don't get that. She's asked all this stuff about us, and I don't want to lie, but I don't want to be honest either. I'm sure that doesn't make sense, but I don't want to give her the chance to come between us. And it feels…false? Intrusive? I don't know."

She hadn't wanted to get in the middle of Victoria and Sophie as they tried to put their relationship back together, but with every meeting they had, the more of Victoria she lost. "Do you need some time away to figure all this out?" It was like getting a blow to the head with a bat, finally realizing that might be what was weighing on Victoria. She wanted out and was having a hard time telling her. "Is that what you're afraid to tell me?"

"What? No." Victoria grabbed the front of her shirt and pulled. "I just know she's asking because she's going to use whatever I say to get to you somehow. She uses people, and I can't imagine losing you now."

The answer made her shake her head. "Why would you think that, baby? You have a lot of history with your mom, and not so much with me, but I found in you the one person I want to be with. And I want that for a long time. Nothing your mom would do could change that."

"What do you mean?"

"I haven't said anything so I wouldn't scare you, but I'm in this for the long haul. You're the one who fits, and I want you in my life. I'm not going to force you into something you don't want, but I'm going to fight like hell to keep you."

"That's what I feel for you, and it scares the hell out of me."

"Why? Tell me what you're afraid of."

"Maybe you'll get tired of all this drama. I wouldn't blame you, and even I think it's too much. And she'll always be around. It's not like you can have me without having her around in some way too."

"There's so much I could say, but they're only words." She moved Victoria so she was straddling her legs. "The proof of my love for you won't come through words, but through simply loving you. If you aren't there yet, I'll give you time, but if you don't want it, tell me now so I can start dealing with it."

The way Victoria looked at her shut her up, and she accepted her kiss. "I want all of you." Victoria started on the buttons of her blouse and kissed her again. "Did you lock the door?"

"Will it make me seem calculating if I said yes?" She laughed when Victoria stopped with her buttons and ripped Mason's shirt open, sending a few buttons flying.

"Thanks for reminding me of us," Victoria said as she dropped her blouse behind her. She popped the buttons of her jeans and moved Mason's hand inside.

"That's what I'm here for." She moaned along with Victoria when she felt how wet she was, and Victoria slid her jeans down enough to position her hand and fingers. "Fuck, baby."

Victoria wasn't as vocal as usual thanks to thin office walls, but she moved her hips with her thrusts, and her breathing picked up close to her ear. That heavy breathing and the way Victoria held on to her were driving her crazy, and her pants felt three sizes too small. "Come for me, baby."

The command made Victoria moan, and her movements got clumsy. She felt Victoria's sex squeeze her fingers, and she covered Victoria's mouth with hers to keep her from getting too loud.

"Oh, I'm coming," Victoria said, pulling away from her and biting her bottom lip. "I'm coming."

She put her other hand at the small of Victoria's back and held her in place. "Give me what I want, baby. I've got you."

Victoria took a deep breath, and she felt a few more spasms go through her body.

"I'm sorry for freaking out on you…again," Victoria whispered after she'd fallen on top of her and exhaled. "You probably think I'm nuts."

"It's more like you're on overload, and you're being pulled in one too many directions." She stopped talking when Victoria ran her tongue along her bottom lip. It was so easy to get lost in what Victoria did to her, how she made her feel pretty much everything she hadn't before, so she relaxed, ready to follow wherever she was willing to lead.

"Why is it you understand me better than anyone else?" Victoria unclasped her bra. It was a good move if her intention was to keep Mason stupid for the rest of the afternoon. The reptilian part of her brain that channeled a teenage boy had a problem stringing words together when confronted with perfect breasts.

"That's an easy one." She reluctantly looked up when Victoria put her fingers under her chin and forced her head up. "It's because I love you."

"Good answer."

Victoria wrapped her fingers around her wrist and guided her hand away, and she shook her head, not ready to stop making love to Victoria.

"Don't pout, honey, you're not done, but I need to take my pants off."

She watched Victoria strip and wondered if she'd ever get tired of the sight. Victoria wasn't simply perfect because of every feminine curve, but also because of the way she looked at her. Her gaze when they were intimate was best described as predatory, the kind of stare that made her both hard and wanted. Add the perfect breasts, and it was a fantastic combination.

"Stop daydreaming about my tits and take your jeans off."

That was all it took to make her desperate, and there was only one way to ease the crazy over-the-top desire. She needed Victoria's mouth on her and these damn jeans off. Of course, the sight of Victoria's white lace panties was doing things to her coordination, and in the back of her mind, she wondered what possessed her to go with the button fly jeans today.

"Jesus." She wasn't loud, but it was certainly time to praise God and whoever else was responsible for the gift of Victoria kneeling between her legs.

"Can you come quietly?"

The way Victoria asked made her want to laugh, but she went with simply nodding. It was hard to form words her clit was so hard, and she blamed the way Victoria did justice to those panties and how hard her nipples were.

"Promise?"

"I promise," she said before Victoria's mouth became the center of her universe. It was so good she wanted it to last, but it turned out Victoria's secret wasn't sexy underwear, but reducing her to a hair trigger and no sense of control.

The orgasm swept over her, and she clamped her mouth shut as her body tensed. Victoria didn't let up until she was so sensitive she croaked out, "Stop."

She felt the feather kisses to her inner thigh as she tried to control her breathing, and all it did was make her want more. Victoria laughed when she picked her up, walked to the desk, and laid her down. "Can *you* come quietly?"

"I'm not making any promises."

After today, she'd never be able to control her smile when she sat at her desk and thought about Victoria lying there with her feet on the arms of her chair, legs spread, waiting for her to touch her. This time she went slow and ran her tongue gently over Vic's hard clit until she was desperate.

"Harder, baby, much harder." Victoria lifted her hips and pulled on her hair to bring her mouth down on her clit. It turned out she *could* orgasm quietly after all.

Victoria seemed much better by the time they shared a shower in her private bath and found her a new shirt with all the buttons attached. "Do you think anyone out there knows what we were doing?" Victoria asked.

"I doubt it, but the size of my smile might give us away." She held Victoria before they opened the door, knowing she wouldn't get another chance until their long day was over.

"You do know how to give a rousing pep talk, honey. If anything was bothering me, I have no idea what it was."

When they returned to the studio, she kissed Victoria before they started again, smiling at the whistles coming from the band. "Will you do something for me?"

"For you, anything." Victoria massaged the side of her neck as she kissed the skin where her shirt parted.

"Sing to me."

And Victoria did.

CHAPTER NINETEEN

Mason worked through the month's sales figures from the office of the river house while Victoria was gone for the morning. She'd offered to go with her to get more clothes from her apartment, as she was tired of wearing the basics she'd brought when they'd arrived here a few months ago, but Victoria wanted her to finish work so they'd have the night free. They were planning to spend the night enjoying the band on Josette's last day behind the bar, so she did her best to clear her paperwork.

"Hello." The number on her phone was from the main house.

"Hey," Belle said. "I hate to bother you, but Sophie would like to meet with you. It's all she's talked about all morning. You aren't exactly part of her recovery, so it's okay to say no."

"Is it okay to say I've had an ass full of Sophie and wish she'd drop off the face of the planet?"

Belle laughed, but she wasn't exactly kidding. "Perfectly okay, but what do you want me to tell her?" She could be wrong, but Belle sounded uncertain, which was unusual in itself. "She really does seem to want to talk to you."

"Can I come up now? Vic ran home to get some stuff, so she should be a few hours. Every time she wanders up there, she's in the dumps for the rest of the night, so I don't want to add to her load." Her stacks of paper lost their appeal as her curiosity took over.

"We'll be waiting."

She had to walk, having let Victoria take the Gator up to her car, but the morning air gave her the opportunity to calm down. Sophie Roddy's music had been something she'd enjoyed through the years, but she'd never really had to deal with Sophie. That had been her father's domain.

Authenticity in the music business only came behind closed doors, and only a precious few got to see the transformation. Up until her dad sent her to deal with the cluster Sophie had gotten herself into, Mason had thought her nice enough. From the little Victoria had told her about their talks, and the bits of Sophie she'd had to deal with in that time, that was no longer the case. In truth, if it were her choice, she'd cut Sophie loose, and she'd be someone else's problem. The only roadblock to that fantasy was that Sophie was Victoria's mother, and despite her being an asshole, Victoria loved her. Familial complexities could make for shitty companions.

Sophie was waiting outside alone, and her aggravation spilled over to Belle. If this was some sort of setup she'd head right back down the hill. "Good morning."

"Depends on how you look at it." Sophie didn't get up and she only glanced at her briefly as she made her way to sit across from her. "This is some place you have here. Makes me wonder where your manners are."

"My manners?" A morning of mind games with an angry woman who thought she was the center of the universe wasn't her idea of a hot time. "What exactly have I failed to do?"

"It's people like me who built this place, so the least you can do is say thank you."

Sophie pointed at her but the table between them kept her finger from poking her in the chest. Had she done that, Mason was sure she'd have snapped it off and poked her in the eye with it.

"Instead you stripped me of everything."

"What exactly have I taken from you that you haven't willingly given away? And you have nothing to do with my life. My father pays me for the bands I represent, and you're not on that list." She took a breath before she got loud, not wanting to get in the mud with Sophie. "If *you* had any manners, you'd send my father a thank-you note for not dropping you. He's well within his rights to do so because of everything you've put Banu through."

"You cut my tour short, and you've turned Victoria against me. You're fucking crazy if you think she's going to pick you over me. It's never going to happen." Sophie snapped her fingers, then laughed.

"She'll come running when I get home, and that should be in about an hour. Weston's coming to pick me up, and I'll call the cops if you try to stop me."

"You're going back to that asshole, and you think *I* turned Victoria against you?" She rubbed her face with both hands. How did you help someone who didn't want it, or reason with total insanity? "At least have the decency to wait until Victoria gets back, and tell her yourself. If you expect her to keep saving you, go ahead and tell her all this was a fucking waste of time."

"Mason, you don't have as much experience as your father, so let me explain an important fact." Sophie snapped her fingers again, and it was starting to aggravate her. "Victoria's going back to work starting tomorrow, and I'm going to make sure she has nothing to do with you or your family. I won't have her, or my career, tarnished over a relationship with you. This ain't that kind of town."

"Does it matter to you that I love her?" She gripped the arms of the chair, and she could hear Fred barking close by. It was a shame she'd never taught him to attack on command. "Because I do love her, and it's my goal to share my life with her if I can get her to agree."

"Get new goals in life, because my daughter is off-limits. I won't have her labeled some kind of pervert."

"Your daughter can make her own decisions."

Mason turned around, surprised to see Victoria standing by the kitchen door, her chin lifted in defiance.

"We both agreed I wasn't going to work for you, and Mason is nonnegotiable." She walked over and put her hands on Mason's shoulders. "Why are you even talking about this?"

"Your mom called Weston, and he's coming to get her."

Sophie's face twisted into a classic snarl at her announcement, but she also looked away like she was caught doing something naughty. From the look of it, the alcohol and pills weren't the only things Sophie was addicted to. That Weston was on his way meant he'd been waiting for Sophie to come to her senses. She wasn't trying to work on her problems—she was running as fast as she could back to them. Or maybe she'd seen things in her therapy she simply couldn't face, and going back to self-destruction was easier. Either way, it was a fucking waste.

"Are you kidding? Haven't you figured out how dangerous that is?" Victoria's voice rose, and she sounded disgusted. "You're going to sit here and disapprove of Mason, but you're going with Weston?"

"Weston is a man. A man who wants to take care of me and won't make people whisper behind my back. That's what you need in your life—not this."

"Then make sure you're okay with your decision. I think you need more time with Belle and her team, but you don't care what I think, do you? All that talk about wanting to try again with me, about being sorry…what was that about? Just lies."

Victoria dug her fingers into her shoulders to the point of pain, but Mason didn't move. Hearing Victoria stand up for herself this way was intoxicating.

"You think I'm some pathetic little girl, and that's fine. I'm not going to change your mind about that, but I found something special in Mason and I'm not giving it up."

"Sophie, you have a guest," Belle said, her professional mask firmly in place, though there was no mistaking her tense body language.

A young guy with scraggly hair and bad skin pushed Belle out of the way and walked quickly to Sophie. He hugged her so hard he lifted her off the ground and twirled her in a circle.

"Let's go, babe. We got so much to catch up on." Weston held Sophie's hand tightly but studied the area around him like he was casing the joint. Mason was glad Sophie could afford to keep this moron in drugs. If not, he'd be back to break in the first chance he got.

"Mama, please reconsider," Victoria said, and Weston stared at her with open hatred. Mason got up and placed her hand on the small of Victoria's back. "Don't do this."

"This is your last chance to come with me." Sophie didn't wait long after giving Victoria her ultimatum. She never looked back, and Weston seemed thrilled as he followed her out.

"She said her next call was to the police if we didn't let her leave." Mason put her arms around Victoria. "She wasn't thrilled you're with me, as you heard."

"Was there anything else we could've done?" Victoria asked Belle, seeming to ignore an important part of what Sophie had said.

Belle shook her head, looking both tired and defeated. "After this kind of therapy, your mom is going to need meetings to help her cope. She didn't finish, and she fought it all the way, so if she slips, it's on her. You, though, did all you could. Whatever Sophie is either trying to mask or run from, she never told me. I thought we were making progress here and there, but then she'd shut down. Maybe it's getting older or not having a career—we'll probably never know."

"So we wait for her to overdose again?" Victoria wrapped her arms around herself and Mason pulled her tighter.

"We wait for her to ask for help." Belle shrugged but looked compassionate. "My best advice to you is to let go of your guilt, and don't step in and play the role of enabler. That'll be the quickest way to get her to backslide all the way, and you'll lose the ground you've gained by having this time away from her."

"Don't worry—I'm not going back to work for my mom." Victoria rested her head on Mason's shoulder. "Thank you for giving up all your time to do this. I appreciate all you did, no matter what the outcome will be."

"Don't give up on Sophie just yet. She might surprise us all by what she learned in her time here. The fact that she stayed all this time, that she kept talking even when she knew she could leave, means something. I'm not sure what, but something." Belle placed her hand on Victoria's cheek. "And you're welcome. If Sophie changes her mind, I'll be happy to come out of retirement again." She turned to Mason. "I'm going to pack up and head home."

Mason nodded and gave her a hug. "Thank you, Belle. I can't say that enough."

Belle nodded, still looking tired. Mason couldn't imagine how tough it had been to live with Sophie for so long, especially in a therapeutic sense. She owed her big-time. Together, she and Victoria walked back down to the river house.

"I love you," Victoria said when they were alone. "I'm so sorry about what my mom said, but that's not how I feel."

"I love you too, and all that matters to me is what you have to say to me. Sophie's a big part of your life, though, so I want you to be sure." She kissed Victoria's temple and ran her hand up and down her back. "It'll kill me if you regret not having her in your life because you chose me instead."

Victoria gave her a sad smile. "I'm not the one cutting my mother out of my life, honey. She either accepts me for me, and that you're in my life, or she won't. Giving you up isn't an option." She cupped

Mason's face and kissed her softly. "You've helped me let go of the person she wanted me to be so that I can be myself."

Mason wasn't sure what to say to that, and she glanced at the clock. "We can stay in if you want. Talk through this some more."

"You promised me dancing, and Josette will be disappointed if we don't go."

There'd be a crash and burn over all this later, but for now there'd be dancing and whatever else it took to make Victoria forget about the afternoon. "I'll give you whatever you want."

"All I want is you."

"Then start thinking of something else to wish for." She held Victoria and felt her inhale deeply a few times. "Me you have."

❖

Sophie disappeared for the next week, but she was still alive. That Victoria knew from the men Mason hired to watch her, if only for Victoria's piece of mind. Her mom's situation was always niggling at her, but recording had started for the five songs on her new album, and that's what had kept her sane.

"Are you and Josette set for today?"

Mason walked out of the bathroom with a towel wrapped around her waist. They'd moved up to the main house, and while she loved the river house, this place was amazing.

"Do you really think it's necessary?" Everything she was doing was starting to become real. Josette was now her full-time assistant, and they had an appointment with a stylist and a publicist that morning. Mason was building the anticipation, and she gave Victoria final say at every step. Having some control was helping her not freak out, but the reality of her dreams coming true was sometimes overwhelming. Completely out of her mother's shadow, she felt like she could fly.

"I think you're the most incredibly beautiful woman I've ever laid eyes on, but why worry about what to wear?" Mason smiled when she pulled her towel off. "Besides, stuff like today is part of the package, so enjoy it."

"Has anyone ever told you how good you are at compliments?" She kissed the spot over Mason's heart. They'd existed in this blissful bubble that was easy to maintain at Blue Heaven. They worked, took afternoon walks, cooked together, and made love. And woven into all that was the music so important to both of them. "And did you know you're the sexiest person alive?"

"Wow, the sexiest, huh?" Mason lifted Victoria's nightgown off and tossed it behind her.

"Definitely." She wrapped her legs around Mason and kissed her. "Are you super busy today?"

"I cleared my morning."

She inhaled when Mason squeezed her ass. For the first time in her life she felt not only desirable and beautiful, but wanted. Mason didn't act like she kept her around because of what she could do for her, but because she simply loved her.

"I'm looking forward to helping you try on clothes. And then taking them off you."

"You are the love of my life," she said as Mason laid her down. She kept her legs around Mason's waist when she landed on her. "Are you sure we have time?" There was no way she wanted to stop once they started. Living with Mason had taught her a few things about herself, like the fact that she not only loved, but craved sex.

"The most important thing to remember is, from now on, you're the boss." Mason rocked her hips into hers, and it made her so wet she didn't care about anything else. Maybe this was how divas were born, when they didn't care who they kept waiting.

"You know I love you, right? I love the way you touch me, but sometimes I look at you, and all I want is for you to fuck me." She said the words slowly and softly so that Mason completely understood.

The way Mason grunted and brought her hips down made her smile. Mason lifted back up to be able to push her hand between them. "Are you ready for me, baby?" Mason grunted again when she ran her fingers through the wet heat. "Fuck."

"Exactly, go inside. Fuck me." From the first time they'd been intimate, Mason had unshackled her desires and rid her of her inhibitions. There was nothing she couldn't ask Mason for, and the freedom made her want to be naked as often as possible. The biggest turn-on was how much Mason wanted her, wanted to touch her, make her completely insane, and lived to make her come. "Jesus," she said as Mason sucked her in as her fingers slammed in as well.

This time it was fast, firm, and so fucking hot that she couldn't help but scream. "Yes…yes, fuck, baby, yes." The orgasm came as hard as Mason's strokes, and she raked her nails up Mason's back. "Like that, just like that. Fuck me. Oh. My. God." Her body tensed and finally relaxed.

She dropped her feet to the bed and ran her fingers through Mason's hair.

"I didn't hurt you, did I?" Mason lifted herself off her but stayed next to her. "I didn't mean to be so rough."

"You just told me I'm the boss, and you gave me exactly what I asked for." She moved to lie on Mason and kissed her. "That makes you employee of the month."

Mason laughed. "I'd better be the only employee on this list. I'm the jealous type, boss lady."

"You're the only one." She made the easy promise and moved down Mason's body. "Are you ready to come in my mouth?" Mason grunted when she ran her fingers from her clit to her sex. "Does that mean yes?"

"Fuck yes."

It was rather empowering making Mason this nuts, and she loved getting her off. She ran her hard nipple along Mason's sex, liking the outline of Mason's thigh muscles as she gazed down at her. "You want me?"

"More than anything."

She sucked and stroked as Mason kept up those grunting noises. The end, as always, came too soon, but one of the best parts was how Mason held her when she crawled back up. They didn't need words, and Mason felt solid and strong, which Victoria would need to help her navigate what was coming. There was no way she would follow in her mother's footsteps with Mason to depend on.

"You make me want to spend my days writing love songs," Mason said. Sappy wasn't her usual state of being.

"You do write beautifully, but right now you have to help me pick clothes." It was wonderful to find someone you could laugh with no matter what you were doing.

Mason slapped her ass before picking her up again for another shower. As they dried off, she went into professional mode. "Do you need anything from me before we really introduce you to the public?"

"The two main things I need are for you to love me and to keep me from becoming an idiot by being honest."

"You're too nice to ever be an idiot, but I'll be happy to love you and keep you grounded."

They dressed and found Josette in the kitchen with a stack of industry news. She spoke without looking up, though her eyebrows were raised. "That sounded like quite the prayer session. Who knew you were so religious?"

"Shut up," she said as Mason laughed. "There's no way you heard any prayer session down here. We were just getting dressed."

"Keep believing that, sweetie. You've officially been linked because of the stud you're doing all your praying with." Josette spread the papers out and pointed to the lifestyle section of *The Tennessee Tribune*. "Who knew you're powerful enough to tame Liner? Your ass must be magic."

"God, I hope not, and my ass is in no way magic." The big color photo was from their night at Josette's bar, and the short article was about Mason. "I'm fond of her wild side, and this is a good picture of us."

"Do I get a vote on that magic ass thing?" Mason asked.

"No, and you'll notice that my name isn't mentioned anywhere in this article."

"In a few weeks people will be asking, Liner who?" Mason laughed and poured her a cup of coffee. "Aside from Woody, your publicist Jerri is the best in the business, so if this kind of thing bothers you, go over it with her. She should be able to keep it to a minimum."

"You mean deny my relationship with you?" She put her cup down and put her hands on the sides of Mason's face to get her full attention. "That isn't going to happen, and if I only sell a few albums because of it, so be it."

"Are you sure? Your mom's prejudice is shared by a lot of people. Country music isn't known for its forward thinking." Mason was gazing at her with the same lovesick expression in the picture. It was like winning the lesbian lottery.

She could no more deny her than she could stop breathing. "Did you already forget the song you wrote?" Mason smiled and shook her head as she caressed her cheek. "Then Nashville will have to accept that you're mine, and I love you. I won't hide."

"The first accusation will be that you got signed *because* I'm yours."

"As your assistant, I give you permission to tell those people to fuck off," Josette said before she could answer. "Now get moving. If there's a chance I can score free new clothes, I don't want to be late."

"I'm sure there's more than a chance," Mason said. "And I can't wait to take this journey with you."

The boutique Mason drove them to was divided into two sections. One was open to the public with a large selection of boots, jewelry, and clothes, and the other side was for private shoppers, with more upscale choices. A pretty brunette hugged Mason before introducing herself as Selena, her stylist, and the redhead who kissed Mason next was Jerri, her new publicist.

"It's great to meet you, Everly. Or would you prefer Victoria when you're not working?" Selena asked.

"I might as well start getting used to it, so let's go with Everly. Otherwise I might forget to answer to it."

"Great. We need to start with measurements and sizes," Selena said. "Once I have all that on file, I can shop for you and save you the trip." Selena definitely caught Josette's frown at that news. "Or if you love to shop, it'll be fun to do together."

"This is Josette, guys, and she's Everly's assistant," Mason said. "She's going to have to look like she fits in for the stuff that's coming up, so set her up as well."

"I'll need your measurements as well, Josette, and a list of upcoming dates. Once I know what you need and where you'll be, we'll get to it." Selena waved to a worker to roll in a full rack of clothes. "I've got a few more boutiques in mind if we don't find everything here."

"You have to launch two singles," Mason said, her attention squarely on her, "so you should go big. Colt's back in town to launch the duet, and Everly has a single to launch. The best venue to do that in is the Opry, and you've got a date on Saturday night. Think casual chic."

"What?" The word barely got out. "Are you kidding?"

"It's good to be Sonny Liner's kid all the time, but sometimes it's downright awesome. You and Colt will sing together, followed by guest appearances at the Ryman Auditorium. That's his tour stop in Nashville." Mason stopped talking when she jumped on her and kissed her, not caring who was in the room. "Then you have a couple of road trips with him before we start setting up some stuff for you alone."

"This is unbelievable. The last time I was at the Opry was such a disaster."

"Forget about that." Mason cupped her cheek and spoke softly to her. "This is your time."

"And it's time to get dressed," Josette said, tapping on her watch.

The memory of the night she met Mason and how utterly deep her despair had been seemed like some distant horrible nightmare. She was awake now and looking into the eyes that haunted even her daydreams, and they held the answers to questions she hadn't even thought to ask yet.

The night her mother had fallen off that stage and started them on this journey had been the beginning of her salvation. Her return to the Opry would be the start of something that Mason had made possible, and she'd spend a lifetime trying to show her how much that meant to her. In the months they'd known each other, she'd learned that love wasn't blind, stupid, or foolish. Instead, it was the way to see clear into her future with this woman who loved her, and all she saw were happier times.

The one doubt she had left had nothing to do with her talent or performing before the biggest audience she'd probably ever stand in front of, but what her mother would do once she realized what she was doing. She was just beginning, and Sophie Roddy's star was starting to fade. How would she retaliate against her and Mason? Because surely her mother wouldn't just let her have her moment and find her way to happiness. She didn't work that way.

"You ready, darlin'?" Mason asked.

She shoved the maudlin thoughts aside. There was a career to get to, but her first priority would be to protect Mason from her mother's cruelty no matter the cost to her. "For everything, love. For everything."

Chapter Twenty

The river house was where Victoria and the band practiced for the rest of the week, and Mason attended as many of the sessions as she could, but it was time to make some hard decisions. A trip to the office for a meeting with her father couldn't be put off any longer.

She met Vic and Josette in the kitchen for breakfast, knowing they'd get a backstage tour of the Opry today, before their performance the next night. It was something the crew did for newcomers, even if technically Vic had been there with Sophie. She was hoping to be done and tag along, but Josette would be there regardless.

"You know, Vic, I'm a boy-crazy kind of gal, but for that, I'd gladly jump the fence," Josette said, pointing at Mason when she walked in and threw her jacket over a chair. "You're my hero for handling all of this." Mason jumped a little when Josette palmed her ass.

"Uh, keep your hands and your fence jumping away from Mason. Besides, it'd be a huge turnoff when you took those great slacks off her and saw my name tattooed across her ass." Victoria turned her face up for a kiss, then stuck her tongue out at Josette when Mason obliged her.

"You two set for today?" The housekeeper had fixed her a plate, so she sat by Victoria, giving her full attention.

"You're coming, aren't you?" Victoria appeared slightly panicked. "I know it's stupid, but I need you there."

"I'm going in early to meet with my father, which hopefully gives me time to come back and get you. If not, I'll meet you there." She pushed away from the table when Victoria moved to her lap. "I'll send a car for you if I'm running late."

"I know you've got a million things going on, but I want you there if you can swing it." Vic fed her some eggs, and she laughed at the gagging noises Josette was making.

"I'm about to change my mind. She's like a big hungry teddy bear." Josette followed that by more gagging noises.

"She is, but she can totally rock my world."

Mason choked a little at Victoria's words, but that was good to know. "Let me up before I start blushing."

Vic did, but not before kissing her to the point of almost making her moan.

"Stay out of trouble, and I'll see you later." Mason watched the ranch disappear in her rearview mirror and spent the drive thinking about how life had changed.

She was confident in what she could do for Victoria career wise, but it was what came after that worried her. Even the best of relationships sometimes died under the glare of the bright lights of fame. Love had already kicked her ass when Natalie had thrown her away for the fast-paced life of drugs and excitement, but she had to have faith it wouldn't happen again.

Victoria loved her, she knew that, but the future was promised to no one. That didn't scare her enough to let Vic go. She never would, so it was time to put all her gloomy thoughts back in their box and get on with what had to be done.

To end her ruminating, she called the office and Scarlet brought her up to date on her entire schedule. "One of the morning shows wants to do a spot with Colt and Everly. I played them a preview of the song, and they promised to do it for their Sunday morning segment. It's their most watched spot, so it's good for Colt and Victoria."

"Good. Every show is sold out, but we have the option to add a few dates if there's enough interest." She stopped and waited for the doughnuts Josette had ordered for her. The clerk was nice enough to come out and put them in the back seat. They'd be the brightest spot of her father's morning. "Anything on Sophie?"

"You aren't planning to blindside Victoria, are you? Telling Sophie anything about this show will make Victoria super crazy nervous."

"Do I look insane? I don't need that crazy bitch doing something to mess Vic's night up."

Scarlet sighed. "I have to say, boss, you're awesome in love, and Sophie's been quiet. If she's using again, she's taking it slow and is doing it in private. None of the guys have seen anything, and she hasn't left the house since Weston came and picked her up."

She knew there was something more from the way Scarlet's voice died away. "What?"

"Your buddy at the paper called and gave me a heads-up about Sophie."

Maybe she needed to join a gym. One where there were plenty of things she could hit repeatedly with no one getting hurt. It would bleed her urge to beat people like Sophie into a pulp. "Are you hesitating for dramatic effect or to drive me completely insane?"

"Don't be mean to me, or I won't give you an alibi when you kill Sophie."

"What did she want with the paper?" It wasn't good news but Scarlet had a talent for making her laugh.

"She was shopping out an exposé on you and Sonny. Seems you and your father ruined her life as well as turned Victoria against her before you turned her into a raving lesbian."

"What the actual fuck?"

"You did say she was totally insane, but you didn't emphasize what a total bitch she is. The reality is, if not that paper, someone's going to bite. Family drama sells. One of the gossip rags is bound to jump on it."

She turned into the parking lot and took deep breaths to try to avoid a headache. "I'm here."

"I know, and I'm waiting for you."

She laughed, and sure enough, there was Scarlet with a tablet next to her parking spot. "Please don't tell me how you always know where I am, and maybe schedule a doctor's appointment to check my heart. If I stroke out because of Sophie, make sure you take out a contract on her."

The cold whoosh of air from the lobby managed to calm her a little.

"Sure, but what about the paper?" Scarlet followed her in, her heels clicking along the wood floor.

"Put out our own warning that whoever prints the story will not only get a firm rebuttal from us, but will also be blackballed from any breaking news coming out of Banu. If they print one inaccuracy, they'd better be prepared to go to court. I'm not letting anything slide on this one." She checked her phone as they entered the elevator. "But on a brighter note, I'll have to send Sophie a thank-you note for this."

"That's interesting."

"She made part of my decision easy to make."

"What decision?" Scarlet followed her to her father's office, and she trusted Scarlet to take the notes and handle whatever came of their meeting.

"There are a couple."

Her father hugged her and kissed both her cheeks. Considering what was on their agenda, she wasn't surprised to see her mom there too.

"If there's anything but fruit in that box, you're in big trouble," her mom said.

"There's fruit in the fillings, so we're good."

"Uh-huh." Amelia kissed her next and treated Scarlet to the same greeting. "How's Victoria? She sounded frazzled when I talked to her yesterday. Isn't her run-through today?"

"She's heading out after lunch, and I have it under control. Trust me, I'll make it special for her." The flowers she'd ordered, along with a makeup and hair team, would get to the house in an hour. "Did Scarlet give you the latest on Sophie?"

"Scarlet told us about Sophie and her new hobby of contacting the media," her father said before biting into a chocolate doughnut with peanut sprinkles. "I also talked to Belle for her opinion."

"Belle gave you a report?" That surprised her.

"Belle sent me a bill and told me that's all the information she could share with me." Sonny laughed as he tossed the bill at her. It took effort not to appear shocked when she saw the total. "Do you think it was a worthwhile investment?"

"We owed it to Sophie to try, and we can show we did all we could for her." Mason's opinion shouldn't have a bearing on what her recommendation was, and she'd reviewed it a dozen times before she'd come to a conclusion she could live with and try to sell to her parents. But her final decision had more to do with Victoria than Sophie, so it wouldn't ever come across as anything but biased. "The next step should be up to you."

"Come on, tell us what you think," Amelia said.

"My gut tells me our lives would be better off if we cut our ties with her, and I admit I told Victoria she'd never do another album for Banu. But there's two important reasons not to drop her." She grinned when her mother did.

"One of those reasons better be singing at the Opry tomorrow," Amelia said. "I'll deny having anything to do with your upbringing if it isn't."

"That's the main reason, and I'm going to have to tell her about what her mother's up to. I hope she forgives me, but I'm not doing that until after tomorrow night. Vic doesn't need the extra pressure of dealing with her mother's crap before then." She stood, poured two cups of coffee, and handed Scarlet one. "The other reason is dropping her would only fuel what she's trying to do. It's hard to sell this kind of story when we can counter with a new tour schedule now that she's okay. *If* she is."

"You're going to take care of that?" Sonny asked.

Mason shook her head and held up her hands. "No way. Sophie Roddy is all yours, Pop, and you're the owner of Banu. That statement will carry the most weight if it's coming from you." She looked at Scarlet, who was picking up a doughnut and nodding as Mason spoke. "Because I love you, though, Scarlet and I will do the grunt work, and when I say Scarlet and I, I totally mean Scarlet."

"Smart-ass." Scarlet stuck a Bavarian cream coated tongue out at her.

"If you give me the okay, I'll start putting a schedule together for Sophie's approval. I'll also put her recording plans back on track. We'll start with smaller venues and put someone with her to help keep her sober. I'm sure Belle can recommend someone."

"That sounds good and proves to me you don't have anything else to learn from us," Sonny said.

"I still have plenty to learn, but maybe the next lesson I'm interested in is how to be a good spouse."

"That's easy, Buckaroo. You do everything Victoria tells you to do, like I do with your mama." Sonny leaned back in his chair with another doughnut.

"Yes, as you can see, he does that all the time." Amelia shook her head, and she took the box away from him. "And if you can't tell, I'm thrilled that you're figuring it out without some major hints. Victoria is a wonderful choice, and we love her."

"Thank you." She kissed them before going back and starting what was probably the last work they'd do for Sophie. Unless she really surprised her, Sophie wouldn't be able to help herself, and she'd go ahead with her plans to lash out no matter what they did for her. The likelihood was that she'd self-destruct again, but without Victoria there to pick up the pieces, she'd have no choice but to sink under the weight of her own mess. And no one would blame Victoria for not being there.

Hopefully she was completely wrong, and she also accepted that the version of herself before she met the Roddys would've dropped Sophie like a fucking hot rock. Maybe she really was becoming a mature adult. All that was left now was her need and responsibility to protect Victoria. To have her hurt by the one person who was supposed to love her unconditionally was unacceptable, and she'd do whatever she could to shield her from that.

"So single no more, huh?" Scarlet asked and bumped shoulders with her.

"Hard to believe, but as aggravating as I find Sophie, I owe her the world for being such a mess."

They had a rough outline a few hours later, and Scarlet promised to keep making calls so she could get back home. This wasn't the first time she'd shared a debut night with an artist, but it was the first time she was nearly as excited as the person she represented. Victoria was one of those rare talents that no one expected to find strictly by accident. Usually you walked into a bar or were at a wedding, and there they were, someone who'd been paying their dues until someone blessed them with a contract. They wanted it, were hungry for it, and would do anything for that one big break.

By accident meant a woman singing in her house because someone twisted her arm to do it. That was Victoria, the reluctant star, but tomorrow she had no doubt the world would fall in love with Everly. She'd worked to get her there, but she'd have to wait to see if once that happened, she'd get to keep the woman she'd fallen in love with.

"You never know what's coming, do you?" Fame changed people

and sometimes not for the good. She turned onto her property and glanced at herself in the rearview mirror. "No matter what, you let her fly." It was the only pep talk she had time to give herself.

Josette was in the den with a tablet like Scarlet's, and Scarlet had obviously told her it must be in hand at all times. She was studying it like there'd be a test later. "Getting a head start on your homework?"

"Hey." Josette barely glanced up. "I'm trying to get a handle on this schedule you put together and everything I'm supposed to do with it. I don't want to get fired on my first week."

"Scarlet is going to tag along for as long as you need her, and she's good at on-the-job training. According to her, that's what she's been doing for me since she started working at Banu."

"I love you." Josette put the device down and hugged her. "I was scared I'd miss something and screw all this up."

"I'll be around for you too, so just ask if you want to know something. Where is the woman with the golden voice?"

"She's upstairs with Selena going through some shoe selections."

Josette followed her into the kitchen and accepted a Pellegrino.

"You didn't need new shoes and boots?"

"If there's time, Selena promised to set me up." Josette glanced at the door. "Thank you, Mason," she said, lowering her voice. "You're the best thing that's ever happened to Victoria, and she deserves better than she's had. Please don't do anything to screw this up."

"I promise I won't do anything that messes up your chances at swag." She put her fingers up in the Scout's oath.

"Believe me, I love me some swag, but I love Victoria, and I like seeing her this happy. That piece of work mother of hers really did a number on her, but with you she's happy and in love. It's been too long in coming, but you've finally arrived, and I want her to keep you."

They were sweet words, and they made Mason's heart sing. "I promise she'll always be okay with me, and we want the same things for her."

She heard talking on the stairs and hugged Josette one more time. "I'm counting on you to be there for her through all of this, starting today."

"You know it."

They headed back to the den, and she had to swallow a few times when Victoria turned and faced her. That she was beautiful was never a question, but Selena's gift was creating simple elegance, and she'd come through again. The maxi-dress accented Victoria's coloring and was stylish without being formal.

"Wow." She put her drink down when Victoria walked into her arms and gazed up at her. "You're beautiful."

"Thank you." Victoria's cheeks pinked up a little, and she shook her head as if to make her embarrassment fade away. "You don't think it's too much?"

"Do you like it?" Mason asked. Victoria nodded. "Are you uncomfortable?"

"No."

"Then think of it as work clothes, a uniform of sorts, and to me you're beautiful no matter what." She smiled when the blush deepened. "Let me go change, and Selena can finish with you. She gets a raise for not putting anything on your lips just yet."

"I left your stuff on the door of the closet, and I'll take my bonus in Godiva," Selena said.

"I'll come up and help." Victoria took her hand and blushed one more time when Selena warned her about getting wrinkles in her outfit. "Thanks for the flowers, honey."

The vase on Victoria's side of the bed was full of pink roses, and Mason ran her finger along the petals of one before she sat on the bed. "I want you to always know how special you are to me, and how proud I am of you. Are you ready for all this?"

"I hope so. It's still weirdly surreal, but it's been fun."

She stripped with Victoria watching and wished they had more time.

"The next couple of days I don't think will change much, but I'm glad I did it."

"You're going to have to trust me on what happens next, but you're never going to be alone."

"Promise?"

"With all my heart." She slipped into her boots and held her hand out. "Let the adventures begin."

❖

The backstage manager was effusive as he took Victoria around and gave her the type of tour that only a privileged few got to see. Mason had been on a few of these, but she could tell when the manager truly liked someone, and from the sound of it, he couldn't wait to see Everly again.

"Don't worry about a thing tomorrow, and I'll be around if you need absolutely anything," he said, holding Victoria's hand between his. "I'm sure you'll be a regular if Mason has any say."

"Thank you, and I appreciate your time today." Victoria smiled and placed her free hand in the crook of Mason's arm as if giving her new admirer a hint it was time to let go.

"Excuse me a moment," Mason said when her phone started buzzing, and she saw it was her father. "Josette, go ahead and take Everly to the car, and I'll be right behind you."

"Buckaroo, are you done?" her dad said when she could answer.

"We just wrapped up, and I'm taking the girls to dinner." She pinched the bridge of her nose when she realized Victoria was still there. She winked and said, "It's just Dad with some last-minute stuff. I'll be right behind you."

As Victoria left, her father's voice blasted in her ear. "Make your excuses, Mason. I need you to head to the hospital."

"Are you fucking kidding me?" She wasn't loud but was still glad there wasn't anyone around.

"Don't let your mama hear you talk like that, but I totally agree with you. I need you to get there before the media does. Jesus Christ won't be able to revive Sophie's career if they catch this story."

"All right but let me see Vic off, and I'll cab it over there."

"I sent another car, and it should be there in about five minutes. Don't linger. I want this kept quiet."

"Okay, Pop, I'll call you."

If Victoria saw her there was no way she would buy some bullshit story, so she called Josette and had her hand Victoria the phone. "I have to head back to the office, baby, so go ahead and keep the reservation. If I'm too late for dinner, I'll call you."

"Is everything okay?" Victoria sounded worried.

"Just some contract stuff Dad wants me to fix before it's finalized, and it really can't wait. Enjoy yourself and relax."

"Okay. I love you."

"I love you too, and you're going to be awesome tomorrow." She'd do anything to give Victoria a great opening night, even if she had to kill Sophie to put all of them out of her misery.

She scanned the news and social media, hoping to keep whatever had happened from Victoria until after tomorrow night. All her notifications were quiet, thankfully, so she texted Scarlet to be on alert and to call if she found anything. The service she'd hired had a guy waiting outside when she arrived, and he led her to the emergency department as he explained what had happened.

"Ms. Roddy called 9-1-1 thirty minutes ago, and the ambulance just rolled in. We haven't confirmed exactly what's going on—"

"Wait, Sophie called 9-1-1?"

"Yes, ma'am. They found Weston Cagle unresponsive when they rolled up on the scene. Ms. Roddy rode in with him once they had him loaded."

"Please tell me she's not high or drunk."

"We haven't been able to confirm that, but we're trying."

"Thanks." She walked into the emergency room and searched the electronic roster by the nurses' station for Weston's name. It wasn't there, which gave her no option but to ask. She was shown to a private consulting room instead of getting the order to leave.

Sophie stood when she walked in, and the next surprise of the night was her genuine relief at the sight of her. "Mason, thank God. They called the police."

"Why, exactly?" she asked the nurse, and Sophie was clinging to her like she'd disappear if she let go.

"The gentleman Ms. Roddy brought in overdosed and passed away. It's standard procedure to call the authorities," the nurse said.

"Thanks, and we'll be waiting." She sat Sophie down and called Woody while Sophie sobbed. "Get over here and threaten whoever you have to, but keep Sophie out of this."

"Give me twenty minutes. Sonny already called me. I've put things in place, and I'm on my way."

She loved that Woody was always raring to go.

"He's dead, Mason, dead." Sophie sounded sober, which was a bonus if they had to involve the police.

"Tell me what happened." It took some time for Sophie to get through her story, but it sounded like Weston had bought from the wrong dealer and paid the price of the poison he'd injected. "Sophie, listen to me."

"It wasn't my fault. You have to believe me."

"I do believe you, but you have to listen to me. Tell that exact story and nothing more. If the police ask, offer to give them Weston's stash, but that's it. Do not volunteer more than you have to." She wiped Sophie's face, not quite believing how lost she sounded. "I'm just glad you didn't take anything."

"Even after everything I've put you through?" Sophie let out a short laugh that sounded wounded.

"Victoria loves you, and I love her. I'm smart enough to know you come as part of the package, and it would've killed something vital in her if this had been you and not Weston." She could see her as a vulnerable, wounded soul for the first time. "Maybe the two of you have a ways to go, but you have an amazing daughter, and she cares about you even after all you've put her through."

"Is she the only reason you're here?"

"Maybe now isn't the time for total honesty." That got a smile from Sophie. "But honestly, no. We still represent you, and I still think you have so much more to do."

The police took Sophie's statement, and Mason was glad she stayed calm. Mason didn't dispute her account of how Weston was a houseguest and she'd had no idea he brought heroin into her home. Maybe that was the only way Sophie could deal with the loss—by denying their connection.

"Do you know where Mr. Cagle would've purchased the drugs?" the younger cop asked gently.

"I couldn't begin to guess. Why do you ask?" Sophie held Mason's hand in a painful grip, but her voice stayed steady.

"This is the third callout about a fatal OD we've had this shift, and we need to find the dealer before someone else dies."

"If we find anything in the stuff he left at the house, I'll contact you if you leave me your card." Mason pocketed the guy's information and led Sophie out. Woody was in the car outside and told them he'd taken care of Weston's last needs.

"I can't go back there." Sophie hadn't let go of her hand, so maybe she was more freaked out than Mason gave her credit for. "I can't."

"Don't worry, you won't be alone, but we need to talk about where you can stay." She explained what Victoria was getting ready to do and why she didn't want to burden her with something that would stress her. "It's asking a lot, but after tomorrow night I'll move you in myself if you want to come back to Blue Heaven."

"The Opry? You think she's good?" Sophie was staring at her like she'd grown horns and had gotten a full-face tattoo.

"I want you to see for yourself, but she has the potential to be legendary. You gave her more than you know, some good, some bad, but through it all she's loved you." She faced Sophie and spoke from the heart that now belonged to Victoria completely. "What I want is for you to spend some time really seeing her for who she is. Her talent is something that will blow you away, but her compassion isn't something you should neglect any longer. You have no right to continue treating her the way you have, which has been truly horrendous. It's not okay, and if you lose her, you're not only missing out, but it will be entirely your fault." Mason didn't care if it hurt Sophie's feelings or if it didn't help her recovery. She needed to hear the truth as clearly as Mason could say it.

"Can I come tomorrow? I know it's last-minute, but I'd like to be there." Sophie had actual tears in her eyes, and Mason smiled. Maybe Sophie's time at the ranch had done some good after all. She was finally seeing herself in that mirror Belle had been holding up for months.

"I got you a ticket just in case, and my parents will pick you up, but tonight I think the best person you could stay with is the one who's been trying to help you all along." Woody drove them to the address she'd texted him, and she prayed Sophie would keep it together. "If you give me the night, we'll figure it out together, you have my word."

"I've been cursing you for weeks, Mason Liner, and I've accused you of plenty of things."

Mason braced herself for some more of the same now the pressure was off.

Sophie's eyes were swollen from crying, but they were clear and strangely empty of the usual malice she looked at the world with. "I'm still not sure a relationship with you is the best thing for Victoria, but I owe you my thanks. After everything, had the roles been reversed, I would've told you to fuck off."

"I'm not sure she should have a relationship with you, either, so we're on even ground there. All I ask is that you think before you say anything to Victoria. Talk to me however you like, but remember, she's your child, and I love her. I'll do whatever I have to in order to keep her safe and happy. And if that means dropping you in a hole somewhere, so be it. Deal?"

The car stopped, and Belle was waiting in front of her house. "Okay, you got a deal, and thanks for understanding me."

"Try listening to Belle this time," she said as she opened the door. Belle was wearing yellow shorts and a sixties-style halter top, and the outfit made her appear younger than Mason had ever seen her. "She knows what she's talking about."

"At least someone does."

CHAPTER TWENTY-ONE

The sun wasn't up when Victoria opened her eyes, and she took the time to assess what had woken her. Mason was spooned behind her, and that meant they hadn't moved since falling asleep. She'd been disappointed that Mason couldn't make dinner, but it'd been nice cooking something for her when she got home.

Her life had never revolved around any type of domesticity, and it probably wouldn't considering what she was getting ready to do, but she'd discovered something about herself. Being with Mason, taking care of her, was something she truly enjoyed. The other thing she loved was having Mason reciprocate.

There was enough moonlight from outside to see the roses Mason had sent, which had sent Selena into a panic when she'd started crying. Josette had understood, though, and let her cry over the surprise of the first flowers she'd ever received. Then there were the simple things like Mason making her coffee the way she liked it, and holding her hand whenever she could. All that was nice.

"It's too early for you to be awake." The low deep burr of Mason's voice made her shiver, and it hardened her nipples. "You okay?"

"I was thinking, not worrying." She turned and Mason lifted her so she was lying on top of her.

"What's running around up here?" Mason tapped the side of her head and kissed her.

"Domestic things." A sudden but brief look of shock, or maybe fear, crossed Mason's face. "Good things," she added, not wanting to upset her.

Mason kissed her and ran her hands through Victoria's hair. "We haven't talked about our permanent arrangements, but if it's not rushing you, I'd like you to move in. If it makes you more comfortable, keep your place, but I want to wake up with you every day. I want that even if it's at a weird early hour that beats even Ivan the rooster." Mason's hands slowly slid down her back and stopped at the slope of her butt.

"Are you sure?" She kissed Mason with all the lust that built when they slept skin to skin. "Once that happens, I'm not going to leave."

"You think that's going to scare me into changing my mind?" The way Mason's nose flared when she exhaled deeply made her press her knee harder into Mason's center.

"Can you tell me one thing?"

Mason's enthusiastic nodding made her certain she could ask anything.

"Why me? Considering who you are, you could've had anyone."

"My mother has always preached to me that the universe creates one perfect match for everyone. It's only when you meet them that you'll know. You'll know because their heart can't deny you."

"I love when you get philosophical." She ran her fingers along the top of Mason's cheek, then the other. "And I'll never deny you any part of me."

"I love you, darlin', and my heart knows you." Mason rolled them over. "You're my match."

"Then I should ask you to help me pack the rest of my stuff."

"You shouldn't tease the animal if you don't mean to feed it." Mason kissed her before starting down her body. Her head dropped to the pillow when Mason sucked in a nipple, making her feel it in her clit.

"Are you teasing me?" Mason let her go with a pop and asked the question before moving to the other nipple "Are you?"

"No." She barely heard her own answer, but the center of her world was focused between her legs. "Yes," she said slightly louder when Mason bit down gently.

"Is that a no or yes?" Mason moved lower with the question, and Victoria bit her lip.

The pulsing in her clit was quickly driving her mad, but Mason was in no hurry.

"Do you know what I want?" She had to suck in her bottom lip when Mason flicked her tongue rapidly over her clit with a feather touch.

"What's that?" Mason asked, and Victoria wanted to cry when Mason had to lift her head to answer.

"I'd like a housewarming gift, and what I want is for you to put your mouth right here." She reached down and put her hand between her legs. The move was an on switch for Mason, and this time she didn't stop. There was no doubt she loved Mason, and the added bonus was how she made her feel.

She bent her knees and grabbed the top of Mason's head. "So good, baby." Mason lifted up a little and put her fingers in, and Victoria felt her moan against her sex. "Harder. Give it to me."

Mason gave her what she wanted, and the moan she released against her sex turned her on even more until she felt the tightening in her abdomen. "Oh…yes…*shit*." She clamped her legs shut, trapping Mason in place as she reached her peak.

They didn't move for a long while and floated in the blissful relaxation, only rousing a little bit when Mason moved up and held her. "Close your eyes, and I'll be right here with you."

It was selfish not to touch Mason, but a wave of lethargy hit her full force, and she drifted off. The room was filled with light when she woke up again, but Mason was right where she'd promised to be and was still sleeping.

Victoria got up slowly and tried not to wake her. She took a few minutes in the bathroom before putting her robe on and heading downstairs. Mason's housekeeper was already in the kitchen and flipped the coffee on when she saw her. Jeb was also in there having breakfast, and she'd come to really enjoy his company.

"Good morning." She ate a piece of bacon off the plate by the stove and smiled when the housekeeper shook her finger at her. "Do either of you know a good mover?"

"It's about damn time the kid got it right," Jeb said with a big smile.

Victoria could tell he was genuinely happy for them both because he loved Mason. They were family, and Jeb loved Blue Heaven and all the animals in his care as much as Mason did.

"Make sure you don't settle—make her put a big old ring on it."

That made her laugh. "Hopefully you'll be as big a fan of mine as you are of Queen Bee."

"You know it, but I also want grandbabies to spoil, and then I'll have an excuse to buy ponies."

"Let's ease her into having me around all the time before we start filling up some bedrooms upstairs." She took two mugs and paused, remembering something. "The photographer should be here today."

"We're on it, sweetie," the housekeeper said. "Enjoy your morning while you can."

"Thanks." She made it back to the bedroom before Mason woke up, so she dropped the robe and got back in bed. "Good morning, my love." Mason grunted when she kissed the back of her shoulder, then grunted again. "Ready for coffee?"

Mason rolled over and sat up, giving her room to straddle her lap. It was a position she enjoyed. She had Mason's full attention, and she was close enough to touch everywhere.

"You're spoiling me."

"I plan to." They shared a cup. "Do you really want me to move in?" Old insecurities died hard.

"Baby, you already agreed, and there's no take back policy." Mason moved to the side of the bed and put her feet down. "You also have people coming over who want to take your picture, and you have to be squeaky clean to do it. Hang on."

"Now who's spoiling who?"

"For the rest of my life."

"I'm holding you to that." She thought about what Jeb had said that morning, and it didn't seem like such a far-fetched fantasy now. "And we need to buy a pony."

❖

The photographer Mason hired made the two-hour-long session fun for Victoria, and Selena was on hand to make sure she looked good in every shot. It was an afternoon of coming out of the shadows in spectacular form. She also enjoyed the quiet for a few hours with Mason as they finally went for a horseback ride.

"This place is beautiful," she said as she sat on a rock overlooking the lake.

Mason hadn't gone far and hadn't kept her in the saddle long, not wanting her to be sore on her big night. "I fell in love with the whole thing when I first walked it and probably paid too much, but it reminded me of Mom and Dad's place."

"It'll be nice to call home."

"I can't wait, and you're free to change whatever you like. I want you to feel at home here."

"There's nothing I want to change about the place or the owner."

"Are you ready for tonight?"

Mason's hand felt so good in hers, and it was the best comfort right before the storm.

"After it's done, your life will never be the same."

"My life isn't the same now." It was a strange change of perspective to be this happy all the time, and not be afraid it would change. "I believe I can handle anything if I don't lose this." She lifted their joined hands and kissed Mason's knuckles.

"I intend to keep all my promises to you, but I also want you to fly, love. You're something special, and you're going to be successful."

The things Mason said to her had a way of building her confidence like nothing else ever had.

"That means you can stand on your own no matter what, which makes me lucky that you want to be with me when you'll have the world at your feet."

"You really think that? There are way better performers out there, honey." It was in no way a fishing expedition for compliments, but she really didn't believe her career would be much more than what she was doing now. It was an exciting moment in time, and it would pass.

"Everly is who you'll be for years to come, and the only way that won't happen is if you decide to retire." Mason tugged on her hand and kissed her. "I can't explain it, but I've been doing this long enough to know. You have *it*, and the audience will know that tonight and every night for as long as you want to share your voice with the world."

"That sounds good, as long as I get to be just Victoria here with you."

"Tonight, and every night." Mason stood and helped her to her feet. "Right now, it's time to get started."

Selena was waiting for them when they got back, and Victoria set her up in the room Mason had put her in the first night she spent in the house. She wanted to share a shower with Mason before they started the process of putting her together. It was the Opry, so she wanted to look nice but not too fancy.

"Josette was right about one thing," she said as Mason turned and rinsed the shampoo out of her hair.

"What's that?" Mason wiped her face and turned back toward her.

"You're a sexy beast, Liner, and you're all mine." She patted Mason on the ass before stepping out and grabbing a towel. "See you in a bit." She put her robe on and headed next door.

"Have fun."

"Pray I remember all the lyrics."

She smiled as she left Mason chuckling and noticed a small gift-wrapped box on the bed with a card on top. It explained why Mason had come back to supposedly check to see if the bedroom door was locked before their shower. The pale pink wrapping and the satin bow made her smile, and the smile widened when she saw her name spelled out in Mason's messy handwriting.

Soon the world will know how beautiful you are, and how beautifully you sing. This is just a little something to remind you that I'm not only in love with you, but I think you're sexy as hell.

She'd never gotten underwear as a gift, but that Mason had gone out of her way to shop for her put a dent in her nervousness. Mason was right—life would never be the same, but that had nothing to do with her career. It was the woman she shared a life with and how she made her feel.

Victoria slipped on the navy-blue matching set, glad it was a perfect fit. "I'm not sure how she managed that, but they're nice."

"They're more than nice, and Selena has all your sizes—*all* of them," Mason said with an appreciative expression on her face. "You're beautiful, and I hope you don't mind the gift. I promise I'm not a creeper or a chauvinist, but I believe beauty should be appreciated in layers."

"Honey, you can buy me panties whenever you like as long as you keep looking at me like this."

"That will never be a hardship." Mason helped her on with her robe and held her. "Let me kiss you before someone slaps me if I mess up your lipstick."

The hairdresser left her hair down, and her makeup was light per her request. Selena had found a vintage peasant top that contrasted well with the tight-fitting jeans she was wearing. The brown boots didn't have that shiny new feel about them even though they were, and the whole outfit had that relaxed but put together look she was comfortable with.

Mason and Wilbur whistled when she came down, and she blinked as her ears got warm. Wilbur was riding in with them, and she smiled at his nervous chatter. They were escorted to the backstage doors forty minutes later and spent some time talking to Colt.

"Colt's going to start with the single he released in New York, and then he's going to introduce you." Mason went through the schedule one more time as the starting acts performed. "You're going to do 'Talk to Me,' followed by the duet."

"And at the end we'll do the number we rehearsed with everyone performing tonight," Colt said. "It'll go by in a second, and you'll be fine."

"Thanks." She nodded to him before he finally stepped out to a cheering crowd. She had to take some deep breaths to keep herself steady. Sonny and Amelia were in the front row, and the lights prevented her from seeing exactly where they were, but she was thankful they were there to cheer her on.

"You got this, love. Just remember to enjoy it." Mason put her hands on her shoulders and squeezed. "I'll be waiting right here when you're done."

"Ladies and gentlemen," Colt said, and all she saw was Wilbur smiling onstage at her. "It's not often you get the chance to see the beginning of something beautiful, but you will tonight. I fell in love with her voice the first time I heard it, and we'll be sharing a song with you in a moment, but first, with her debut song...Everly."

She walked out to applause, but nothing like what Colt had gotten, and she remembered her mother right then. Her mom always said it was her responsibility to give the people what they paid to see, and that was her best. She was sad Sophie—both the performer and her mom—wouldn't be there to see this, but she'd give these people her best.

The piano had a spotlight on it, and Wilbur was close by, ready to play. "Hello, everyone, thank you for having us." She put her hands on the keys and waited for Wilbur to count them off. When she started playing, she forgot the audience and everything else except Mason, close by and listening. That's who she sang to, poured her heart out to, and she tried to do justice to the words Mason had written.

She held the last note, and her voice faded away right before the music ended, and she wanted to laugh from the relief of not screwing this up. That's when it hit her. She'd just made her debut at the Opry. The audience was on its feet and there were plenty of yells, so she stood and took a bow.

"Everly, ladies and gentlemen," Colt said, clapping with them.

She bowed again with her hands pressed together and stared out at the audience. When her eyes adjusted, she saw Sonny and Amelia still on their feet, but she came close to stumbling when she saw her mom right next to them. She could be wrong, but her mom actually appeared proud as she clapped, her hands over her head and a huge smile on her face.

Colt put his hands back on his guitar and was introducing their duet, but she glanced to the wings, trying to find Mason. When she spotted her, Mason pointed out to the crowd to get her head back in the game.

She started them off with the piano intro and Colt started playing when she began singing. Halfway through, Colt handed off his guitar and stood next to the piano with a handheld microphone. Like before, the crowd was on its feet, so she stood as well. Colt's next move surprised her so much she froze with her hands on his chest. He moved in close, his head bent toward hers.

To the audience it must've looked like two lovers kissing after a love song, and the shouts were louder now, followed by the flashing of cameras. "What are you doing?" she whispered to Colt, trying to keep a smile on her face.

"Giving the people what they want." He waved to the crowd as he took her hand and walked her off the stage.

Mason looked furious as Victoria pulled her hand out of Colt's grip, and if there wasn't the finale to get through, she would have hauled back and hit the idiot herself. What he'd done was way beyond inappropriate, and she didn't appreciate it.

"What'd you think, boss?" Colt asked. He acted like he was on top of the world, and he expected the world to join in on his high.

"Excuse me, I have a call." Mason turned and walked away, and Victoria physically hurt.

"Don't ever do that again." She was having a hard time keeping the anger out of her voice, and Colt seemed to realize that something was very wrong.

"We're single people, Victoria, and the audience loved it. What's the big deal?" He looked genuinely confused.

"I'm with someone is the big deal, and even if I wasn't, you don't get to do that without asking first. What the hell is the matter with you? Do you not know what year it is? Mason isn't going to appreciate what you did, either."

"Look, I'm sorry. Maybe I got carried away, but I didn't mean anything by it. There's no reason to drag Mason into this—it's you I owe the apology to." He was talking fast, but he sounded sincere.

She walked away in search of Mason, not caring about anything else. Thankfully she wasn't that far away, and she was actually on the phone. She stood and waited, relief hitting her when Mason held her hand out. The call was short and sounded like business.

"You were fantastic," Mason said once she was done.

"I'm so sorry—" she started, but Mason put a finger to her lips.

"You don't need to apologize, and I doubt you agreed to that."

"Don't ever think that." She moved closer and put her arms around Mason. "You're the only one in my life I want kissing me."

"Then pretty boy Colt owes you an apology."

"He already said sorry, and later I'll give him an update on my love life, but I don't want to talk about him."

"From the crowd's approval, you have a hit on your hands." Mason kissed her forehead and whispered in her ear, "I love you, and I'm so proud of you."

"That's everything, then, isn't it?" She kissed the side of Mason's neck, smiling at the little bit of lipstick she left behind. "Was I hallucinating, or was my mother sitting next to your parents?"

"She was totally real, and I need you to forgive me for not saying anything earlier. I knew how nervous you were, and I didn't want to add one more thing to stress you out, but yeah, I knew she was going to be there."

"I probably sound childish, but I'm thrilled with how tonight went. It's like a dream, and having her there listening and then clapping when I was done was probably the most wonderfully surreal part. She actually looked kind of proud."

Mason rubbed her thumbs along her sides as she held her. "She's your mom, darlin', so you're not being selfish at all. I'm glad she was here to see what an awesome person you are."

"There's a first time for everything, huh?"

"I can't believe I'm going to say this, but we need to give Sophie another shot. Her pride might've been buried deep, but it was there all along. It can't be anything other than that when she has a child as wonderful as you."

She laughed and kissed Mason's lips. "My God, you're good at seeing the bright side of things. Thank you for that and for everything you've done to get both me and my mother to this wonderful place. I'm so lucky." She kissed Mason again and took a deep breath, ready to face whatever came next. She was loved by this wonderful woman, and that put a spear into the fear that had been such a big part of her life until now. "You are everything to me."

CHAPTER TWENTY-TWO

The show ended, and Mason guided her back to the car and drove them to the L27 Rooftop Lounge where she'd booked the entire space to celebrate Victoria's night. Her parents took Josette and Wilbur, as well as Sophie, with knowing smiles. She wanted a few minutes alone with Victoria, and Victoria seemed to want the same thing.

"The reviews are in already?" Victoria asked as soon as the door closed.

"Baby, I'm not lying just because I'm madly in love with you. Try to accept that you and that voice of yours are going to take country music and knock it on its head." She took the opportunity to kiss Victoria, the joy of seeing her succeed making her almost dizzy. "Once you do that, then you can concentrate on the fact that I'm madly in love with you, and that I can't wait to see that underwear again."

"I'm glad." Victoria kissed her again. "Did you invite Mom to this too?"

"I did, and we have to talk about something before we get there. I'll never keep anything from you, but this was the exception." The story of what had happened to Weston made Victoria go pale. "She accepted my help, and I left her with Belle. I'm sorry I didn't tell you sooner, but I didn't want you freaking out right before this performance."

"Are you sure she's going to be here tonight?"

"She's coming with my parents, and they promised to deliver one Sophie Roddy." She twirled a strand of Victoria's hair around her finger and wished this ride would last longer.

"You're something else."

"I keep telling you how wonderful I am, so that's not news." She grinned. "But your mom was blown away by you tonight. I hope you know that." She'd watched Sophie while Victoria sang, and she could've sworn she was crying. How the woman had missed the treasure she'd had with her all those years was unbelievable, but tonight seemed like an opening for both of them.

Victoria had discovered herself, and Sophie discovered she was a parent to a strong, talented woman. Or, at least, that's what Mason wanted to believe. Time would tell.

"I'm not sure about that, or how to deal with this." They sat in each other's arms until the car stopped in front of the bar.

"How about you concentrate on celebrating your night? That's all you need to do because you deserve it. Deal with other things tomorrow."

"As long as you're there, I'll be fine." Victoria leaned back and took her hand.

Victoria really was a strong, capable woman, and Mason was sure she saw herself that way *most* of the time these days. That she had stood up to Sophie and told her to fuck off taught her she was all right, but everyone had a trigger that made you forget your strength. Sophie had much to make up for, and she hoped she did, but she'd stand and hold Vic's hand until Sophie came to her senses, and Vic realized her mother didn't have any power over her. Not anymore.

"Let's go have fun, and we'll leave when you've had enough."

The crowd at the party included a few people from the office, the songwriters, her parents, the band, and Belle and Sophie, and they all applauded when they walked in. Jerri had also taken care to have the music media there to cover Vic's awesome start, since the single dropped the second she stepped onstage. The band came up and hugged Victoria. This had been their first time at the Opry too, and now they were on their way as well.

"Vic!" Wilbur lifted her off the ground as he jumped over and over. "They've been playing your single on the radio every five minutes."

"That's great."

Victoria kissed his cheek, but Mason could tell her eyes were on Sophie. Vic's mom was standing back with Belle and had a glass of something gripped in her hand.

Mason left Victoria in the midst of the people she'd be spending most of her time with in the future to go and feel Sophie out. If her attitude had changed dramatically from asking for a ticket to Victoria's show, she'd ask her to go. The change in Sophie was noticeable, though, from her new short haircut to her subdued outfit and her clear, alert eyes.

"Thank you for coming," she said, kissing Belle's cheek, then Sophie's. "You doing okay?"

"It's more like I'm surviving, but this one assures me I'll live." Sophie pointed at Belle and smiled. "Weston's death…" She swallowed hard. "What I learned last night was that I really fucked my life up, but I'm still here to try to fix it. I've got a lot to make up for."

Victoria slipped her hand into Mason's as Sophie finished her enlightened statement. "Mama."

"I'm not staying long." Sophie's fingers whitened around the glass. "This is your night, and you should enjoy it, but I wanted to tell you how wonderful I thought you were. That performance will be remembered forever, and you might not believe me, but I'm so proud of you."

"Thank you." Victoria's eyes were glassy with tears, but she appeared happy. "It's silly, but I'm so happy you were there—that you're here. Please stay."

"It's me that should be thanking you. I never deserved you, but I'll work on that if you'll allow me." She sighed, looking tired. "And I mean it this time."

"That's all I've ever wanted, and I'm sorry about Weston. I know you cared for him." Victoria stepped forward and put her arms around Sophie, and the move made Sophie cry, but she appeared grateful.

Mason didn't need to be convinced of Victoria's grace, but she proved it on a daily basis. It was time for her to give a little as well. "Your mom doesn't want to go back to her house, so I thought we could help her with that until she settles somewhere." She hoped she was right to offer.

"You know," Victoria said, letting Sophie go and putting her arm around Mason's waist, "I found my life in a house by the river. Maybe you'll have the same luck."

"Mason's not my type." Sophie's joke put the first crack in the awkward atmosphere and everyone laughed.

"Mason's taken, but the river house is a magical place where you and the guys can find some of the music that made you happy. I know Bryce would love to hear from you."

"I'm sure Bryce has moved on, and happily so." Sophie put her glass down and pressed her hands together. "Belle keeps talking about these twelve steps, but I screwed up so much that my list probably has a hundred more, and then some."

"You always were a lousy guesser."

A big grizzly bear of a man walked up beside them, and Mason recognized him from Sophie's hospital room.

"We've been waiting on you to stop losing your mind."

"Bryce, thank you for coming," Victoria said, letting Mason go and throwing her arms around him.

"You're crazy if you thought I'd miss this. I have no words to tell you how good you are." He hugged her tightly and smiled down at her.

"Thank you. Honey, this is Mama's lead guitar, Bryce Benton." Mason took Bryce's hand and smiled. "Bryce, this is Mason Liner."

"You look like your dad," Bryce said. "And like your dad, you're damn lucky in love. Congratulations."

"Thanks. My mom always says it's never too late." She let his hand go and winked. Maybe Bryce Benton had been waiting for Sophie to do more than stop losing her mind. The look in his eyes when he looked at Sophie had a hell of a lot more emotion than went with a job prospect.

"Keep this one around, Vicky. She's smarter than your average music executive."

They heard some cheering from downstairs, and Mason knew who'd arrived. "Excuse me a second, everyone, I'll be right back."

She waited a few steps from the landing to the first floor and waved the server off. There was no way she wanted an audience for this. Colt hesitated, then said something to the people with him. He held his hands up and smiled as he started climbing.

"Hey, Mason, I think we have a solid hit with that duet. Thank you for introducing me to Victoria."

She smiled and nodded. "That we do, but remember to keep your hands to yourself unless the lady tells you otherwise. Vic doesn't need my help fighting her battles, but"—she took another deep breath—"don't do it again. And that goes for any other women you work with. Be professional, Colt. Don't assume you have the right."

"I hear you, I swear. She already gave me the lecture, and I really didn't mean anything by it. I had no idea she was seeing someone."

They both turned when they spotted Victoria at the top of the steps. "She is seeing someone, and I'm absolutely crazy about her."

His eyes widened and he looked truly abashed. "Wow, sorry, boss, and congratulations."

"Thanks, now let's go celebrate. You two sounded awesome tonight, so there's plenty to be happy about." Colt went up first and hugged Victoria like she was his sister and pointed down at Mason before leaving her to join the other guests.

"Victoria's in good hands," Sophie said when she joined her on the landing.

"And she always will be."

"I'm counting on it, but more importantly, so is she. Don't let either of us down."

"There's no chance of that. Ever." That was the easiest promise she'd ever made.

❖

Victoria watched Mason head for the stairs, and it was Josette's expression that made her follow. She was happy to see Mason and Colt shaking hands and smiling.

Colt turned to her and said, "I'm sorry again, and good for you and Mason. Like I said, she's made all my dreams come true, but with you, I'm sure she's going to deliver in spectacular form. Congratulations," Colt said. "I hope we can work together again, and it'll be nice having you along for part of the tour."

"Thank you, and I'd love to. I appreciate your taking a chance on me, and call me if any great duets come along."

"That goes both ways, Everly. I'm not the only one who's going to sell out some arenas in the future, and I was proud to share the stage with you."

"Thanks." She turned back to Mason when Colt walked off and

his band finally made it upstairs. "You having fun, honey?" She rested her head on Mason's chest when she joined her and was glad to be on the sidelines for a minute.

"This has been one special night, and I'm so glad I got to share it with you."

"Can I admit something to you?" She glanced up at her and smiled.

"Sure."

"This could be the only time I get to sing in front of an audience, and I'd be okay with that because you love me. I know that sounds sappy, but the music isn't why I feel so blessed."

"The good thing about life is that you can have both, or anything else you want. All you have to do is tell me if I'm ever falling down on either job. And I'm glad the thing with Colt resolved easily. I'd have hated to break his pretty nose."

"The fact that I got another apology and an offer to work with him again means you're doing both jobs really well, and your bit of jealousy is the sexiest thing I've ever witnessed."

"It's good to pull his head out of the music every so often and give him a clue," Mason said and laughed. "I did tell you I'm the jealous type, just not the crazed punch-you-in-the-face type. Unless it's warranted."

She laughed too when Mason gave her that big smile. "These damn dimples. They're going to be your get out of jail free card for the rest of your life."

"Talk to Me" came over the speakers, and Mason took her hand. "Dance with me."

There were joined by Sophie and Bryce, Mason's parents, and the others, but they could've been alone for all Victoria noticed. She felt Mason shiver when she sang to her, and she was ready to go once the song was over. If this really was the start of a new career and life, it certainly had been memorable.

No one took long in wishing them good night, and Victoria was grateful for the car service. Mason's wandering hands and all the kissing made her want to yell at the driver to speed it up. She needed to get naked and feel Mason pressed up against her.

"Can we spend the night down the hill?"

Mason nodded and pointed to the utility vehicle. "I was going to ask."

She wanted to be where it had all started, and she realized Mason had anticipated her, when she saw the candles and champagne in the bedroom. "You are a gift."

They didn't need any more words as Mason undressed her while she did the same for Mason. They went slow, but the passion was there, always there. It was hot, needy, and fulfilling, but through it all she felt cherished. Mason loved her and that would carry her wherever she went without fear.

That was her last thought as she fell asleep, not waking until she smelled coffee the next morning. She pressed against Mason when she lay back down and handed her a cup. "I love you so much."

"Do you love me enough to throw on something and sit on the deck with me? It's a beautiful morning." Mason had on a robe and nothing else.

"I'd love to."

"If that's your answer to everything, the morning will be perfect."

She smiled when they shared a lounger, and she stared out at the water. There were only a few early fishermen out, but none of them were looking up. "What time does your mom want us over?"

"Late lunch, she said." Mason kissed her as she pressed her hand to her cheek "My mom was right," Mason said softly as she moved her hand to the side of her neck.

"About what?"

"Before you I was content, drifting from contract to contract, but not really passionate about a whole lot. Then there was you, and you woke something up in me and made me face the music. At least, you made me face that there was more to life than work and drifting."

"Are you okay with all this? It's big, sweeping changes, and I don't want you to feel obligated to something that won't make you happy." She couldn't help the creeping self-doubt that might always make its presence known.

"You know what will make me happy?" Mason reached into her pocket and came out with a box. "If you'll say yes."

"Buh…" Her brain froze as she stared at the archetypal box.

"Will you marry me?" The box creaked open to reveal a beautiful ring. "I don't want another day to go by without you knowing not only how much I love you, but how much I want to spend the rest of my life with you."

"Yes. Yes!" The answer made Mason smile and slip the ring on her finger.

"I can't wait for what comes next." Mason kissed the ring. "It's going to be awesome."

"It will be, because it's forever."

EPILOGUE

A Year Later

"The crowds have been gathering outside the Staples Center since early this afternoon for tonight's Grammys," the entertainment reporter said.

Victoria watched the coverage from the car, not really believing she was here at all.

Their last year had been a whirlwind of performances, a wedding, and the start of another album. Everything Mason had promised had happened, only it had been bigger than Victoria could have imagined. The album had done so well that she couldn't simply run out for doughnuts on Sunday mornings, and she was having a hard time adjusting to the fame. It wasn't that she was unhappy, but she'd always thought she'd just play piano in the background. This was so, so much more than that.

Through it all Mason had been right there making sure it was all fun, and it had been. They laughed and played and were looking forward to the coming months at home. Even her mother was taking time off from her tour schedule to come home to Blue Heaven and the river house she and Bryce had adopted as theirs. Her relationship with her mom was better, though it would never be terribly close, and her mom had continued into the twelve-step program. Bryce helped keep her on the straight and narrow, and though her audiences would never be as big as they once were, she was happy and holding steady. Victoria knew her mom was genuinely proud of her success, if a little jealous, and the meanness seemed to have gone out of her with Weston's death. It was enough.

"This is something." She gripped her purse in her hands as she watched the small television. "It's surreal, and I doubt I'll win."

"You'd better be wrong." Mason looked good in the dark suit she'd worn with old cowboy boots. She would've pushed for something dressier, but Mason had said all she was tonight was background support for the great Everly. "I've got money riding on this. Belle's burlesque troop has thrown money in the pot too. I'll make enough to retire when you win. You ready?"

Victoria nodded, though she wasn't sure she was ready at all. Mason gave her a quick kiss.

"Everly, over here!" the photographers yelled when the door opened, and Mason got out to give her a hand.

She prayed she didn't make a fool of herself on national television by falling on her face. They smiled as they started toward the arena, but Mason let her go forward alone as she stopped for the obligatory fashion shots.

"Are you excited?" the reporter she'd been watching asked her.

Did anyone ever answer no to that question? "I am, and it's a real honor to be nominated in such great company." It was what everyone said, but considering her competition, she really meant it.

"What's next?"

"I'm starting a new album, and Mason and I are working on a new project together."

Their relationship had turned some people off, but for the majority of her fans, her marriage to Mason had been happy news. If she had been a one-and-done artist, she would've been fine with that, but folks wanted more.

"Anything you want to share?"

The woman appeared almost giddy, and they'd decided tonight was as good a night as any to make their announcement.

"We're four months pregnant," she said, and the woman glanced between them, appearing confused. "*I'm* four months along and we're thrilled." That would get social media going again, but you couldn't hide a baby.

"Let's get you inside," Mason said when the paparazzi's shouting began in earnest, and she smiled at Mason's protective streak. It had gotten more focused when she'd gotten pregnant.

The starting act was good, and she held Mason's hand as the show finally got underway. One of the first awards was for best new artist, and she'd been shocked when she'd been nominated, given the competition. Now, the presenter went through the list of nominees as the cameras panned the audience.

"This year's winner is..." The presenter paused for effect. "Everly."

It was Mason's kiss that finally brought her out of her shock, and she stood to make her way to the stage. She accepted the award and thanked all the appropriate people before trying to find Mason in the audience. When she made eye contact she could breathe again.

"Nothing in life is sweeter than finding the one person who's your match. The only one who fits and understands you, and for me, that's my wife, Mason. Thank you, honey, for giving me a chance and showing me what true happiness means. I love you."

She made two more trips to the stage that night, winning best country song and best country album. One of the most incredible parts of her night was performing "Talk to Me" with Wilbur accompanying her, and he smiled so much she thought his face should hurt.

It wasn't until later when she and Mason went to bed that she finally relaxed and really took it all in. "Can you believe this?"

Mason lay beside her with her hand on her abdomen. "Totally. I'm in love with you, baby, but I'm also good at my job. I know talent when I see it, and I signed it."

"What else are you good at?"

"Happily ever afters."

She rolled over and kissed Mason with all the love she had to share. "That you are, my love. That you are."

About the Author

Ali Vali is the author of the long-running Cain Casey Devil series and the Genesis Clan Forces series, as well as numerous standalone romances including two Lambda Literary Award finalists, *Calling the Dead* and *Love Match*, and her 2020 release *The Inheritance*. Ali also has a novella in the collection *Girls with Guns*.

Originally from Cuba, Ali has retained much of her family's traditions and language and uses them frequently in her stories. Having her father read her stories and poetry before bed every night as a child infused her with a love of reading, which she carries till today. Ali currently lives outside New Orleans, Louisiana, and she has discovered that living in Louisiana provides plenty of material to draw from in creating her novels and short stories.

Books Available From Bold Strokes Books

Face the Music by Ali Vali. Sweet music is the last thing that happens when Nashville music producer Mason Liner and daughter of country royalty Victoria Roddy are thrown together in an effort to save country star Sophie Roddy's career. (978-1-63555-532-5)

Flavor of the Month by Georgia Beers. What happens when baker Charlie and chef Emma realize their differing paths have led them right back to each other? (978-1-63555-616-2)

Mending Fences by Angie Williams. Rancher Bobbie Del Rey and veterinarian Grace Hammond are about to discover if heartbreaks of the past can ever truly be mended. (978-1-63555-708-4)

Silk and Leather: Lesbian Erotica with an Edge, edited by Victoria Villaseñor. This collection of stories by award-winning authors offers fantasies as soft as silk and tough as leather. The only question is: How far will you go to make your deepest desires come true? (978-1-63555-587-5)

The Last Place You Look by Aurora Rey. Dumped by her wife and looking for anything but love, Julia Pierce retreats to her hometown only to rediscover high school friend Taylor Winslow, who's secretly crushed on her for years. (978-1-63555-574-5)

The Mortician's Daughter by Nan Higgins. A singer on the verge of stardom discovers she must give up her dreams to live a life in service to ghosts. (978-1-63555-594-3)

The Real Thing by Laney Webber. When passion flares between actress Virginia Green and masseuse Allison McDonald, can they be sure it's the real thing? (978-1-63555-478-6)

What the Heart Remembers Most by M. Ullrich. For college sweethearts Jax Levine and Gretchen Mills, could an accident be the second chance neither knew they wanted? (978-1-63555-401-4)

White Horse Point by Andrews & Austin. Mystery writer Taylor James finds herself falling for the mysterious woman on White Horse Point who lives alone, protecting a secret she can't share about a murderer who walks among them. (978-1-63555-695-7)

Femme Tales by Anne Shade. Six women find themselves in their own real-life fairy tales when true love finds them in the most unexpected ways. (978-1-63555-657-5)

Jellicle Girl by Stevie Mikayne. One dark summer night, Beth and Jackie go out to the canoe dock. Two years later, Beth is still carrying the weight of what happened to Jackie. (978-1-63555-691-9)

My Date with a Wendigo by Genevieve McCluer. Elizabeth Rosseau finds her long-lost love and the secret community of fiends she's now a part of. (978-1-63555-679-7)

On the Run by Charlotte Greene. Even when they're cute blondes, it's stupid to pick up hitchhikers, especially when they've just broken out of prison, but doing so is about to change Gwen's life forever. (978-1-63555-682-7)

Perfect Timing by Dena Blake. The choice between love and family has never been so difficult, and Lynn's and Maggie's different visions of the future may end their romance before it's begun. (978-1-63555-466-3)

The Mail Order Bride by R. Kent. When a mail order bride is thrust on Austin, he must choose between the bride he never wanted or the dream he lives for. (978-1-63555-678-0)

Through Love's Eyes by C.A. Popovich. When fate reunites Brittany Yardin and Amy Jansons, can they move beyond the pain of their past to find love? (978-1-63555-629-2)

To the Moon and Back by Melissa Brayden. Film actress Carly Daniel thinks that stage work is boring and unexciting, but when she accepts a lead role in a new play, stage manager Lauren Prescott tests both her heart and her ability to share the limelight. (978-1-63555-618-6)

Tokyo Love by Diana Jean. When Kathleen Schmitt is given the opportunity to be on the cutting edge of AI technology, she never thought a failed robotic love companion would bring her closer to her neighbor, Yuriko Velucci, and finding love in unexpected places. (978-1-63555-681-0)

Brooklyn Summer by Maggie Cummings. When opposites attract, can a summer of passion and adventure lead to a lifetime of love? (978-1-63555-578-3)

City Kitty and Country Mouse by Alyssa Linn Palmer. Pulled in two different directions, can a city kitty and a country mouse fall in love and make it work? (978-1-63555-553-0)

Elimination by Jackie D. When a dangerous homegrown terrorist seeks refuge with the Russian mafia, the team will be put to the ultimate test. (978-1-63555-570-7)

In the Shadow of Darkness by Nicole Stiling. Angeline Vallencourt is a reluctant vampire who must decide what she wants more—obscurity, revenge, or the woman who makes her feel alive. (978-1-63555-624-7)

On Second Thought by C. Spencer. Madisen is falling hard for Rae. Even single life and co-parenting are beginning to click. At least, that is, until her ex-wife begins to have second thoughts. (978-1-63555-415-1)

Out of Practice by Carsen Taite. When attorney Abby Keane discovers the wedding blogger tormenting her client is the woman she had a passionate, anonymous vacation fling with, sparks and subpoenas fly. Legal Affairs: one law firm, three best friends, three chances to fall in love. (978-1-63555-359-8)

Providence by Leigh Hays. With every click of the shutter, photographer Rebekiah Kearns finds it harder and harder to keep Lindsey Blackwell in focus without getting too close. (978-1-63555-620-9)

Taking a Shot at Love by KC Richardson. When academic and athletic worlds collide, will English professor Celeste Bouchard and basketball coach Lisa Tobias ignore their attraction to achieve their professional goals? (978-1-63555-549-3)

Flight to the Horizon by Julie Tizard. Airline captain Kerri Sullivan and flight attendant Janine Case struggle to survive an emergency water landing and overcome dark secrets to give love a chance to fly. (978-1-63555-331-4)

In Helen's Hands by Nanisi Barrett D'Arnuk. As her mistress, Helen pushes Mickey to her sensual limits, delivering the pleasure only a BDSM lifestyle can provide her. (978-1-63555-639-1)

Jamis Bachman, Ghost Hunter by Jen Jensen. In Sage Creek, Utah, a poltergeist stirs to life and past secrets emerge. (978-1-63555-605-6)

Moon Shadow by Suzie Clarke. Add betrayal, season with survival, then serve revenge smokin' hot with a sharp knife. (978-1-63555-584-4)

Spellbound by Jean Copeland and Jackie D. When the supernatural worlds of good and evil face off, love might be what saves them all. (978-1-63555-564-6)

Temptation by Kris Bryant. Can experienced nanny Cassie Miller deny her growing attraction and keep her relationship with her boss professional? Or will they sidestep propriety and give in to temptation? (978-1-63555-508-0)

The Inheritance by Ali Vali. Family ties bring Tucker Delacroix and Willow Vernon together, but they could also tear them, and any chance they have at love, apart. (978-1-63555-303-1)

Thief of the Heart by MJ Williamz. Kit Hanson makes a living seducing rich women in casinos and relieving them of the expensive jewelry most won't even miss. But her streak ends when she meets beautiful FBI agent Savannah Brown. (978-1-63555-572-1)

Face Off by PJ Trebelhorn. Hockey player Savannah Wells rarely spends more than a night with any one woman, but when photographer Madison Scott buys the house next door, she's forced to rethink what she expects out of life. (978-1-63555-480-9)

Hot Ice by Aurora Rey, Elle Spencer, and Erin Zak. Can falling in love melt the hearts of the iciest ice queens? Join Aurora Rey, Elle Spencer, and Erin Zak to find out! A contemporary romance novella collection. (978-1-63555-513-4)

Line of Duty by VK Powell. Dr. Dylan Carlyle's professional and personal life is turned upside down when a tragic event at Fairview

Station pits her against ambitious, handsome police officer Finley Masters. ((978-1-63555-486-1)

London Undone by Nan Higgins. London Craft reinvents her life after reading a childhood letter to her future self and, in doing so, finds the love she truly wants. (978-1-63555-562-2)

Lunar Eclipse by Gun Brooke. Moon De Cruz lives alone on an uninhabited planet after being shipwrecked in space. Her life changes forever when Captain Beaux Lestarion's arrival threatens the planet and Moon's freedom. (978-1-63555-460-1)

One Small Step by MA Binfield. In this contemporary romance, Iris and Cam discover the meaning of taking chances and following your heart, even if it means getting hurt. (978-1-63555-596-7)

Shadows of a Dream by Nicole Disney. Rainn has the talent to take her rock band all the way, but falling in love is a powerful distraction, and her new girlfriend's meth addiction might just take them both down. 978-1-63555-598-1)

Someone to Love by Jenny Frame. When Davina Trent is given an unexpected family, can she let nanny Wendy Darling teach her to open her heart to the children and to Wendy? (978-1-63555-468-7)

Uncharted by Robyn Nyx. As Rayne Marcellus and Chase Stinsen track the legendary Golden Trinity, they must learn to put their differences aside and depend on one another to survive. (978-1-63555-325-3)

Where We Are by Annie McDonald. A sensual account of two women who discover a way to walk on the same path together with the help of an Indigenous tale, a Canadian art movement, and the mysterious appearance of dimes. (978-1-63555-581-3)